SCORPION STING

A DAN ROY THRILLER

DAN ROY SERIES 9

MICK BOSE

D1526100

Copyright © 2018 by Mick Bose

All rights reserved.

If you got this ebook without buying it, remember that is a breach of Copyright law. Thank you for supporting the author's hard work.

No part of this book may be reproduced in any form or by any electronic or

mechanical means, including information storage and retrieval systems, without

permission in writing from the author.

This book is a work of fiction. Names, characters, places, and incidents either are

products of the author's imagination or are used fictitiously. Any resemblance to actual

persons, living or dead, events, or locales is entirely coincidental.

*****

PRAISE FOR THE DAN ROY SERIES:

Mick Bose is the standard bearer of a new generation of thriller writers. Complex plots, vivid descriptions of exotic locations, and an emotional core to an action driven story. - Hera B, Editor.

Mick Bose, you have done the impossible. Finally, I've found a hero who is equal to Jason Bourne. Just sit back and enjoy - this is thrill ride! - Mark Earls, ARC Reader.

Fans of Reacher, Rapp, Baldacci - Rejoice!! Dan Roy is up there with the best. So worth reading this series! - John Arlington, Amazon Reviewer.

The definition of a page turner. I found myself right there with Dan and the Scorpion, twisting and turning. I stayed up all night just to read! - Maddy Graves, Amazon Reviewer.

What a stunning thriller! I devoured this book in one day. Please write more. - Karl Cox, Goodreads Reviewer.

Can't wait for the next one! A long series, hopefully!! - Emmy Mccabe

A white knuckled ride that swept me away! Pure adrenaline pulses through this book, I couldn't believe it. - Goodreads Reviewer

Utter, sheer, unbelievable entertainment. Mick Bose, you are here to stay!! - Amazon Reviewer

...And that ending took my breath away! - Polly Hughes

I am still holding the book and thinking, wow, just WOW! Do yourself a favor and get yourself a copy today! - Sue Nicole

HAVE YOU READ THEM ALL?

ALL BOOKS AVAILABLE IN AMAZON ONLY – VISIT AMAZON ONLINE

(Each book can be read as a stand-alone)

Special offer: Save 40% when you get the box sets!! 3 full length novels in one book!

VISIT AMAZON ONLINE TO BUY BOTH PAPERBACK AND EBOOK

The Dan Roy Series Box Set: Books 1-3

The Dan Roy Series Box Set: Books 4-6

Table of Contents

CHAPTER 1

Tver City

North-east of Moscow

Ten Years Ago

It was Natasha Karmen's wedding day, so she strapped a Makarov pistol to her thigh length stocking.

She wasn't expecting trouble on her special day. But old habits die hard. Ever since she had graduated from the Red Chamber, the female only, ultra-secretive special operations group run by the KGB, she had packed a weapon before any social occasion. It was like a smoker reaching for a cigarette in the morning. Killer habit.

And one she couldn't do without. Of course, like any bride-to-be, she wanted this day to be normal in the purest sense of the word. To be full of happiness and laughter, like any wedding day. Surely, she deserved that. After all the conflict and hardship she had seen in her life, one golden day of happiness must be due to her?

Outside her second-story window, sunlight streamed in from a blue sky. It shone on the packed ice on the pavement, dazzled on the white rooftop of houses. Natasha was in Tver, a city by the Volga river, 80 kilometers northeast of Moscow. It was her husband-to-be, Vladimir's, hometown. A medium sized city, Tver had direct links to the capital, and its yellow and pastel colored buildings hugged the banks of the mighty Volga as the river curled gracefully around the city.

Natasha stood in front of the full-length mirror, checking her underwear. It was all black, a color Vladimir liked. She walked around the room, the butt of the snub-nosed pistol was small enough for her to move with ease.

She slipped on the waist length camisole over which she would wear her white wedding dress. The dress was hanging from a hook on the dresser next to the mirror. There was a knock on the door, and her bridesmaid Dominika entered.

"Such a nice day," she trilled, putting down a bouquet of flowers on the table next to the bed, then looking at Natasha appreciatively. "You look good."

Natasha smiled. "With hardly any clothes on, you mean?"

Dominika's eyes fell on the gun. She clicked her tongue on the roof of her mouth and pointed to the weapon. "Even today?"

Natasha shrugged. "You never know." The truth, which she didn't like to think about too much, was that her enemies were everywhere. She was an assassin for hire, officially employed by the Russian Government, but with the freedom to accept contracts from third parties. Most of these third parties were foreign governments who didn't want to use their own agents in case an operation went south. They, the grey masked men who did the ordering, would never be exposed.

But Natasha, or the Scorpion as she was nicknamed, was exposed. That was the problem with fame in the murky world she inhabited. She made a living killing targets, but her skill made her a target, too.

Dominika picked up a hairbrush and comb. Natasha put her dressing gown on and sat down facing the mirror.

Dominika moved the brush in rhythmic strokes down the back of Natasha's shoulder length brown hair.

"No need to worry, honey," Dominika said. "You're wearing white today, not black."

Dominika was also a graduate of the Red Chamber. She had been on multiple missions with Natasha in the past. Just by looking at each other, they often knew what the other was thinking. Apart from Vladimir, Dom was the closest friend Natasha had.

"Besides, we're all here," Dom continued as she brushed her friend's hair. "Only a small group, close," she stopped herself, then said quickly, "Friends."

"It's okay, you can say family. You guys are my family." Natasha's mother died, and she had never known her father.

"Vlad's parents will be here," Dominika said. "We'll have them covered, don't worry."

"I know," Natasha said, her head tilted backwards as the brush untangled knots. "But I like to be prepared just in case. You know that."

Dominika's face was a mask of concentration as she wrapped several strands into a curl. "Well, honey, there's nothing like starting a marriage with a bang."

*****

The blue dome of the Russian Orthodox church rose up into a similar colored sky. The gold cross at the top twinkled, winking like it knew all of life, marriage, death was just a mirage, a blink in the ocean of existence.

The train of Natasha's long dress was held up by two bridesmaids, lest it draped over the snow. A bearded priest, dressed in the traditional grey smock, held a rosary bead to his chest and smiled at Natasha. She entered the church and noises from the street outside faded.

Vladimir, her groom, was waiting at the altar. He turned to look at her and nodded. Natasha lowered her eyes to the tiled floor. The lace veil came over her face, disturbing her vision. She didn't like it, but like Dominika said all she had to do today was embrace happiness.

Dominika walked alongside her, as she had no father, or male relative to accompany her down the aisle. It seemed to take a long time. Her dress slowed her down, but so did the slow steps they were supposed to take. She could feel the faint brush of the Makarov as she got to the end and turned to face Vladimir.

He was a soldier, and they had met at a ball for service men thrown by the FSB, the KGB's successor. His sculpted jawline and large eyes had drawn her attention. Along with the fact that he spoke English, as she was trained to do, like a native speaker without any accents. It was a requirement of anyone graduating from the Red Chamber.

But most importantly, Vladimir was untainted by the grime that masked her, the cloak of dirt which covered people who worked in lies and subterfuge. Vladimir was a front-line soldier, no more. One who had seen active combat, but not the machinations that went on behind the scenes.

He would never know the darkness she had fumbled around in. She liked that.

The priest was standing in front of them, and both bride and groom turned slightly to face him. Vladimir was still holding both her hands in his. The veil still bothered her vision. But she knew everyone else apart from the three of them were seated now. Only three rows of the pews behind her were taken. This wasn't going to be a long ceremony.

Vladimir lifted her veil, and they faced each other, smiling but nervous. They repeated the vows with the priest. Then he leaned over to kiss her, and applause sounded from the benches. The noise seemed strangely loud and hollow in the nave of the large church, most of it empty.

The bridesmaids stepped in behind her when it was all done. As practiced, they filed outside through the side entrance. A brick path had been cleared of snow. The sky was still blue, thankfully.

Vladimir gripped her hand and whispered in her ear, "I'm the happiest man in the world." He kissed her cheek.

Natasha blushed and grinned at him.

A burly, middle aged man, camera hanging from his neck, came forward. Natasha's smile faltered when she saw his face. The skin was leathery, loose, hanging from the jowls. His eyes were dark, so small they were almost slits. But what bothered her was the flicker of recognition. Where had she seen that face before?

There was movement around her. Vladmir leaned toward her again. "It's the photographer. You saw him earlier outside."

Natasha nodded, slightlty relieved. She looked around for Dominika but couldn't see her in the small huddle of the guests. The priest had come outside as well, speaking to the wedding party.

"Line up against the wall please," the photographer said.

Natasha stood smiling, next to her husband, ready for a photo she would keep for the rest of her life.

The photographer set his camera up on the tripod and put his face to it. Then he gestured with his hand. "Closer please."

Natasha did as she was told. A hand raised from behind the camera. "Ready, one, two…"

The last word was drowned in an explosion. A yellow orange fireball boomed from the right, where the guests were standing. Natasha felt a sudden jerk, a push sent her sprawling to the ground. Warm blood splattered over her dress, ugly, red streaks disfiguring the pristine whiteness.

As if in slow motion, she turned to look at Vladimir. Not much remained of him. His face was blown off, barely hanging from the neck. His body was turned to the side, facing her, the legs still jerking. Time moved through a dense fog as more explosions sounded. The photographer lay on the ground, his dead eyes staring towards heaven.

Natasha screamed but there was hardly any sound. She rolled over, snow sticking to her dress, and reached for the weapon in her stocking. She pulled the gun out, flicked safety off and scanned around. Her shocked, dazed mind couldn't make her eyes focus. It was so slow, dreary, like it wasn't happening. Like she was watching herself in a bad dream.

Bodies littered the ground, red blood seeping into the snow, turning darker shades of crimson. She could figure out the priest, his robe black and bloodied, and some of the guests. Guilt, panic, fear gripped her in a seizure, a spasm of the senses that left her shaking and wide-mouthed.

She didn't hear the crunch of boots on snow. It came from behind her.

"We meet at last, Scorpion."

She whirled around, weapon pointed at the voice. A tall man stood in front of her with two other men flanking him, holding Uzi sub machine guns.

She didn't know the face. "This is for my son, Adham Marutov."

Natasha's eyes widened. She snarled. She fired, but it was too late. The Uzi's blasted first, smashing the weapon out of her hand.

CHAPTER 2

Moscow

Present Day

The Scorpion's eyes flew open. Her breath came in gasps. But she didn't make a sound. Her mouth opened, and she breathed heavily. Sweat trickled down the side of her face, drenched her back, giving her that uncomfortable, sticky sensation of the sheets adhering to her skin. But she didn't move a muscle save the ones already being used.

It wasn't a dream. Vladimir was dead. But it was a long time ago when youth still cast the ever-present glow of optimism over her life. Funny, how quickly that faded as she got older. Now in her mid-thirties, she felt ancient. Too old to be living this life. Too old to wake up in the middle of the night, a steam train hammering through her head, sheets soaking wet. But that wasn't all.

There was someone in the room.

She felt it, despite the room being dark. It was still night outside. Natasha wanted to reach under her pillow, but the movement would betray her intentions. Without lifting her head, she did her best to look around the room. There, in the corner opposite the window, a dense black shadow. Sitting on her armchair. It had to be a man, judging by the size. He too, sat perfectly still, watching her.

Neither of them spoke for a while. Then Natasha said softly, "Borislov."

The figure shifted in the armchair, and sighed. He coughed, an old, rheumatic sound, emanating from a smoker's chest.

"Didn't know you could see in the dark," Borislov said.

Natasha sat up, then put her feet on the ground. Borislov was her old handler at the KGB. Every Red Chamber graduate had a handler, but Natasha had moved to new pastures. Nevertheless, she knew Borislov would always know where to find her.

She didn't mind facing him without a weapon. If he wanted her dead, she would be already.

"I'm going to turn the light on," Natasha said. "But I'll go to the bathroom first. Are you alone?"

"Yes."

She didn't bother asking him how he got inside. He probably had a team waiting outside on the freezing Ulitsa Prospekt. It was her own fault to come back to Moscow. She should have delayed selling this apartment for a few more months.

When she emerged from the bathroom and walked down the hallway, the bedroom light was on, and Borislov hadn't moved. His hair was going white, and his thin, pinched face was gaunter with the passing of years. She wondered if he was sick, then decided against asking him.

She sat on the edge of the bed, wrapping the dressing gown loosely around her. She wanted to disguise her hand that slipped down the edge of the mattress. She could reach her Makarov PM with ease. All the time, she didn't take her eyes off Borislov.

"May I smoke?" the old man asked.

"No. What do you want?"

"I need you to do a job for us."

They stared at each other, neither looking away. Borislov was the first one to break the silence. "Ali Marutov."

Natasha drew her breath in sharply. Her lips pressed together in a thin line. "I'm listening."

"He's surfaced in Naxos. An island in Greece."

"Who told you? We don't have assets on the Greek islands."

"He was recognized when he landed at Athens airport. Then tracked."

Natasha digested this in silence. Seven years ago, she had killed Adham, the son of Ali Marutov, notorious Islamist terrorist. In revenge, Ali had massacred her wedding day two years later.

She squeezed her eyes shut as the memories assaulted her again.

"This is your chance. Make him pay," Borislov said.

"What's in it for you?"

"He's lining up with the Chechens. We have enough trouble in Chechnya. Last thing we need is an alliance of Marutov and them."

Natasha smirked. "Plenty of Chechen hitmen in the ranks of the FSB. You guys recruit them actively. What's the problem?"

"We do, but not when they threaten to blow up our subways."

Natasha was quiet for a while. "So, you want a clean kill, and that's it?"

"I need proof as well. Photos. If you can get documents from his safe, any intel that will be helpful."

"Which makes my getaway harder."

"Take it or leave it."

Natasha said, "This come from higher up, right? What's he really done?"

Borislov remained silent. "You could send anyone to kill him. Why me?" Natasha asked.

"Because you're the best close contact assassin we have. Not saying that to boost your ego." He shrugged. "Plus, you have a vendetta. But you're not emotional, at least I hope you won't be. That could–"

"I never let emotions cloud my judgement," Natasha snapped. "But you still haven't told me the real reason."

"Only good terrorist is a dead one."

"Unless you use them, like you do with the Chechens," Natasha said. "Okay, whatever. I get intel from the usual place?"

There was a locker in a Moscow bus station where a USB flash drive would be left for her in a waterproof, sealed packet. She would destroy it after use. The dead drop point changed, but for the last two operations, it had remained the same.

"Yes."

CHAPTER 3

Dan Roy didn't like going south of the river. Not when he was in London city, anyway.

The main reason was his unfamiliarity with the territory. He had to rely on his GPS and map, and he hated looking like a tourist. He was well versed in London's many hued life, having lived here for a few months when he was taking time off Intercept, the black ops organization that had recruited him from Delta. Dan had never gone back to Intercept, but Intercept had come back to him, several times. Including that time he was living in London. A time when things came undone in spectacular fashion. Dan shook his head at the memory. The US Embassy in London was still standing, luckily.

He had been back since, mainly on transit. London was surprisingly international, and felt surprisingly small for a city that was larger than NYC. Its narrow-cobbled streets and old pubs on street corners were a lot like London from the Victorian times. Dan knew Brits were like that, they liked the old stuff, loved to preserve things as they used to be, even when they were on the brink of falling down. In fact, the older and more decrepit some buildings and institutions got, the more the Brits loved them.

Mad dogs and Englishmen, he thought wryly.

Still, he liked them. They were a funny lot, no doubt. They loved a drink. Not to drink in England was like not having a burger in New York. Brits were polite to a fault, but behind their niceties hide secrets they guarded with their lives. Secrets no outsider would ever know.

The thought made Dan wonder about the man he was on the way to meet.

Mr. Jeff Pearce. McBride, Dan's former handler at Intercept, had requested Dan to see him. Jeff worked at MI6, UK's equivalent of the CIA. A tiny fraction of the CIA's size and often nicknamed Six by English servicemen, it nevertheless punched far above its weight. After all, Military Intelligence is what had caused Britain to spread its tentacles all around the world, including America. Love it or hate it, facts were facts. If an MI6 agent told a CIA agent they needed to have a chat, it was organized fast.

Only in this instance, the MI6 made a peculiar request. They wanted the man who had saved the US Embassy in London from a rogue terrorist bomb, and thereby almost certainly prevented a global war.

"Why me?" Dan had asked McBride on the phone.

The old man was apologetic. "It's about an American in the US Embassy in London. They think he's being developed as an asset by our friends in Moscow."

"So? Happens all the time, right? The CIA's office in London can handle that easily. Why the hell do they need me?"

"Because you know the place. You've worked with the SAS."

"Bullshit. What's going on, McBride? Intercept has an angle on this, right?"

McBride let out a deep sigh. "For once, I actually think they don't. Jeff approached me directly. I was stationed with him in Shackleton Barracks when he was in the Royal Marines. They want someone who's discreet. Not a known face or official CIA agent."

"Someone they can ditch at the first sign of trouble. Did this guy ask you about me? Or did you tell him?"

There was a pause. Dan knew McBride was crafty as hell, but Dan trusted him. An old dog couldn't be taught new tricks, and Jim McBride had seen most of them. He was like a father figure to Dan.

So when he said it, Dan knew he was speaking the truth.

"He asked me. I was surprised, didn't expect him to know about you."

Dan frowned. "And you don't think it's a huge fucking coincidence he just *happens* to call you, my old handler?"

McBride was quiet. "The thought did occur to me. But I knew him, son. Sure, people can change. But Jeff isn't a dancer."

Dan snorted. "He's a Six agent. If you don't trust the CIA, why the hell should you trust him?"

"For one, I saved the guy's ass once in Iraq. He knows that and owes me. Second, what you did in London two years ago is still hot talk. You saved the Brits a load of trouble. They don't forget these things easy. To be honest, I'm surprised they haven't tried to contact you before."

Both were quiet for a while, and Dan could sense the unease in McBride seeping down the line.

McBride said, "Still, I know it's kinda odd. But to get to the bottom of it, best to find out more. We need to know what the Brits want. Jeff wouldn't say any more over the phone. Besides I checked with the CIA. This agent is causing trouble in London, Dan. He's been seen in public with known SVR agents."

"Can't be much of a spy then," Dan said drily.

"Guess not. But you're not a known face in the intelligence circles, so it won't hurt to check it out. Right?"

Now, as Dan walked down Waterloo Bridge, the wind whipping at his ears, he remembered McBride's words. He sensed the Brits had an ulterior motive in calling him. A reason they didn't disclosed to McBride. That intrigued Dan. He was a lone operator and had been for a long time since his retirement from Intercept. True, Intercept kept calling him back via McBride. Dan had long learnt to distrust the shadowy black ops organization. The first trigger had been when he refused to blow up a bus full of children in Yemen. Dan could never do that. He was through with deniable missions. The leaders of Intercept, unknown faces in the Pentagon and Capitol Hill, wanted to play devious games, that was fine. But they should have the guts to stand up and take responsibility when the shit hit the fan. Instead, they blamed operatives like Dan.

Dan took the subway from Waterloo, and headed further down south towards Wimbledon. If he was a tourist, he would have visited the hallowed tennis courts. But it was getting dark, the perennial rain was on its way, and Dan had little interest in tourist attractions.

Dan walked up the hill from the station, heading toward a vast wooden area called the Wimbledon Common. His destination was a pub at the edge of the Common.

The whispering rain arrived as he walked. The thin drops made no sound as they fell. Dan went the opposite way first, stopped several times and got lost on purpose. If he had any followers, the surveillance detection route must've worked because he saw no one save pedestrians.

He was glad for his hat and coat, and cursed himself for not buying an umbrella at the station. By the time he got to the pub, his coat had a sheen of rain covering it.

Darkness covered the Common. The glow from the streetlights showed the rain. Warm yellow light shone dully from the pub windows as he stood opposite. It was very quiet, even for a weekday, even so close to the woodlands.

Dan watched the pub for a while. A couple came out and hurried to their car parked opposite. A man came out to smoke, joined by his friend. Their shoulders were relaxed, they talked loudly, probably the effect of a few beers. No danger there. Dan walked up when the men went inside.

The pub was typical of many Dan had been to in England. An old building with low wooden beams that almost touched his head. He had to lower his neck, nodded at the bar staff and made his way to the rear as he had been instructed. Jeff would be wearing a brown sweater and grey raincoat, and Dan knew he would make an effort to look as normal as possible, blend in with the locals.

He clocked Jeff sitting in the corner from where the main door was visible, and the spot was also close to a side exit. No one else was sitting apart from an almost balding man in his fifties wearing a brown sweater and grey coat.

Dan went up to him and said, "The Spaniards won't give up Gibraltar without a fight."

The man called Jeff Pearce said, "Unless we reach a deal for Brexit."

At least the password was correct.

Dan grabbed a chair and sat down. He removed his beanie and put it in his pocket but didn't take his coat off. The side exit was two paces to his left, and he also had a view of the main door. Jeff hadn't been in eye contact with anyone else in the pub. A few people were scattered around, but the place wasn't especially busy.

"It's okay. I'm alone," Jeff said. Dan looked at him closely. Jeff's hazel eyes were large and observant, his cheeks sunken and

26

slightly saggy. He picked up his glass and sipped from his beer. Dan saw the wedding ring, and fingers that held pens and beer glasses but nothing more. Some nicotine stains in his nails but nothing else. He lowered his eyes as he put the glass down.

"Made your assumptions about me, Mr. Roy?" Jeff asked. Slight twang in his vowels made Dan think of an accent from North England.

"What would they be?" Dan asked.

Jeff smiled. "If I told you I'd have to kill you."

"And what assumptions have you made about me?" Dan asked.

Jeff wasn't smiling any more. "Not assumptions. Just facts."

"And they are?"

Jeff fixed Dan with a stare. "You're a wanted man."

CHAPTER 4

Dubai

United Arab Emirates

One year ago

Rashid Al-Falaj stared blankly as his Ferrari Testarossa drove past the glittering needle of the world's tallest tower. The Burj Khalifa, standing at 832 meters, was the highest any structure built by human hands. Rashid used to feel a twinge of pride as he drove past it. Lines of tourists came to see it every day of the year, to marvel at the needle reaching the lower edges of the atmosphere. Soon, he knew, the Burj Khalifa would be replaced by the The Dubai Creek Harbor Tower, which would rise in three years' time to a full 1,000 meters tall.

Rashid used to feel pride, but now he only felt emptiness. The Royal Family of Dubai had decided to take this path thirty years ago, and the whole of the Emirates had grown rich as a result. So had Rashid's family, the Al-Falaj conglomerate supplying the oil rigs with their machinery, and now also into construction. He glimpsed the name Falaj glowing in giant red letters against a huge building, another luminous needle in the forest of incandescent high rises. American tourists said Dubai put New York's skyline to shame, and as he visited USA often he knew there was some truth to the story. Dubai was brand spanking new, a product of the petro dollars used to create a tax-free haven for business and individuals. The zero tax lured masses of corporates and rich individuals.

To Rashid's mind, it also corrupted the Wahabi fundamentalism he so desperately wished to be instilled in the hearts and minds of every Arab. True, Rashid came from Riyadh, Saudi Arabia, and while the Saudi's respected and cooperated with the Emiratis, they were also secret rivals. Riyadh and Jeddah, two of the largest Saudi cities, also had zero tax for foreigners. But they didn't have the glamour or style of Dubai.

The reason of course was the relaxed style of Islam practiced in the Emirates.

Muslim women dressed modestly and covered up, but white women were allowed to wear shorts and skirts. So did all the brown skinned foreign women.

Rashid despised that. He despised the lax morality of these foreigners, and the fact that the Emiratis turned a blind eye to it. Yes, it had made Dubai a tourist and business hotspot, but at what price?

To his mind, it was Waleed who had paid the price. His brave cousin who had taken the fight to the Americans last year. Waleed had asked Rashid for help, but Rashid was too busy with business to take jihad too seriously. Now he knew it had been a mistake. With his support, Waleed might have succeeded. And that would have been *Qayamat.*

The Final Judgement.

But Waleed, his dear cousin, had failed, and the guilt was now eating Rashid up. He was angry, and he wanted vengeance.

He rolled the window down a bit and told the driver to slow down. Like many Arabs, he had a driver for his expensive sports car.

"How much further, Abdul?" Rashid asked.

"Not long, sayidi. We are almost there. Another five minutes." Abdul, his trusted bodyguard, was sat in the front next to the driver.

Rashid's mood brightened when he thought of what lay ahead. A firangi, white man, had been caught snooping around the Al-Falaj Dubai office. The office was a sumptuous, twenty story high rise, as eye-catching as the rest of the buildings in Dubai. Rashid was the head of the family now, and he made sure the building was well-manned and guarded. But none of the real decisions were made in Dubai. That was in Riyadh, where there comparatively fewer foreigners, and markedly lesser Americans. It was safer, as despite the billion-dollar business they now had, Rashid was still secretly supporting the jihadi groups in Yemen, Syria, and Pakistan. His ardor for a Wahabi lifestyle was always strong, and the puritanical zeal of jihad made his desire intense, burning like the first desert star.

Waleed had not died in vain. Memories of his shahid, or martyred cousin, came to his mind. They had grown up together, skipped school, learnt the strict ways of the madrassah.

Tears crept into his eyes, a black shadow of grief engulfed his heart. He tried to swallow the leaden weight of sadness in his throat and failed.

The Ferrari rolled through the open gates of a large compound near the Saudi German Hospital.

Rashid gathered himself, then stepped out of the car as the driver opened the door for him and saluted.

The warehouse like structure was used by his construction company. The guards at the massive automatic gates pressed a button and the structure rose, sheet steel rolling upwards. Rashid

30

stepped into a space the size of an airplane hangar but lit with dim lights. Only one corner was illuminated. He strode quickly in that direction.

A man was tied to a chair, black bag over his head. His feet were also tied together, hand tied in front, and body strapped to the chair. The man's face was puffed with bruises. The black bag moved as the man sensed someone approaching and the men around him moving.

Rashid knew the man had been in solitary confinement for three days. No light, only water. Naked, no heating. Whenever he fell asleep loud music blared in his ears. Hence no sleep either. It was called sensory deprivation, coupled with sensory overload.

24 hours broke many men, but 72 hours? Rashid hadn't seen anyone survive that long. The CIA practiced this on the jihadists in their so called black jails. Rashid had to smile wryly to himself. Well, it was time the roles were reversed.

The man had cracked a few hours ago, hence Rashid was called. Originally, he had said his name was Andrew Wakefield, and he was a tourist. On the second day, it changed to Grant Pearson. On the third day, he confessed that he was trying to recruit one of the receptionists as an asset.

Rashid stood in front of the man. The stench of humid sweat, stale urine, and feces assaulted his nostrils. He pressed his nostrils together, then unfurled the silk handkerchief with his name on it, and pressed it on his nose. He tied it around his face, and then put his sunglasses on. He stepped back.

"Take the bag off," Rashid said.

The man blinked, then screwed his eyes shut as the light hurt his eyes. His face was twisted, small stubble on his cheeks. Deep shadows marked the hollow under his eyes. He leaned forward and retched. Nothing came out but saliva. His head hung over his chest.

"Look at me," Rashid ordered. The man didn't move. One of Rashid's men stepped forward, but he waved the man back.

"Grant," Rashid said in his Oxbridge accent. It wasn't fake, Rashid had been to St Balliol College in Oxford for his undergraduate degree in English Literature.

"Grant!" Rashid raised his voice. "I don't have much time. If you don't look at me now, you're going back in the hole for another three days."

Grant raised his head. His face was creased in pain as he tried to open his eyes.

Rashid stepped forward. "Why were you at my office?"

"I told you. I told you everything. Please, let me go."

"Tell me again."

"I came to get an asset inside your organization."

"Who sent you?"

Grant's head sank down on his chest.

"Take him back to the hole," Rashid said.

Grant howled like a wounded animal. He thrashed and moved in his chair, but two men gripped him hard. One started to drag the chair backwards.

"Please," Grant wailed. "Please!" Rashid held his eyes as he was dragged off.

He was almost out of the door that led to the basement.

"Stop," Rashid said. He came forward. He put a long, manicured finger inside his silver colored silk suit and took out a photograph. It showed Grant, a woman and a child in a park. All were smiling and sunlight danced on their faces.

Grant took one look at the photo, then his face sunk down again. He started to sob.

Rashid said, "There are too many Grant Pearson's in the USA. So, we asked our Russian friends to search for those in the CIA. And guess what? You're the only CIA agent called Grant Pearson."

Grant's face was contorted with pain, eyes wild with fear. Spittle foamed at the corner of his lips.

"What... What do you want?"

Rashid knelt on one knee, glad the bandana was masking his smell.

"Last year, a man called Waleed Al-Falaj was killed in USA. That's why you are here, after all. Waleed's death was a very big event. But the FBI kept it as quiet as they could. Details were hidden from the media. I want to know who killed Waleed."

Rashid saw a light in Grant's eyes, like a switch had been turned on inside. He nodded.

"If I tell you, will you let me go?"

Rashid smiled under the hanky. "I ask the questions. But yes, I will certainly consider it."

Grant's chest heaved, and his eyes closed. He seemed tired, all his energy spent in the few words he had spoken.

"I want a name, Grant."

Grant opened his eyes. "Dan Roy."

"Who is he?"

"A black ops operative. He's retired but used to work for Intercept, a black ops group. A file was made on him after Waleed's death. I read it."

"You sure?"

Grant nodded, too exhausted to speak again.

Rashid stood. He inspected Grant, thoughts running through his head. This was the first time a real flesh and blood CIA agent had landed in his lap. Right when he was getting disillusioned with jihad. Right when the desire for revenge was running like a lava flow in his blood.

Subhan Allah. God is perfect.

"What else can you tell me?" Rashid asked.

Grant looked at him, his eyes yellow with jaundice. "About Dan Roy?"

Rashid ground his teeth together. "No. That bastard is a dead man. You are CIA. There must be something you know that is worth the price of your family's survival?"

Grant swallowed and his eyes bulged out. He strained the ropes as he leaned forward. His voice was hoarse. "You said you would let me go."

Rashid stood. "Maybe. But I never mentioned your family."

"You can't do this. Leave my family alone."

Rashid shrugged. "Killing Iraqi civilians is normal for the US Army. Why shouldn't I kill your family? Collateral damage, as you say."

"That is not true," Grant protested. "We never knowingly killed any–"

"Enough," Rashid barked. "Tell me something worth knowing. Or you go back into the hole, but more importantly your wife and son dies."

Grant started weeping. Tears ran down his grime covered cheeks. Eventually, he raised his head. "You have to promise. Promise in Allah's name you will leave my family alone?"

The men around them stood straighter at the name of their God. Rashid himself was taken aback.

A kafir, unbeliever, just used Allah's name. Of course, being a CIA agent, Rashid suspected Grant spoke Arabic.

He gestured to one of his men. The ropes were removed from Grant's body. He was helped into a new chair, and a glass of water handed to him. A man arrived with a table, and another with a tray. Grant was given a plate of humus and pitta bread. He didn't touch the food.

Rashid came forward, tore off a piece of the bread and dipped it in the humus. Then he lifted his hanky and put it in his mouth.

"Eat," he said to Grant.

If Grant had four hands he would have eaten with all of them. He finished, licked his fingers, burped, and sat back in the chair.

Rashid was observing him quietly. *"Inshallah,* you have survived. *Alhamdulillah,* he brought you to me."

Around Rashid his men murmured Ameen and lowered their heads.

Grant nodded. *"Shukran."* Thank you, in Arabic.

"Now," Rashid said, "Tell me what you know"

Grant spoke. When he finished, Rashid stared at him for a very long time. Then he removed his glasses. Took his handkerchief off.

He looked Grant in the eyes and said, "Are you sure about this?"

Grant nodded. "I swear on the life of my wife and son. If this is the price I have to pay for their lives then so be it." Grant's voice was stronger, but once again tears spilled out of his eyes. He sniffed and wiped his cheeks.

Rashid shook his head slowly, trying to believe what he just heard. He said to Gant, "My men will help you to find accommodation, and you will be my guest. Then travel to London and await my instructions. Your family will be safe as long as you follow my orders."

Rashid closed his eyes and looked skywards. What had he done to deserve such a great prize? The angels of Gabriel were looking down on him today.

"Bismillah Rahman ir Rahim," he whispered fervently. "I will change the course of history."

CHAPTER 5

Podolsk,

Russia

One year ago

The new US President, Bertram Ryan and his decade and a half younger, glamorous wife, Janice, had just taken residence inside the White House, and their photo was posted over the front page of the Washington Post.

Sat inside the Zil limousine, Rashid stared at the photo of the First Couple as the car raced down the M2, the three lane highway that connected Moscow to Podolsk. Podolsk was an industrial town, ringed by factories with residence and offices in the center.

Rashid turned to his fellow passenger, Borislov Medvedev, the former KGB and now SVR Colonel, Chief of the First Directorate. The First Directorate still dealt with all matters relating to the USA and Canada, the department's name a throwback to the KGB days.

Borislov was also holding the same newspaper in his hands, staring at the same photo. He swore under his breath.

"What do you think?" Rashid asked Borislov.

Whereas Rashid always looked smart, Borislow managed to look crumpled despite his uniform. White hair stuck out of his nostrils, and his shoulders were always stooped. But a hard, glittering pair of dark eyes danced inside their bushy, eye browed orbits. Eyes that missed very little.

His grey-white hair was still plentiful and fell over his forehead, Rashid noted with some jealousy.

Borislov continued to stare at the photo, shaking his head. "I can't believe it."

Rashid nodded, and looked out the window at the speeding landscape. Green hills rose in both directions, resplendent in the summer heat. Moscow Oblast, the region surrounding Moscow ,and Russia in general, was freezing in winter and boiling in summer. *Now the blue sky and white sailboat of clouds made the country look nice*, Rashid thought.

Within half an hour, they had arrived at their destination. They sat for a while, looking at the row of two story houses that formed an entire block of residences for the factory workers. Nondescript and yellow walled, all of them looked the same. It was late afternoon, and the workers were coming home. Some on bicycles, now that it was summer, others in their Lada and Skoda cars, still the mainstay of passenger vehicles outside Moscow.

The driver pointed to a figure on the pavement. "There she is, sir."

They watched the woman, dressed in a light blue coat and brown pants, her hair tied back in a ponytail, approach an apartment and produce a set of keys to open the door. Borislov and Rashid alighted. Borisloe knocked on the door, and after a while, the woman opened. They knew the woman lived alone. Her parents were dead, and she was a Communist Party worker and taught english language to middle grade students in school.

Her eyes widened when she saw Borislov's uniform. Rashid saw a pale skinned face, the nose small, eyes large and blue, hair light brown. An attractive face and also familiar.

"Anna Ramitorva?" Borislov asked. He held his hands up after the woman nodded. "Don't be scared. We are not here to cause trouble." He tried to smile, but on his face it looked like a hyena baring its teeth.

"What do you want?" Anna asked.

"Can we please come in?" Borislov asked. "You are not in any danger, but we wouldn't be here if your country didn't need you."

Rashid remembered a line from Oscar Wilde. *Patriotism is the last refuge of the scoundrel.*

But it seemed to work on Anna. She opened the door wider.

They went inside. It was a simple, but well decorated *kvartira*, or apartment, they stepped into. Framed photos of Lenin and Marx adorned the walls. The sound of a Russian news channel came from the TV. Anna turned it off and walked to the kitchen, motioning her guests to take a seat at the table.

Rashid couldn't help staring at her when she came back with a tray and three cups of coffee. So was Borislov. The two men simply gaped at her.

Anna was a simple woman, it was plain to see. The only makeup she wore was mascara. That alone was enough to make her large eyes stand out, framed by the high cheekbones. It was a beautiful face.

Anna returned their scrutiny with an impassive face, then dropped her gaze to the floor. She scratched her neck.

"What do you want from me?"

Borislov and Rashid glanced at each other. It was the Russian who spoke. "I, we, the Motherland, wants you to perform in a theatre."

Anna's expressive face creased, the smooth forehead wrinkling in the middle. "Theatre? Why?"

"You have taken part in the Bolshevik Theatre in Podolsk, haven't you?"

Anna was taken aback, but then she recovered. After all, even today, the Party knew everything about everyone. *Perestroika* and *Glasnost* were distant memories.

"I have, yes. So is this the national chapter of the Bolshevik Theatre?"

Borislov rubbed his hands together and exhaled. "Not quite, no, *Debushka.* Why don't you sit down?"

*****

Once they were back in the Zil speeding back towards Moscow, Rashid spoke. "So then. Will you help me?"

Borislov looked at him critically. "Tell me."

"I need to find an American called Dan Roy."

"I will activate the usual channels. Do you want him dead?"

Rashid clenched his jaws. "No. He will die by my hands."

40

CHAPTER 6

Eight months ago

Geneva

Switzerland

Lake Geneva sparkled like crystal under a perfect blue sky. Along the eastern shore was a sleek modernist building, contrasting with surrounding forested mountains and the medieval turrets of nearby Chillon Castle. A silver Bentley Continental GT approached the building, winding its way past triangular buildings along the lakeshore. It pulled onto the premises as the roar of its engine faded, leaving only the sound of birdsong and gently lapping water.

A valet waved the driver through a darkened archway into an underground garage. Inside the garage was a superb collection of luxury cars. The valet opened the passenger side door of the Bentley and Anna Ramitorva stepped out. A floral headscarf obscured most of her face but revealed a few dark curls. Anna looked around briefly, her eyes passing over a yellow Lamborghini Aventador and a Koenigsegg Agera R in black. She turned her head gracefully and went through a discreet doorway.

Anna barely looked like the woman from Podolsk. Her slouched posture and plain face had gone. There was a spring in her steps, heels clicking on the floor. She wore heavy makeup, and her hair, loose around her shoulders, was done up by the finest salon in Moscow's Tverskaya district.

The clinic she had entered was private in every sense of the word. It was known among the uber wealthy as being one of the finest plastic surgery clinics in the world. Its discretion and level of service came with a price tag that fewer than one percent of people could ever hope to pay.

Not satisfied that even that level of quality would ensure the expertise she needed, Anna refused to see anyone but the best surgeon working at the clinic. Dr Mettler had 30 years of experience in facial plastic surgery and was assigned to the task.

That sunny morning was his third meeting with Anna. Like the previous two visits, she came alone.

"Wonderful to see you again, madam," he said, pulling out her seat as she sat down in his office. The white, streamlined room was decorated with a single contemporary sculpture of twisted metal.

"Now," Dr Mettler said. "As we discussed, your requirements are very specific. Nothing wrong with that, of course. But I want to make sure we're absolutely clear before we proceed."

"It would concern me if you are not absolutely clear already," Anna replied.

"I can assure you I know what's required," the surgeon told her, using his thumb and ring finger to smooth down his already pristine moustache. "This is simply a final meeting to make sure you haven't changed your mind about any aspect of the surgery and to see if you have any further questions."

"I do not."

"Then we'll begin tomorrow as planned."

*****

Two days later, after the surgery, they were sitting in the same office. This time, Anna's face was swollen and heavily bandaged, and only her remarkably dark eyes were visible.

"As you know, we went in behind the ears and at the frontal hairline," Dr Mettler said. "The sutures are as discreet as our clinic itself. No one will ever know you had surgery."

Anna nodded.

"In two weeks, you'll notice significant recovery. In four weeks, you can live your life and forget this ever took place."

There was silence as a clock's ticking echoed around the room.

"Is there anything we can do for you in the meantime?" the surgeon added.

"Yes. I want you to delete all the files you have on me," Anna replied.

"Madam. This is the most discreet clinic in Europe. We have…"

"Delete the files, then give me the device they were stored on. Or people in all kinds of circles you like to think you're part of will hear that your secret neurological disorder has meant you've been botching surgery for the last two years."

"What do you... I have no such disorder…," the doctor said, his brow furrowed and his eyes searching Anna's face for answers. She was expressionless.

"Give me the laptop, and it'll stay that way."

In a state of shock, the surgeon told his confused receptionist to hand over a laptop to the woman.

*****

Two weeks later, Anna returned to the clinic. The doctor noticed immediately that her dressing had been replaced.

"Who did your new dressing, madam, if you don't mind me asking?"

"I did it myself."

"Well, I must say, it's been done perfectly."

After removing the dressing, he told her she had completely healed. Much quicker than expected. The job had been simple, in the end. The nasal bridge was lifted by quarter of an inch, a four-inch stitch was applied at the top of the neck at the back, and the eyebrows were lifted slightly.

People came to Dr Mettler for far more complex facial plastic surgery. He wondered once again why this woman had come here, and who she really was. Her need for secrecy was extreme. Dr Mettler had operated on Hollywood A list celebrities and signed forty page NDA's. But he never had to hand over his laptop.

"You've done your job well then, doctor," Anna told him. "Thank you. I'd also like to thank all of your staff personally if you wouldn't mind."

"Certainly," Dr Mettler said, pushing down on a button and calling the staff on duty to his office. The receptionist and two female nurses in light pink uniforms stood next to Dr Mettler, smiling and clasping their hands behind their backs.

There was knock on the door.

"I'll be back in a minute," Anna. said. Without a word, she opened the door and then stepped outside the room. Anna strode down the corridor, and then down the stairs into the courtyard.

Another woman stepped in, roughly the same age as Anna. A suppressed Glock 22 appeared in the woman's hand like magic.

With surgical precision, the woman put a bullet in the foreheads of each person. She ended with the receptionist, who was the only one of them to start screaming. The door was shut. She listened with one ear to the wood for a sound then opened it a crack. The gleaming clinical hallway was empty. The clinic had a minimal number of staff, which helped. She slipped out, closed the door and went rapidly, but silently, down the stairs. Anna was waiting for her in the silver Bentley. No one saw her start the car and leave.

CHAPTER 7

Present Day

London

Dan stared back at Jeff impassively. He didn't reply or show any emotion. It tended to disconcert people, but Jeff merely held his eyes, then looked away, stretching his legs.

Was that a signal?

Dan glanced all around him. No one in the pub had moved. Dan was sitting with his back to the wall and he had a 180-degree angle covered. Nothing unusual hit his eyes. When he looked back at Jeff, the man had the hint of a smile on his lips.

"You really are paranoid, aren't you?" Jeff said.

For some reason, Dan didn't like the guy. He was acting far too casual for someone with bad news. Either he was bluffing or trying to play it cool. But Dan brushed the feeling aside. What he felt was not important. His gut told him something much bigger was going down here tonight.

"You just told me I was a wanted man. Now you expect me not to be paranoid?"

Jeff nodded. "What I mean is there's no danger here. That's why I chose this place and not one in central London. You weren't followed?"

"Don't think so. How about you?"

"Ditto. Anyone who came in after me has been in a group or a couple. No suspects."

Dan nodded, letting his eyes roam around the place once again.

Then he asked, "Can you explain what you meant?"

Jeff licked his lips. "Jim McBride is a friend of mine. I owed him from my Army days."

"Right, I know that."

"I knew about you as well, obviously, from the US Embassy job a couple of years back. But in certain circles, it is also known that to get to you we have to go through an agent."

"That's the way it works with most lone operators."

"Yes. In your case, McBride is the best link we have. By the way, where are my manners? You need a drink. Let me get you one."

"A diet coke please. No alcohol."

"Nonsense. It's cold outside. A beer will warm you up."

Dan wanted to argue, but Jeff was already gone. Again, Dan watched him closely. He acted normally, ordering a drink, then leaning against the bar. Dan didn't trust him. He was trying hard to be friendly.

Jeff came back with a pint. Dan took a sip, and his love of English craft beer was immediately rekindled. But he put the glass down.

"Carry on."

"You know how the CIA denies it has a base in UK?"

"Yup."

"But there are scores of CIA agents in the Embassy. Well, we sometimes have parties at the Embassy in Grosvenor Square. Thrown by Her Majesty's Secret Service, or us, to meet everyone."

"Where you Brits pretend to drink and laugh, but actually you're checking out the American Embassy officials and agents. Yeah, I know. So what?"

"Your reputation precedes you, Mr. Roy. Yes, you are entirely correct. It's the special relationship at work, you see. But we need to be sure we are having the relationship with the right people."

"So you check them out. Got that."

"A man approached me. Name of Grant, from Idaho. Ring any bells? He's an Embassy official so that has to be his real name."

Dan searched his mind and came up with a blank. "No."

"He started talking about the Embassy attack, and how an unknown black ops agent saved the day. I realized after a while he was trying to get information out of me."

Dan narrowed his eyes. "What did you tell him?"

"Nothing. He took my number, then got back to me the next day. His job title is cultural attache which means absolute piffle, as you know."

"You think he's an agent."

"I know so. He more or less confessed. He does contract work at the Central European research desk in Langley. He told me that as a barter. He exposes himself a little, and I tell him what I know of you."

"And did you?"

Jeff took a long sip and smacked his lips. "I asked him why he wants to know. Of course, when I said that he guessed I know your true identity, or I wouldn't be, as you say in America, playing hardball."

Dan flexed his jaws. He didn't like where this was going. "I think he knew already. That's why he approached you at the Embassy party. Probably was waiting for a suitable opportunity."

"Correct." After a pause, Jeff said, "Anyway, I pressed him for why he wanted to know. You'll never guess his answer."

Jeff paused and the crow's feet at the corner of his eyes crinkled. He spoke slowly, with deliberate effect. *"You are a threat to national security."*

Dan leaned back against the wall, breath suddenly leaving his chest in a rush. Truth was, he wasn't completely surprised. He had done and seen things that could bring down a lot of powerful people. But so had three hundred or so other special forces operatives. Why was he being singled out?

"Did he say why?" Dan managed to ask.

"No. What he did say was more than enough though."

Dan passed a hand over his face. "This guy, Grant, must've known you'll pass the information onto McBride, right?"

"I thought so too, yes."

"Then me being here is a risk. I'm under surveillance already." Dan's eyebrows knotted together. "And you knew that would be the case. Then why did you call me?"

Jeff breathed out. "Because the guy we suspect of being a double agent is also Grant."

CHAPTER 8

By the time Dan left the pub, it was close to midnight. It was closing time, and the bartenders were going around, claning up empty glasses from vacant tables. Jeff had left, but Dan had stayed back to have some pub food as he was starving. He had booked a hotel in central London, near Soho in Leicester Square. The place held memories from last time.

Dan left a tip, despite knowing it wasn't what you did in a pub in England. But the fish and chips had been good. He didn't drink any more, he felt he needed his wits about him. He also needed a weapon, but Jeff was coy about that. It wasn't easy to get hold of weapons in this country, unless one had contacts. Dan knew that from previous experience. He had a couple of numbers he could call, all of them underground.

The drizzle had stopped when he came out of the pub. Streetlights glistened on rain slicked roads. Dan headed back the way he had come, heading for the train station. The black expanse of the Common lay to his left.

He picked up the first tail five minutes into his walk. Footsteps behind him, and the man was making no attempts to hide himself. If it was a man. Dan crossed the road. He felt the footsteps do the same. He was now on the side of the Common, the knotted clots of huge shadowed trees just a stone's throw away. Ahead of him, on the deserted road, he saw a shadow separate itself from the streetlamp and stand still. Another man. He turned until he was facing Dan.

Dan slowed his steps. From the corner of his eye, he saw another shape crossed the road slowly to his right.

He heard a rustling sound from his left. A figure broke in through the undergrowth, breath heaving with the exertion. Must be a big guy, judging by the sound.

Dan came to a stop. He was surrounded in all four directions. He glanced behind him and saw the man following him about ten yards behind. The guy to his left was the closest, and also the biggest. Dan could barely see him, his hulking shape half hidden in the bush.

The man ahead of him walked towards Dan. He stopped roughly ten yards away. "Dan Roy?" he called out.

Dan said nothing. How many more were hiding? Where was the car?

To his left, across the Common, lay the Royal Borough of Putney. But not for miles. All he had was cold grassland. At least it would be dark.

All four of them came closer. Dan stood stock still. These guys would be carrying, he was sure. He didn't have a weapon, not even a knife.

"You need to come with us." The man in front of him seemed to be the leader. He came closer, but stopped a couple of yards away. Light hair, likely blonde, longish. The accent was odd. Not English or American. Eastern European, Dan guessed.

Dan sensed the big guy to his left get closer. He glanced toward him. The head was lost in the shadows cast by the trees. The legs were like tree trunk. Dan was six three, two hundred ten after he lost some weight recently. This guy must be way over six five, Dan guessed.

Dan remained like a statue. The three men now formed a semicircle around him. The leader stepped closer, a gun appearing in his hand. A large handgun, 0.45 caliber. Maybe a Colt M1911, favored by many of Dan's friends. Personally, he liked the Sig P226.

"This doesn't have to end this way, Dan. We just want to talk," the leader said.

If he wanted to kill me, Dan thought, *he would've done it already.*

The guy from behind, and the one to his right were now by his elbows. An arm's length away. The big guy was at an angle to the left. Dan knew what they were waiting for. They wanted him to make the first move. He wouldn't give them that pleasure.

"Okay," Dan said. "Who are you?"

The gun remained pointed at his chest. "Friends. Sorry about the gun. But you have a reputation."

"I'll come," Dan said.

"Good," Mr. Blond said. "This way." He pointed the gun to the right. Dan knew he was in a rush. Guns are unusual in England, and showing it on a street was asking for trouble. Dan waited, relaxed.

He heard a sound to his right. All heads turned to the sound. It was a man, walking his dog. The little terrier strained at the leash, making his owner walk faster.

Dan cleared his throat. "Hey John," he shouted. The man stopped, and turned toward them. It wasn't hard to see something was weird here. Four men almost surrounding one guy.

"John, it's me, Barry." Dan said, still in a loud voice, hoping to attract more attention.

The man was on the road, trying to get his dog back on the pavement. He seemed confused. "I'm not John. You must have me confused."

Dan turned to cross the road. "Sure, you do, pal."

He bumped against the man to his right, who was blocking his way. Dan hugged the man to himself, hard. The man flinched, expecting trouble.

He didn't expect a hug.

First rule of combat. Always do the unexpected.

No movement is possible in a close embrace. The hands are useless. Dan could feel the man's weapon in the shoulder holster. Too bad he couldn't reach it.

Dan gripped the man to his own chest, holding him tight around the waist. He propelled the guy backwards. Dan craned his neck back and brought his wide forehead slamming down on the man's nose. He howled in agony. Dan repeated the process, and the guy went limp.

Dan felt a blow from behind, jarring his head. He turned, holding the guy as a shield, driving him backwards against his attacker.

They crashed into the undergrowth, Dan falling on top of them both.

Then he was up and running into the dark, rain swept expanse of the Common.

CHAPTER 9

His boots were made for walking, and better than sneakers on wet grass. Dan pumped his legs, hurtling down a muddy path with trees on either side. He sensed a clearing up ahead and strained his ears for the sound of traffic. Instead, he heard footsteps. Before he could judge how close they were, a shape crashed into him from behind.

The body was heavy, and Dan felt his breath whoosh out of his chest as he fell sideway, ribs crushing on the ground. Luckily the ground was wet. Despite his size, Dan kept himself agile with Yoga and running. But this guy who had caught up him with was fit, too, or else he wouldn't have caught up with him.

Dan rolled on the ground, mud and water splashing into his face. His attacker lost his grip, and Dan folded his knees and kicked out viciously. He heard a grunt as his feet slammed into the guy's chest. He went sprawling backwards. It was Dan's turn to attack, which he did in one fluid, almost graceful motion, catapulting himself at the man.

Dan's shoulders cannoned into the guy's chest just as he was trying to get up. He crashed back down, and Dan straddled him. He tried to punch Dan, but he was feeble now. Two sharp punches rocked his head back. Dan was off him immediately, scurrying into the bushes. He hid, his eyes having grown used to the dark.

Two men came running. One held a gun and Dan recognized the leader, who swore in a foreign tongue when he saw the shape on the ground. They had a quick conversation in raised voices. Giving their position away. Not seeking cover.

They were hired muscle, nothing special. Not even basic army level. They were competent thugs, men who made a living out of intimidation and violence, but no match for a black ops, special forces trained operative like Dan.

Dan breathed in relief. He was worried at first, but barring the gun, he had no real need for concern.

While the two men argued, Dan stole out from the brush, uncoiling himself like a serpent. Darkness afforded him protection. He grabbed the leader by the knees from behind, bringing him down. At the same time, his fingers closed around the wrist holding the gun. Dan held the gun arm away from him while he stomped on the shoulder of the man on the floor hard enough to dislocate the joint. The man screamed.

The speed of Dan's movements took the other guy by surprise. Dan was kicking with his leg, sliding on the ground, almost losing control of the gun hand.

The other guy slipped, falling heavily. The gun fired, the loud blast like an explosion in the silent night. Dan bent his elbow and drove into the leader's face. He had to do it twice before the gun came loose in his hands.

The other guy got to his feet, and they circled each other. The man's hand dived inside his jacket, and Dan didn't wait. He fired, aiming for center mass. The man fell backwards, arms cartwheeling. He fell, and this time lay still.

The leader was still half conscious. The other guy was out cold. Third one was dead. And they had left the fourth guy by the road, Dan guessed.

Dan knelt, and slapped the leader across the face. The man moaned, eyes shut in pain. Dan pressed his knuckles into the man's sternum, rubbing hard. The man squirmed, then shouted in pain.

"Who sent you?" Dan asked. He got no answer.

Dan patted the man's pockets. He found a cigarette packet, a lighter, and a knife. He held a flame to the tip of the knife, keeping an eye on the unconscious man as well as looking around him. The flame would be like a beacon to anyone watching. As soon as the tip of the knife glowed red hot Dan turned the flame off. He grabbed the leader by the neck, slapped him twice, then pulled his head up.

The man's eyes widened when he saw the gleaming blade. Dan moved it closer to his face.

"No, please," the guy mumbled.

"What's your name?"

The man stared at the glowing tip, then at Dan's face, which he couldn't possibly see.

"Name?" Dan repeated.

"Ric...Ricky."

"Where are you from Ricky?"

"Romania."

"Who sent you after me?"

"I... I don't know."

Dan moved the knife tip closer to the man's eyes. He thrashed and fought, but he was weak, and Dan was holding him down by the neck.

"What did he look like? Where did you meet him?" Dan knew this man wouldn't know much. He was the lowest on the food chain. But something was better than nothing.

"If you don't tell me, this knife is going in your eye. Shall I start with the right or left?"

"Wait!" the man gasped. "A warehouse in the east... east London."

"Give me a location."

"Plaisstow."

Dan got the name of the street off Ricky, then stood. Bullets were a waste on him, and he was nothing anyway. Dan kicked his head twice, and Ricky was out cold once again.

Dan shivered. The night was getting colder. He frisked the men quickly and took their weapons. Then he set off at a brisk jog back to the road near the pub. The man he had knocked out was still lying flat. A search on him revealed nothing, not even a gun.

At Wimbledon town center, his watch said past 1am, and he had just missed the last train to Waterloo. He took an Uber back to his hotel, surprised to find the owner still at his desk.

Dan was aware he looked weird in his wet, mud splattered clothes. But that didn't seem to bother Mr. Belchamber much. He was in his sixties and was every bit the English gentleman in his pinstripe suit which he wore every day. He had been the owner three years ago, when Dan had last been to London.

He said, "How nice to see you, Mr. Roy."

Dan halted. He wasn't accustomed to others knowing his name, and it bugged him. He liked being invisible. But Mr. Belchamber had checked him in this morning after his night flight arrived from Washington Dulles.

"Nice to see you too," Dan said. He didn't get too close to the counter behind which Mr. Belchamber was sitting. He wanted to get up to his room, shower, then go to sleep. He was exhausted, that bone aching, deep tiredness that comes after a long flight and a sudden encounter with four murderous thugs.

"Stay for a nightcap?" Mr. Belchamber said, pulling out a bottle of Drambuie from the counter. "When the Queen Mother was alive, this was her favorite nocturnal tipple." He winked.

"Thanks, but not tonight." Dan lifted his palms. "I'm shattered."

"No problem. By the way, there was a call for you."

Dan stopped and turned, instantly alert. "From who?"

"He didn't leave his name. English chap. Said it was about Gibraltar remaining in Spanish hands after Brexit."

Jeff Pearce. Gibraltar was the code they were using.

Dan wondered if Jeff knew about what happened tonight.

"Thank you," he said, and went up the stairs.

CHAPTER 10

The Scorpion pressed herself into the shadows. She was outside a massive estate in Weybridge, Surrey. She had followed Ali Marutov from his extravagant villa in Greece to this place, his base in England. The neoclassical mansion on the outskirts of the town was no less impressive than Marutov's home in Greece, but it seemed a million miles away in the pale English twilight.

Natasha moved softly with every step as she made her way across the grounds. Cold air filled her lungs as she tried to control her breathing, which inevitably grew heavier no matter how many times she'd been in this kind of situation.

As she got close to the mansion, she crouched down among the wet bushes on the edge of the garden. A light was on in one of the mansion's many windows. That was worth noting. But more significant was the presence by the back entrance. Two guards were on duty, positioned under a porch between stone columns. One guard was standing, looking alert as his head swiveled on square shoulders to observe the grounds. The other appeared less interested in doing his job and was slumped in a chair. Both wore coats big enough to be concealing weapons.

Natasha made a quick decision to break in rather than take the guards on. It was possible she could get to Marutov without the guards ever knowing she'd been there. Dressed in skin-tight black clothes, the Scorpion made the increasing darkness her ally. She moved rapidly and silently, half-crouching, to a corner of the mansion. She could see that the right side of the property wasn't used for anything aesthetic. It was unlit and lined with industrial-sized waste containers.

She assessed her options. There were no windows open. She could break one, but she would have to make at least some noise doing it. There was a small door with a lock that looked as if it could be picked, but that would take time. Then fate handed her the answer. A drop of good luck trying to counterbalance the ocean of bad luck she'd had during her life.

A woman who looked like catering staff opened the door and was leaving it open as she brought out one bag of trash after another.

Following this woman in was a good move. She might have to be put out of action temporarily if she spotted Natasha. But only unconscious, not permanently damaged. That was worst case scenario.

Natasha pushed herself fully against the smooth wall, the open door obscuring her from view. She waited to hear the shuffling of feet and the rustling of bags. When that noise stopped, Natasha peeked between door hinges and saw the woman turn to walk back inside. The Scorpion paused for a moment. She slipped round the door and followed the catering lady inside.

The woman was just disappearing around a corner but stopped suddenly and looked back as Natasha slipped into an alcove filled with cleaning gear. Her heart pounded as she waited for the woman to come back, notice her, and for all hell to break loose. But she never came.

Forgetting the close call, Natasha made her way carefully into the heart of the mansion. She knew she would have to go up, away from the staff quarters. The room with the light on was the obvious place to aim for.

She made her way up a stone staircase and, gently pushing a door open, found herself in an astonishing room. Nobody was in here –

it was filled only with splendor. Intricate floral patterns in gold leaf framed walls of red velvet, and huge chandeliers hung over it all. She thought back briefly to the squalor she had lived in as a child. Then, as she had long ago been trained to do, checked herself and removed any thoughts other than the task at hand.

She headed up another staircase, this one much grander than the first. And much more open. She felt very exposed, but it seemed like 90 per cent of the rooms in this house weren't occupied. This could be easy, she thought. She was wrong.

Approaching the top of the stairs, Natasha could see the room she assumed Marutov to be in. She'd observed him going into the house earlier in the day so she knew he was home. The presence of two sturdy guards outside the room all but confirmed Marutov would be in there. She should have known the guards downstairs wouldn't be the only ones. But this time she had an advantage. She was approaching from behind. That meant she could get in close before they knew she was there, which was exactly how she liked it.

She knew she could dispose of one of the guards immediately. The other would fight, but she was confident. Her hand moved towards her belt, the hard metal of a handle slipping into her hand. The needles that had become her weapon of choice were perfect for this sort of situation, and she had several concealed around her waist.

She leapt up the final two stairs and across the corridor in one move, pulling out the needle by its handle and driving it into the neck of a guard. The Scorpion knew exactly where to put it – below the angle of the jaw where the carotid artery and jugular vein are found. The guard made almost no sound, just a sharp intake of breath and a blood-filled gurgle.

It was enough to draw the attention of the second guard, who spun around to face her as he was still assessing what the hell was going on. Natasha shattered his shin with a kick to his left leg as her hands let the first guard's body slip to the floor.

The not-yet-dead guard reached for his gun. Natasha pulled another needle from her belt, this time with her left hand and thrust it into his chest with brutal power. A fist punch with a sting. She gently lowered his body to the ground, the scent of his sweat filling her nostrils as he drew his last breath. She had made so little noise Marutov might not even know he was no longer guarded.

Opening the door slowly would give him warning, so she kicked it open hard.

Marutov was sitting in an armchair facing her. His spine jerked upright as Scorpion stepped inside the room and kicked the door shut.

He froze for a moment, staring into the Scorpion's green eyes dilated with adrenaline. He pulled a gun from beneath the blanket. Natasha ran two paces then went to ground, sliding across the polished floor and along the side of the armchair. She straightened up behind the chair and yanked Marutov's hair back with her left hand. Her right held her kukri knife to his throat. The Nepalese knife with its curved 11-inch blade was enough to terrify even the most hardened terrorist.

"I've waited for this moment a long time," she whispered.

Suddenly weak, this wealthy and feared man pleaded in a shaking voice.

"Wait. Please," Marutov said. "I can help you."

"Can you?" Natasha asked, whispering menacingly in his ear.

"Yes. There's something you need to know."

As Natasha battled the feeling that she should believe him, a door creaked open. At the side of the room stood a woman and a young girl. The girl was about ten, dressed in pajamas. She was ready for bed; not for the horrific scene she was now witnessing.

Natasha knew they were Marutov's wife and daughter. She had never killed women or children, despite there having been times when it would have made her life much easier. But they had seen her face, and that was a problem. Normally, anyone who might identify her would be killed.

Her stomach tightened as she wrestled with the dilemma.

"Ask yourself. How did I know you were getting married?" Marutov said. "Who let me into your wedding when it was so closely guarded?" Natasha looked into his eyes, right beneath hers.

"People closest to you are your biggest threat, not me," he added.

"Who is?" she hissed, pulling his hair violently. He yelled in pain.

"Trust no one," Marutov whispered. "If you want to know more you'll have to keep me alive."

Natasha saw the wife had disappeared from the room, she presumed to get help. She was out of time.

She ran out of the room, past the bodies of the guards and down the magnificent staircase. Out into the cold night.

She jumped into her car, tucked away beside a quiet field near the estate.

She made her way through leafy country lanes, trying to keep her speed down, but knowing she was going too fast to keep a low profile. Suddenly, she noticed a car going even faster than hers. It was approaching from behind at ridiculous speed.

Without any doubt it was chasing her, she put her foot down. Past quaint houses with well-kept gardens and families inside watching

TV, she tore through the quiet streets of Weybridge, zig-zagging between cars parked along the street.

She went through a red light, clipping the rear bumper of a car. As she slowed down momentarily, the car chasing her rammed into her side. She managed to keep going and take a side street as the other car continued on the bigger road. She exited the side street and headed for a secluded street opposite, but another collision, this time harder, sent her car careering onto its side and then its top. The sound of shattering glass was the last thing she heard before she passed out.

CHAPTER 11

Natasha was brought slowly back to consciousness by the rhythmic beeping of hospital machinery. The first thing she noticed was that her mouth was completely dry and her lips stuck together. Strangely, that was the physical sensation she was aware of before the awful throbbing in her head. She tried to raise her left hand up toward her hair, which felt matted and wet on one side. Something prevented her from moving. She realized she was attached to some kind of equipment that may or may not have been keeping her alive.

She lay in the stillness of the hospital ward, trying to remember what had happened. She could recall being chased at high-speed. But she had no idea who was driving the other car or how the chase ended in a crash.

She also thought back to Marutov's mansion, and in particular what had happened when she found him. She hadn't managed to kill him or find out what he was talking about when he said she should trust no one. Including people close to her. She hadn't even managed to steal intel from his home. More than all of that, she couldn't help thinking about the look on the little girl's face. It wasn't fear; it was bewilderment. Someone trying to completely recalibrate their understanding of the world they live in. *It'd be surprising to most people to learn an assassin has compassion and principles*, she thought to herself. *And it should be surprising because most don't.*

Her musing on morality was interrupted by the door opening. A male nurse walked in.

"How are we doing?"

"Who's *we*?" Natasha asked. A meaningless sarcastic response was better than giving something away unnecessarily. It might help her to say she was doing either 'just fine' or 'terribly' depending on what the situation turned out to be.

"I'm only doing good if you're doing good, so I guess *we* is both of us," the nurse replied. Nice. He turned to face Natasha. He gave her a smile that was charming enough to momentarily make the pain stop.

He came closer and adjusted the drip on her arm. She noticed that the forearm sticking out of his uniform was wide and strong.

"Do you know what happened to you?" he asked her. This time, she chose silence as a means of avoidance.

"You were in a car accident," he volunteered. "A passing car saw it and called the police." 'Police' was never a good word to hear, but she figured it was standard to call the police after a traffic accident.

"Anyway, get some rest," the nurse told her.

The next morning, Natasha woke up feeling only slightly better. She was in a room with four beds, but she noted that, like yesterday, she was the only patient. She felt hungry and hoped the strong-armed nurse would bring her breakfast. He arrived a short time later looking much more appealing than the breakfast.

"You again?" she said, smiling at him as he checked her over.

"Me again," he replied. "I'm gonna help you get moving a little today if you're good with that. The doctor says there's no major head injury. But you hurt your leg pretty bad so there'll have to be some rehabilitation on that."

"Fine. Thanks," Natasha said. She looked up at his face, and the soft, black hair falling in short curls over his square forehead. She thought he looked more like a Hollywood actor pretending to be a nurse.

When the nurse had left, the Scorpion lay back and thought to herself. She decided there was no advantage in getting out fast. Getting to Marutov would be much more difficult now. He would also likely be trying to get to her. She might not be any safer out in broad daylight and hardly able to move, than she was in here.

Just as she was getting used to being cared for by the cute nurse – nurse Delgado to give him his official name – things took a turn for the worse. Two police officers showed up wanting to talk to her.

The female officer was short and plump, and her small, glittering eyes bore into Scorpion's skull. She did most of the talking.

"Dark night in a quiet town, a car is seen doing F1 speeds driven by a woman dressed all in black," she said to Natasha. She was standing next to the bed. A male officer was sitting down looking at a phone. Scorpion said nothing.

"So, what's the story?" the dumpy officer asked her.

"I think you've covered it there," Natasha replied.

"Oh, good," the officer said. "Come on, Webster. We're finished here." The male officer stood.

"Great," he said, getting ready to leave while still looking at the phone.

"Sit down, Webster," the woman said. "Of course, we're not finished here." Webster looked at her and shook his head. He sat back down.

"I'd like to know why you were doing almost double the speed limit," the female officer said, turning back to Natasha. "I'm definitely within my rights to ask that. I'd also quite like to know who you are, and what you'd been doing leading up to the accident. And I'd love to know how you decided on your outfit."

"Is this the right place for this?" Natasha asked. "In a hospital where I'm still recovering from head injuries. Confused and

67

maybe capable of saying something to incriminate myself even though I've done nothing wrong? I'd be happy to come to a station when I've recovered to answer your questions. With a lawyer."

The officer eyeballed her. They stared at each other as Natasha observed the open mouth of someone who has difficulty breathing even sitting down, the yellow teeth with a gap at the front, and the short hair sticking to the officer's sweating neck just below her ears.

"Just get a statement and let's go," Webster said.

"She's not going to give a statement, Webster."

"Well just get her name and address then."

"The hospital gave us the name. What's your address?" the female officer asked Natasha. "If you refuse to give that, I'd have to say things are looking suspicious."

"11, Fonthill Gardens, Finsbury Park."

"Postcode?"

"N4 3FA."

The dumpy officer stared at Natasha one more time before assessing she wasn't going to get any information easily. The two officers got ready to leave.

"Oh, your passport," the female officer said. "Where is it?"

"At the address I gave you."

"You don't carry your passport with you?" "Do you?" Natasha asked.

Correctly sensing they would get nowhere fast, the two officers left.

CHAPTER 12

Dan stepped out of his hotel onto a lively Soho street. Londoners were sitting and chatting outside pubs and cafes despite the chill in the air. He walked past the Georgian townhouses of Mayfair and into Hyde Park, a leafy landmark that picnicking families, political protestors, and daytime drinkers all shared.

He headed over the gently rippling Serpentine Lake to the western end of the park. Jeff was sitting on a bench in the designated spot. Dan sat down next to him without greeting him. They both stared straight ahead as the aroma from Jeff's coffee mixed with the smell of the park's damp soil.

"This Brexit business doesn't get any easier, does it?" Jeff said.

"I have no desire to talk about Brexit if we don't need to. You all have fun with it thought," Dan replied. Jeff smiled.

Jeff's grey raincoat was folded neatly on the bench between them. Dan effortlessly pulled a folder from under it and slid it into his own jacket. He waited for a second then stood.

"And you have fun with that, buddy," Jeff muttered as Dan walked away.

He continued west to where Kensington Palace came into view on the edge of the park. The 17th century red-brick building, where Prince Charles had lived with Diana after they married, appeared less impressive than many of Europe's royal homes. Dan recalled an old memory of footage showing the oceans of flowers left outside Kensington Palace by inconsolable members of the public when Princess Diana died. *Weird how this country goes crazy in its own little way from time to time,* he thought as he briefly observed the palace.

Dan wanted to get a look at what was in the folder as soon possible. He exited the park into the upmarket Kensington district and found the nearest pub. The Victorian-era Elephant and Castle did just fine. He ordered a diet coke then made his way to the bathroom. Locking himself in a cubicle, he opened the file. Dan wasn't sure he liked Jeff much, but the MI6 agent had done a good job getting this dossier on Grant Pearson together. He left without going back for his drink.

That evening, Dan waited close to the Embassy. It took Grant longer to come out than expected, but eventually he did. Grant unwittingly made the job of following him much easier by quickly getting drunk and suppressing his senses. Dan watched him from a distance as he had three quick drinks alone in a wine bar before meeting a female companion for dinner. Grant and the woman shared a bottle of wine as they ate dinner in an Italian restaurant that was trying to seem more upscale than it was. Wine and dinner complete, they came out and said their goodbyes before walking off in opposite directions.

Grant's next stop was the Knightsbridge area. Home to the famous Harrods department store and to the kind of very wealthy people who can afford to shop there. Dan watched as Grant darted into a door guarded by two extremely well-dressed and very stout doormen. Dan knew from the dossier that the venue was an exclusive members-only nightclub. Grant had been known to visit it at least once before.

Dan did a quick assessment of the building. It was in a row of ornate townhouses and was joined on either side to other properties. Options for entry or even getting a look inside were limited. He removed his beanie and straightened his hair. He made his way toward the nightclub entrance and the doormen.

"Evening, gentlemen," he said to the bouncers.

"It's a private event this evening, sir," one of them said without looking at Dan.

"Oh, yeah? Who's hosting?" Dan said casually.

"It's a mind your own business meeting," the other bouncer replied. Dan grinned.

"Nice," he said. Then he slipped a folded fifty pound note into the jacket pocket of the nearest doorman.

"Fifty more just for a name," Dan said.

Both doormen smiled.

"Is that how it works?" one of them asked. "Old-school?"

"Timeless," Dan replied.

"It's the Al-Falaj clan. Family gathering."

Dan's throat tightened, his nerve-endings tingling in response to the name.

"Thank you, gents," he said, his voice remaining casual. He strolled off, but alarm bells were ringing. It wasn't long ago he'd killed Waleed Al-Falaj. Now, Grant was meeting with Waleed's family. He wanted answers, fast.

When Grant got back to his apartment later that evening, Dan was waiting discreetly across the street. As Grant was clumsily opening the door, Dan marched swiftly up behind him and clamped his hand over his mouth. His other hand held Grant tightly to stop him from moving. But the amount Grant had drunk meant it was more like holding him up.

"Not a fucking word," Dan hissed in his ear. Few people would be able to struggle free once Dan had his strong grip around them, let alone a man who could hardly hold himself upright.

He walked Grant into his apartment and locked the door.

"Can we talk about this another time?" Grant joked. When Dan didn't answer, Grant tried to free himself. Dan span him around and hit him with a crunching right hand to the jaw. Grant collapsed immediately and hit the floor, the back of his head bouncing up off the floor. Dan feared he might have killed him with one punch before he got any information out of him.

He picked Grant up and flung him on the plush sofa. He got his face in close, his knife held flat under Grant's right eye.

"I'll take this eye first, then the next one before morning," Dan said.

"Go on, then," Grant replied, breathing heavily. Adrenaline had kicked in, and Grant was suddenly sober.

Dan slowly dragged the point of his knife under Grant's eye, nicking the skin, allowing a drop of red blood to ooze out. Grant squirmed as Dan held him by the neck.

"Okay, okay," Grant begged. "I'll tell you."

"Damn right you will."

Grant licked his lips, sweat pouring down his face. He croaked, "Rashid Al-Falaj."

They stared at each other, their eyes inches apart. Their breathing echoed around the dark, empty apartment with its high ceilings. Dan felt his mouth go dry, and his pulse surged.

"Did you say Rashid Al-Falaj?" His voice was hoarse.

Grant nodded. "You... You killed his cousin, right?"

"How did you know that?"

"There's a file on you in Langley. You're listed as a black ops contractor."

Dan's fist became lax on Grant's neck as he grappled with the implications of what he was hearing.

Holy hell. He was in deeper shit than he had imagined. His fist tightened again as a snarl split his face. "Is that why you asked Jeff Pearce about me?"

"Pl... Please. They would kill me otherwise."

"What the hell do you think I'll do now?" Dan growled. But both of them knew the answer.

"I'm on your side," Grant whimpered.

"Like hell you are."

"They'll kill my wife and little boy! They had their pictures!"

Dan frowned. "What?"

"Rashid. He had my family photos, man. What was I supposed to do?"

Dan's hand became lax again and he stood, towering over Grant. He bent down quickly and searched Grant before he could stand up. Dan didn't trust him, still. This story could be a ruse to get Dan offtrack.

But if Grant was speaking the truth what the hell was going on? How did Rashid get pictures of a CIA agent's family?

Dan knew of the Al-Falaj family. Sure, they were powerful. Dan had broken up their terrorist cell inside USA last year. But no way could they infiltrate a CIA agent's personal information. Then a thought struck him.

"The woman you met tonight. Who was she?"

Grant was standing now. He tried to smooth his rumpled coat and shirt. He sniffed and wiped his face.

"She's, uh, a friend." His face betrayed the truth.

"You're sleeping with her, right?"

Grant looked to the floor. Dan shook his head. "You fool. I bet you my bottom dollar she's Russian. Where did you meet her? Embassy function? Russian American Business summit?"

Grant sighed. "Business summit. How did you know?"

"Because everyone knows it, asshole. What sort of a CIA agent are you? This is basic workcraft, man!"

"She... She seemed so different. She studied in New York. Oh god, I..."

"Shut up," Dan ground his teeth together. "Stop babbling. You're an idiot. You landed yourself in this position. What's her name?"

"Tatyana Mirov."

"What else do you know about her?"

When Grant said nothing, Dan stepped forward.

"Nothing. I don't know what they're planning. I swear, I don't," Grant whimpered. "They're just giving me instructions day-to-day."

Dan took a fist full of Grant's shirt and shoved him backwards. "Where do you meet her?"

Grant was about to answer when Dan saw a red dot dancing on Grant's chest. A second later, his chest exploded, his insides splattering across Dan's face.

Bullets came raining in thick and fast, hammering against metal and shattering glass. Within a minute, the heavy caliber bullets had demolished the entire room, tearing up the carpet, walls and furniture.

Dan dove behind the sofa, the window behind him. He had shouted at Grant, but it was too late.

Covering his head, Dan moved toward the exit. He got to the main door of the building and shaped to run, but he was tackled from the side. A man in a thick leather jacket was sitting on top of him, his hands around his throat. Dan plunged a thumb into the man's eye, making him shriek and turn his head. After a follow-up jab to the neck, the man shifted his weight enough that Dan could wriggle free.

Two more men came lunging at him. One made a weak attempt at grabbing him and ended up pulling his hair while Dan swung an elbow at lighting speed and smashed it into the attacker's cheekbone. He went down heavily. Dan turned and saw the third man was wearing brass knuckles. As the man tried to throw a punch, Dan blocked his arm and squeezed it, but was disoriented by a headbutt landing on the bridge of his nose.

Managing to stay on his feet, he was locked in a clinch with the attacker. For once, he ignored his own first rule of combat – always do the unexpected – and delivered a classic knee to the groin. The first attacker was getting to his feet, but Dan sprinted away into the night. He ran a few blocks and dived into the first black cab he saw. The driver was eyeing his bleeding nose in the mirror.

"Just drive," Dan said, in no uncertain terms. The driver averted his gaze.

Gathering his thoughts, Dan knew he needed to see Jeff. Quickly. A CIA agent had just been killed. That was a big deal.

CHAPTER 13

The Scorpion awoke to sunlight streaming through the hospital windows. She ran two fingers along the bed frame's cold metal – a texture that was comfortingly familiar. As had become routine, nurse Delgado walked in with breakfast.

"How are we doing?" he asked.

"Much better. Thanks for looking after me." She gave him a smile.

"The doctors are amazed how fast you're getting better," he told her. "It can't be only down to me. You must have good genes or something."

"I'm just stubborn," she said. "I push my body 'til it does what it's told."

Delgado smiled at her and raised his eyebrows. She'd been in the hospital for almost a week, and it had turned out her initial attraction to him wasn't only fleeting.

"Why the smile?" she asked him.

"Nothing," he said, looking at her admiringly. "I was gonna say I'm glad you ended up here, but that sounds weird."

"Yeah, thanks. You're glad I was in a car crash. Don't worry, I know what you meant."

The previous evening, he'd helped her take a walk around the hospital garden. A change of scenery during her rehabilitation. They'd chatted about how he'd decided to move over from Spain to work in the UK. How he hated the weather but enjoyed British humor and liked going to watch stand-up comedy around London. Natasha was looking forward to another afternoon with an arm around his shoulder. Purely for medical reasons, of course.

Later that morning, Natasha heard raised voices outside her room. One of them was Delgado's. The others were revealed when the two police officers from earlier in the week barged back into her ward. She rolled her eyes and faced away from them, resting her head on her pillow.

"Thanks for the fake address," Harris, the female officer said. "We found two decorators in a completely empty flat. They said no one lives there."

"You sure you went to the right place?" Natasha asked.

Harris gave her a *so that's how you want to play it* look.

"You're walking a very thin line. Sorry, hobbling a very thin line. I'll put it simply. Give us your real address, or we'll do you for obstruction," Harris told her.

"That was my address. The last place I lived. I went on holiday for a while and haven't sorted out a new place yet."

"That sounds like absolute tosh to me. How about you, Webster?"

"Pure tosh."

"You've been here a week, and you weren't that bad to begin with," Harris told Natasha. "I think you're more than well enough to come to the station now."

"The hospital decides when I'm well enough to be discharged."

Webster fixed Natasha with a cold stare. It was the first time he looked like he cared what was going on. He closed the door and leaned hard against it.

Harris approached Natasha quickly, reaching for something on her belt. The Scorpion suddenly feared they weren't cops at all, and could be hired assassins. If the hospital agreed to let them take her, she imagined the car they went to would be unmarked and the destination would not be a police station. As Harris reached her bed, there was a solid knock on the door. Harris stood stock still.

"A minute," Webster barked. Another knock came even harder.

"Open up!" Delgado demanded. He opened the door and Webster didn't resist.

"That's enough for today," Delgado told the officers. "She needs her meds then rest."

"We're not done," Harris said.

"If you're not arresting her then you're done," Delgado replied.

Webster tried to use his stare on Delgado as they walked out, but its effect was ruined by him being significantly shorter than the nurse.

"Thanks," Natasha said.

Delgado reached out his arms, handing Natasha her phone and purse.

"You'll need these," he said. "And you'll need to take that call."

Natasha looked at her phone. It was ringing. Delgado left the room and closed the door.

"Hello?" There was a moment's pause.

"The Scorpion," the caller said in a slow, calm voice. A menacing voice. Natasha said nothing. "You failed. Our friend in the big house. What happened?" Still, she said nothing. "Answer me!" the voice barked.

"I don't know if this is a safe line," she said.

"It's more dangerous not to talk. Believe me."

"It didn't make sense to do it there and then," she said.

"Your job was not to make sense. What did you get from him?"

"Nothing."

"You didn't find out anything?"

Natasha paused.

"No. Who are you?" she asked the man. She knew it wasn't Borislov, but guessed it was one of his colleagues. "FSB?"

"Worse than FSB," he told her.

"Worse?"
"We're in every corner of the planet. We have the money to do anything we want. Nothing escapes our knowledge. And no one, you should know."

"That doesn't tell me who you are," Natasha said.

"Cyclone," the man replied.

"Your group? Your group is called Cyclone?"

"You made a big mistake," the man replied. "You failed and you refused to cooperate. You'll pay for that."

The call ended.

Natasha was shaking as Delgado came back into the room. She suddenly felt weak. Pains from her injuries returned. She knew she had to escape. She was now sure the 'cops' were killers, hired by Cyclone, and if they came back a third time it would not end well.

"Everything okay?" Delgado asked.

"You need to help me," she said, looking into his eyes.

"What happened?"

"I can't tell you. But you need to get me out of here. Today."

"You're not ready," he told her.

"Please," she begged him, gently touching his arm. Their eyes met, and she was held captive in his.

He cocked his head to one side. "You know when I told you I came here from Spain?"

"Yeah?"

"You said you're from England, but your accent tells me otherwise."

She lowered her head. She knew she hadn't fooled him, but hoped against hope he would let it slide. He was a sweet guy, and now she would have to lie to him again.

"There are things," she said, "I can't explain."

The bed lowered as he sat down. He was close for her to smell his clean uniform and his body as well. A longing tightened inside the scarred chambers of her heart. When was the last time she had been with a man?

Thoughts of Dan Roy came floating back to her. Was it a coincidence that Delgado's dark hair and dark looks were so compellingly like Dan's?

She swallowed hard and banished the thoughts from her mind. It wasn't easy. Like sunlight peeking in through the blinds, Dan's face kept haunting her. But she forced herself to look back at Delgado.

"You running from something?" he asked gently. "Or someone?"

She looked away from him. The briefest movement of her head could be interpreted as a nod.

"Okay," he replied. "I'll get your things together. Be ready tonight."

That evening, he came into her room with her things. He lifted her out of bed. She put her arm around his shoulders as they walked steadily to the car park.

"Where do you wanna go?" he asked as they got into his car.

"Chelsea," she replied.

"Chelsea it is," he said.

"I really appreciate this," Natasha said to him as they drove. "I'll take you to dinner some time to thank you."

"You don't need to thank me, but dinner sounds great," he told her.

Approaching Wandsworth and the River Thames, Delgado took a right.

"You need to be crossing the river," Natasha told him.

"I know the way," he said.

Natasha looked at his face. She was skilled at reading expressions. His eyes were on the road, face unreadable. A cold dread settled into the pits of her stomach like a block of ice.

Delgado kept on driving, and apart from seeing the occasional slick of water to her right, she couldn't see any road signs.

She had made a mistake. The cops were not the danger. In fact, the worse the cops could have done was stick her in a cell. Now she was going to die.

"How much do they pay you?" she asked.

Delgado sighed. He looked so handsome, his chiseled jawbone lit up in the light from the dashboard.

Why did she always have to attract assassins?

"Enough to get the job done."

"You're good. Very good. You got my guard down, which isn't easy."

"Thank you." His tone was sincere. "Coming from you, that's a compliment. I've heard a lot about you."

She said nothing. The doors were locked already. They were driving down a part of London she had never been to before. She was lost.

"I guess there's no point in asking where you're taking me." she said in a flat voice.

"No, sorry."

His large hands gripped the steering wheel lightly. The car was an automatic. He kept glancing over to her. She figured it couldn't be a long journey due to the risk. Too many variable. She could launch herself at him. Claw his face. But he would simply stop the car and attack back. It would be over in minutes. She was way too weak to fight his tall, muscular frame right now.

But she needed to do something. She asked, "At least tell me this. Are you going to hand me over to them or do it yourself?"

She preferred the latter. She didn't trust this group called the Cyclone. Getting tortured for information, after what she'd just been through didn't bear thinking about.

She could see that he was heading for the river. They bounced over a railway track, and a sign appeared for the Imperial Wharf.

Her eyes swept around the dashboard. A flicker of movement to the right caught her eye. Something was moving by the lower glove compartment. It was below the level of the seat, so she could reach it with her hand, without moving the rest of her arm. It was a ballpoint pen.

Delgado shifted in his seat and looked at her. She froze. She could feel his eyes sweep up and down her body.

"What are you doing?" he asked.

She shrugged. "Nothing."

His eyes stayed on her for a while, and she glanced at him. Then he went back to the road. Immediately her fingers felt for the pen. Her fingers encircled, then lost the narrow shaft of the pen as the car jolted over a bump. She noticed he had sped up. A sign appeared which said *Boats, This Way.*

It was now or never. She had the pen in her hand. She would've loved to release the seat belt, but that would clearly warn him.

Gripping the pen like a knife, she launched herself at him. He saw her coming, and her movements were slow with the injury and weakness. But she knew it was an all or nothing move, so she had given it everything. His right hand left the steering and came up, but her hand had flown over by then. His hand hit her face, but the pen sank into his right eye socket with a squelching sound.

He howled. Both hands came off the steering and the car careened across the road. She didn't waste time on the car. She was dead if he was alive. Simple as that. The car was heading for a wall and the impact would be on his side.

She opened her door and reached to unlock her seatbelt. Delgado grabbed her hand and stopped her from releasing herself. The car swerved on the road as they struggled, the door swaying in the wind. Natasha rolled out of the vehicle as it smashed into a wall.

She tried to run but her leg was badly hurt. A new injury or the old one made worse, she wasn't sure. She stumbled away from the car. The nurse emerged, covering his eye with his left hand and firing a handgun with his right. Natasha leapt over a wall with no idea of the drop on the other side.

It was far enough to send a cutting pain through her leg. Almost instantly, she dealt with that shock like most people never could. She pinned herself to the wall, freezing wind whipping off the river into her face, as she watched Delgado approach the wall.

He peered over the wall, but Natasha was nowhere to be seen. He took his hand from his eye and looked in horror at the blood. Then his world went dark as a sharp object ploughed into his other eye. The Scorpion punched him first with her right hand then her left. She kicked him into the wall, blind and unconscious. She rifled through his pockets and found his phone and wallet. She calmly walked to the car, pulled out her bag and removed her weapons belt. It was like seeing an old friend. She picked out a needle, walked over to Delgado and with a quick, efficient jab stuck it into his throat. She kicked his lifeless body into the river.

As she limped away, she knew more people would be looking for her. She wasn't far from the wharf, and someone would have heard a sound from the crash.

CHAPTER 14

Anna Ramitrova had learned English as a child at school. She had been an adopted child, but her parents, apart from being zealous socialists who believed in the *Sovietski Soyuz*, or Soviet Union, also believed in the Marxist ideal of high thinking and plain living. Not the other way around, her adopted father used to tell her. Yevgeny might have been a adoptive parent, but in every way, he was her real dad. He shared a first name with his favorite poet, Yevgeny Yevtushenko.

Yevgeny, or Papa, as Anna called him, made her read aloud *Babi Yar*, the 1962 poem denouncing the Nazi massacre of 34,000 Jews. Anna was hooked by the words, and she went on to devour the works of other Russian poets, like Anna Akhmatova and Mayakovsky. Russians love their poets like Americans love their film stars. The recitation of poetry is considered a special skill for Russian children, and an adult poet is held in the esteem generally given to a rock star in western society.

By the time she was twelve, Anna could read the works of modern English poets like Ted Hughes and his mercurial poet wife Sylvia Plath. She never saw Yorkshire, the English county whose rain drowsed fields and harsh winters Hughes described so vividly, but imagination ran riot in her mind.

She discovered the American poets like John Ashberry and even avant-garde ones like Allen Ginsburg and Jack Kerouac, the beat generation artists. America came alive in her mind, and so did the conflict with the constant negative propaganda about the Imperialists in her own society.

Papa and her Mama, Rezina, taught her to think freely but also to remain within the bounds of Mother Russia. America might be free, but it was also dangerous. The States didn't look after its people. *It was every man for himself*, Yevgeny said.

Then why did Yevtushenko live there now, as a teacher at Tula University in Oklahoma?

Papa had no answer to that.

When Borislov came knocking on her door, asking her to play a role in an English-speaking theatre, Anna was all but ready. She had read English books all her life, watched whatever English films she could get hold of – many in fact, after the regime change in 1991. Her mind was divided between allegiance to Mother Russia and the so-called democracy of the West. She liked elements of both, but her life was in Russia, and ultimately, so was her heart. But a little voice did always whisper inside her. What would it be like to live in the West?

Were Americans really free as they claimed to be? Free to write, say, and do as they please?

Or did they work, look after their children, then grow old and die one day, like Russians did? What did freedom even mean, anyway?

One day, she would love to find out for herself.

Hence, she fell head long for Borislov's proposition. He wanted to form a western theatre, and for her to play the role of the same heroine, every day. It astonished her, at first. She couldn't believe it. As a socialist, she was also a committed atheist. But for something like this to happen, there must be also be a God.

Borislov seemed to be a man of infinite means. Getting her an apartment in Moscow's nicest street wasn't a problem. Neither were the actors who came to her apartment, to train and challenge her. It was an endless procession. Her acting improved by leaps and bounds, until she was a star of the little theatre she attended. All her parts were in English. American English, to be precise.

She spoke no Russian at all any more. She worked so hard the actors and theatre personnel were the only friends she had. She had no husband or partner, and her mother had retired down to the Crimea by the Black Sea. All her new friends spoke in English with her, and most of them had spent time in USA, one of them even had a proper Texan twang she loved.

All the books she read were in English. She had to read western newspapers only, especially American ones like Washington Post and New York times. She had to watch US news channels like CNN and Fox. She got to know the names of all the news anchors on TV. She enjoyed the coverage on CNN, but she found the views of the Fox news hosts the most interesting. Fox news was rabidly anti-liberal and pro-American, and to her ears, they sounded just like the Russian news channels that denounced America and capitalism, and praised the Soviet Republic.

Anna only ate western breakfasts of porridge, orange juice, Kellogg's cereals. She ate sandwiches, pancakes with maple syrup, pancakes with bacon and eggs – a dish she despised as it was gross. Too filling. As her part demanded, she had to watch her weight, size, and shape. Her daily gym routine was strict. She had a two-mile run, followed by yoga, Pilates, then swimming. It lasted for two hours in the morning, then her rehearsals started, followed by the performance in the evening.

CHAPTER 15

The role Anna played was fixed and focused on the same person. She followed this person's routine, her habits, and mannerisms until she felt she could write a book on her. Her performances moved from one theatre to another, and her audiences were always appreciative.

One evening, after her performance, Borislov met her backstage. Attending with Borislov was a man who needed no introduction. Dimitri Trushenko was a short, stocky man. He came up to her chest. He had a barrel chest, and his eyes were strange, widely spaced apart. They were bright blue, but small, and moved constantly, like he couldn't decide what to look at. But when they came to rest on her, Anna saw his eyes widen and stop moving.

Trushenko was the Russian Premier. Soviet era politics were experiencing a resurgence under him, and the Politburo was under his absolute command, staffed by his cronies. His face was plastered on billboards all over Russia, and Anna felt her heart constrict as the most powerful man in the country focused his tiny, glittering eyes on her.

*****

Borislv looked on anxiously as Trushenko stared at Anna. When Trushenko glanced at him, he saw Trusheko eyes bulging like never before. The Premier wasn't a man given to excesses. He kept his personal life private, emotions under check. Indeed, Trushenko was famous for his poker face. That flat, blank countenance was now replaced by a glow in his weird, wide spaced eyes, and a slack opening of his jaws.

Trushenko took a deep breath and nodded once to Borislov, and that was all the confirmation he needed. Initial relief swept through him. For Borislov, being the chief of the First Directorate, had gone ahead with this project without seeking the Kremlin's approval. The SVR wasn't like the old KGB. SVR section chiefs couldn't do as they please. The SVR was under more direct control of the Kremlin than ever before, partly because Trushenko was a former KGB agent himself.

Trushenko stretched his short, podgy arm and shook Anna's hand lightly. Borislov hoped it was light because Trushenko had a bone crushing grip. Anna's face bore no concern. She was surprised of course, but was taking it in stride. Borislov was getting more used to her. She had a remarkable composure, and her acting had improved so much it was hard to tell if she was acting or being herself.

Trushenko said, "Very nice to meet you, Miss Ramitrov. Your performances are amazing."

Anna did a small courtesy like she was in the presence of royalty. "Thank you, Mr. Premier."

Trushenko asked a few other well-meaning questions before the entourage left. They went upstairs to the street level where armed Spetznaz, or Russian Special Forces, guards lined the street. They got into the Zil limousine and the convoy of three cars took off, headed back to the Kremlin.

Once they were in Trushenko's office, Borislov asked the question. "So, what do you think?"

Trushenko walked to the bar at the side of his gigantic office. He poured two tumblers of Glenmorangie whiskey, his favorite, with some ice. He handed one to Borislov, then sat down opposite.

"Tell me what the plan is."

Borislov did. He knew if this went ahead he wouldn't be a section chief anymore. He would take over the entire SVR, and become a member of the Politburo, the 9-man central committee that ruled Russia. Under the Premier, of course. And everyone knew the head of the SVR had the Premier's ear. He, because it was always a he, was the most influential member of the Politburo.

Trushenko listened in silence, sipping from his tumbler. When Borislov finished, he got up and paced the room, clearly agitated. He stopped eventually and addressed Borislov. "What if this goes wrong? You know what the Americans will do to us? This could cause a war."

Borislov spread his hands. "Why? This isn't an act of aggression. It's espionage. Let's face it, the Americans know as well as we do our governments are riddled with each other's spies."

"They'll release it to their media, and it'll cause a global scandal. We're going to lose face."

"Sir, we are fighting several proxy wars against them right now. Syria is one. Yemen is another. Think of what we can achieve by doing this."

"I know." Trushenko sighed and sat back down. "But don't underestimate the Americans. If they get wind of this there will be hell to pay. I'm just worried about the fallout."

They sat in contemplative silence for a while. Eventually, Trushenko said, "I'm sorry, but tempting as it is, I have to say no. There will be a global outrage if this becomes public. The ramifications are mind-boggling. Even our allies will turn against us."

Borislov was disappointed, but he had been expecting this. He had another ace up his sleeve.

"What if we could get someone else to take responsibility?"

Trushenko frowned. "Who else would agree? We cannot just ask a terrorist group. The Americans will know only state sponsorship can achieve something like this."

"Not a terrorist group. Well, I guess you can call them anything you like. But they are a global power organization, dedicated to bring about the end of democracy in the West, and replace it with dictatorship."

Trushenko's eyebrows shot up. "And I haven't heard of them? Why not?"

"Because they are ultra-secretive. They do not exist online. They don't have a leader, or any hierarchy. Just a group of like-minded people getting together."

"You make it sound like a tea-party."

Borislov smiled. "That's exactly what they are. And they will take responsibility because if this succeeds, they will be happy to reap the benefits. So will we, obviously."

"Who are they?" Trushneko asked after a pause.

"Cyclone," Borislov said quietly.

CHAPTER 16

CIA HQ

Langley, Virginia

From the seventh floor of the George Bush Center for Intelligence, the decision-makers at the CIA were positioned high enough to see the dense expanse of trees surrounding the agency's headquarters. The unpretentious monstrosity of the Original Headquarters Building, which looked ironically like something the Soviets would have built, was also visible. But there was plenty to occupy their minds in the meeting room they had gathered in within the New Headquarters Building.

Susan Harris, the Director, was holding a meeting with her divisional chiefs. They included Martin Shaw, the CIA head in London where the incident they were discussing had taken place. It takes a special kind of person to stand up in front of gathered top dogs of the CIA and tell them off like school kids. Harris was without a doubt that kind of person.

She stood and paced the room, her shoulder-length blonde hair swaying slightly as she turned back and forth, delivering her diatribe. She was tall and looked especially so when she was standing and towering over people as they sat. She power-dressed with style, her tight, blue skirt suit clinging to her well-maintained figure. A figure that many male agents found alluring, but none dared state at. Now in her late 50s, she had 34 years of agency service to back up her unspoken demand for respect. Susan Harris was a classic DC ballbreaker.

"How has a CIA agent wound up dead in London?" Susan fumed. "Not Yemen, not Syria. Freaking London."

The divisional chiefs looked at her, answerless.

"Okay. Let me put it another way. What are we going to do to find out why an agent ended up dead in London?"

More blank looks.

"Anyone?"

It wasn't at all uncommon to see Susan do whatever it took to get answers. But she seemed even more forceful than usual. Angry.

"The positive is that the media still haven't gotten hold of it," Martin said. "MI6 changed Grant Pearson into an American tourist named Matt Lowry who was in the wrong place at the wrong time."

"Poor fictitious guy got it all kinds of wrong," Frank Attler, chief of the South Europe division said. "Not every day an upmarket London apartment gets shot to pieces."

Susan threw him a look that advised no more quips were required.

"Obviously, the media are sniffing round it," Martin said. "But thanks to MI6 they've no idea who was really inside."

"Everything about the whole scene is being kept on a strict need-to-know basis," Susan said. "The embassy used their influence to make sure it's as locked down as possible. Only the UK Special Branch is investigating it, and they aren't doing any forensics."

Susan paused as she thought about the strings she'd had to pull to ensure this was all kept under wraps, and the favors she'd be burdened with returning later. Martin had played his part, but it was mostly on her.

A chair leg scraped jarringly along the floor, bringing her attention back to the meeting.

"The British media know very little so far, but to be honest, so do we," Martin told the room. "We need answers fast."

"Ideally within the next 15 minutes because I've to speak to the DNI," Susan said. The Director of National Intelligence was not someone to keep secrets from, especially on something as important at this. That would basically be keeping secrets from the president, who the DNI reported to.

"We know Grant was at an exclusive members-only nightclub in Knightsbridge not long before he went home," Martin said. "Special Branch are questioning staff and members. We have the CCTV of him coming back to the street where his apartment was, looking a little tipsy but perfectly well."

"We also need to talk to the MI6 agent, Jeff Pearce," Susan interrupted. "Martin, I'll need you on that asap." Martin nodded in agreement as Susan continued, "The week before he died, Grant was seen talking to Jeff at an Embassy party thrown by MI6. Best party planners in the world – weddings, bar mitzvahs, and shitshows." Quips were fine when she did it. As long as they were delivered with acerbic disdain.

"Obviously, the primary thing we need to know is the identity of the man who approached Grant at his door and went into the apartment with him," Martin said.

"The man who we assume killed him," Frank said.

Martin looked out across the canopy of trees that led to Potomac River.

"Not necessarily," he replied. "In fact, not likely. The bullet that killed Grant was found embedded on the floor along with others. Others from a heavy round, fired long distance like a sniper weapon. Not from a short-range weapon."

"We need to get someone on facial recognition immediately," Susan said. "Whoever knows most about the latest shit-hot software in this building, get them on facial recognition."

"Impossible," Martin said. "CCTV only got the guy from behind."

"This is fucking bullshit," Susan said, angry again. "They've got more CCTV cameras per head than any country in the world, and for what? To fine some poor guy caught pissing in the street?"

Susan stopped talking, and the room became so silent they could almost hear the voices of agents past echoing through history. So many renowned agents had sat before them in this room. The silence was broken by the crack of Susan clapping her hands together. It was part frustration, part an attempt to rouse her team.

"Come on! Jesus!" she shouted. "Someone give me something!" A few agents gazed into their coffee cups, others stared into her eyes trying to convince themselves they wouldn't be intimidated. Susan looked at Frank and clocked that his tie was too loose, and his slouch too casual for her liking.

"Right," she said, finally. "Looks like we've got jackshit. Martin, talk to Jeff immediately. And don't let him off lightly."

CHAPTER 17

The East Wing

White House

Washington DC

How fitting it was, Janice Ryan, the First Lady, thought that the East Wing, housing the Office of the First Lady, was built originally to cover up the Presidential Emergency bunker during the second world war.

Janice wanted to go and hide in the bunker at this particular moment because the assembled reporters were giving her a headache. Her Personal Secretary, Jennifer Gilmore, sat next to her on the velvet blue sofa, facing the bank of cameras and media people. Michelle Campbell, the Social Secretary of the White House, and not just of her Office, was standing to her left.

Janice hadn't faced the media in months. She had an ovarian cyst removed, which thankfully turned out to be benign. Bertram Ryan, the President, had done everything possible to keep it a secret. The Press were told the First Lady was keeping a low profile for personal reasons. It was Jenny and Michelle who had done the heavy lifting while she was away, keeping the ever-curious media at bay.

Janice didn't know how they'd managed. True, she was out for one day only, and then started responding to messages as soon as she got back. In this day and age, communication had no barriers, and for Janice, that wasn't a good thing. Jenny controlled her cell phone and social media accounts, and the day she returned, Janice had to respond to over two hundred twitter and FB messages.

"Mrs Ryan, this is Lee Goldstein from the New York Times," a bespectacled male reporter asked. "Can you tell us something more about the Rise Up initiative that you are launching."

Janice could feel both her staff members stir next to her. They were more like her close friends in fact. Jenny in particular, knew almost everything about her life, down to her bra and dress size.

"Certainly," Janice said. "Rise Up is for teenagers who have mental health disorders and feel isolated from school and community. The social media can often be a negative for these children, as they can be bullied, harassed, and form their own groups who become even more isolated. This has to change."

A few flashbulbs snapped, irritating Janice. She kept the plastic smile frozen on her lips, eyebrows and forehead smooth. Several hands went up, and Michelle pointed to a female reporter.

For the next hour, the questions continued. Whenever Janice paused, Michelle stepped in smoothly. She was managing the launch of the charity, along with Janice.

The political questions followed soon, and despite her headache, and the need for a Tylenol Janice knew she couldn't avoid them.

"Are you helping the President prepare for the mid-term elections, Mrs Ryan?"

Janice was looking at the peaceful green expanse of the Jacqueline Kennedy Garden to the left when the question came. She turned back to the reporters quickly.

"If the President asks me to, I shall be happy to do whatever I can."

"Will you be voting yourself?"

Janice played up and laughed slightly. Give them something now so they leave her alone later. "We live in a democracy so I have to vote, yes."

"What do you think about being voted the most popular woman in America today?"

"What is the name of the puppy you bought recently? What type of a dog is he?"

"Will you be supporting any more charities this month?"

"What is your favorite TV show?"

"What is your favorite cuisine? How often do you cook?"

"What is the President's favorite dish?"

The questions just kept coming. Bertram wanted her to be popular, and she had obliged, as it would help his prospects for a second term. She was meant to focus on disadvantaged children from poor social backgrounds. This was devised by the Director of Policy for the First Lady's Office, Jeremy Dunstall, a man Janice didn't like. But given that her husband was a Republican, and since Republican First Lady's softened their husband's image, Jeremy's idea was a sound one. Rise Up was a small step in that direction.

After another half hour, the grilling ended. But the last question was the one that threw her off track the most. The editor of Women's style of the Washington Post finally got her turn.

"Will you be attending the G20 summit with the President next week?"

It was the one question Janice didn't prepared for. The G20 summit was in Moscow, a city she had never visited, but felt an affinity to. Her mother was born in Russia, but raised in USA. Bertram had requested her attendance, but that was before her surgery. She had recovered from the operation completely, and knew she had to make her mind up about the summit soon.

She stiffened, words stuck in her throat. Jenny spoke up. "The G20 Summit is mainly for the leaders of those countries. Mrs Ryan will decide over the coming days whether she will be attending or not."

Thankfully that answer seemed to satiate the hungry mob. Janice shot her secretary a look of unadulterated gratitude.

"What about the conference in Paris about the impact of social media on vulnerable children?"

Now this was a topic that Janice could handle herself. This was an initiative organized by the wives of G8 country leaders, and Janice was one of the leaders. The Paris conference tied in nicely with Rise Up.

She glanced at Jenny and nodded slightly, then spoke up.

"The Paris Conference has been a highlight in my calendar for a long time. I definitely want to attend. Unless the President needs me to be in the country, I will be going, that's for sure."

Pens scribbled on paper. Then the questions resumed. After another half hour, she was all done.

She left the hot seat and stepped out into the garden. She leaned against a colonnade and closed her eyes. Janice was forty, fitter than someone half her age, and looked after herself. But every press conference she did left her drained. She didn't know how the other First Lady's had coped.

Jenny appeared again, a cup of steaming coffee in her hand. "For you," she said. "Looked like you needed it."

"I did, thanks," Janice said, taking the mug. "What's next on the agenda?

"The Yellow Oval Office for photos with the wives of the Senate majority and minority leaders. Then meeting the National School Lunch Committee. After that, the Girl's Speech winner for disadvantaged children."

Janice closed her eyes and sat down on the garden bench. This garden, secluded to one side of the entire White House complex, was the most private space she had. No wonder Jacqueline Kennedy had liked it so much.

"When do I see my mom today?"

"At 16.30. Yes, there will be traffic, but it couldn't be helped."

"We have to drive to AFB Anacostia-Bolling, right?"

"Right. Because Marine One isn't available."

Janice's mood brightened. She hadn't seen her mother in three months. She was an only child and was close to her mother. Her father had died three years ago.

CHAPTER 18

After four hours, and feeling more exhausted than before, Janice and Jenny, with two bodyguards, and a Secret Service escort, had arrived at her mother's home in Silver Springs, Maryland.

Margaret opened the door, leaning on a stick. She was 71 years old, but looked much older. Colon cancer had ravaged her guts, and she was only alive due to two surgeries which had removed most of her large bowel. She reached out to hug Janice. Jenny went back to the car to wait while the First Lady and her mother went inside and shut the door.

Janice stepped inside her mother's small kitchen. The space was four feet by five, and she felt humbled, wondering at how her mother spent her days. Margaret cooked in this kitchen, then took her food to the dining tablet outside. She ate while she watched TV. She had refused Bertram's generous offer to move her somewhere in DC. This was her home, and this is where she would stay.

Janice made two cups of coffee and brought them to the living room where Margaret was watching the news on TV.

Margaret said, "I'm glad you came."

Janice downturned her lips, softened her face. "Oh, Mama. I miss you. Why don't you move closer to us?"

Margaret shook her head, her yellowing eyes looking at the distance. "I'll die here," she said quietly.

"Don't say things like that," Janice said.

Margaret smiled. "When you get to my age, you start accepting more. This is my lot in life."

Janice noted her mother's cheeks were more sunken. The furrows on her top lip and the lines on her forehead were deeper.

She frowned. "Have you lost weight?"

Margaret didn't reply for a while. Janice stared at her mother, who looked at her, then smiled. It was a sad, rueful smile.

Janice felt her chest tighten. A black weight pressed against her neck, and it was hard to swallow. She put the cup down and leaned toward Margaret.

"Mama, what is it? Tell me." She feared the worst, but wouldn't even let herself think it.

"It's come back," Margaret whispered. "This time, its spread to my liver."

Janice felt like she'd been slapped. An iron pair of hands reached inside and broke her heart in two. Her head hung down like it couldn't bear its own weight.

"I don't have much time," Margaret said after a long silence.

Janice looked at her mother. She understood now why the eyes were yellow. Jaundice spreading from the liver.

She got up, sat down next to her mother, and hugged her. Margaret's body was stiff and unyielding. She sat rigid as a surfboard. Janice imagined she was preparing herself for the worst.

Janice wiped her eyes. Her father had died of cancer as well, and she knew when cancer spread, or metastasized, there was little anyone could do.

"What did the doctors say?"

"What can they say? Radiotherapy and chemotherapy again. But I'm so tired of it. It makes me vomit all day, fills my body with pain. I think death is better."

"No, Mama," Janice's voice broke. "Don't say that."

She straightened herself, noting Margaret was still stiff, staring ahead like she was in a trance.

"Mama?"

"I need to tell you something." Margaret sighed and looked down at her hands. They were hard, coarse, wrinkled.

When she spoke, her voice was strong, steady. "But first, can you go up to the loft? There's a trap door that leads downstairs. When you go up, on the right, you'll see a black trunk. Open it. You'll see folded blankets and books. Remove them. At the bottom, there's a red box. It's small. Bring it to me. Don't open it."

Janice stared at her mother. Margaret's eyes were dry. If anything, there was a hardness in them Janice found scary. Margaret turned to look at her daughter. They stared at each other in silence for a while.

"Go," Margaret said. "Now."

Janice got up and climbed the stairs. She felt strange, like she was having an out of body experience. Her heart was hammering against her ribs. She had no idea what was happening, but an ominous, heavy shadow hung over her. Her movements were slow, ponderous.

The trap door creaked as it opened. She went up the dusty, unused stairs and flicked on the light switch. Cobwebs gleamed in the light, hung like drapes over the rafters. She found the black trunk. It opened just like her mother had said it would. And inside, she found the layers of blankets. She removed all of them, and when she got the red box, her hands shook. It was the size of a jewelry box, made of blue felt, soft in her hands.

Janice closed the trunk, turned off the light, and went back to her mother, holding the box.

Margaret was still sitting in the same position when she got back. Janice sat next to her and without a word, gave her the box.

"Open it for me," Margaret said. Her voice shook suddenly, and she screwed her eyes shut. She rocked backwards.

"Mama!" Janice cried in panic.

Margaret steadied herself. "Don't worry. I'm fine. Open the box."

Janice opened the box and stared in surprise. It contained some black and white photos. She picked one up. Suddenly, Janice could feel her head reeling. She shook her head, then tried to refocus her blurring eyes.

"I'm sorry," Margaret whispered. "I'm so sorry, Janice."

CHAPTER 19

Dan had arrived in London with a brooding sense of caution about why Jeff mysteriously wanted to meet him. But he had been calm enough, and he'd enjoyed seeing some of the old sights. Now, calm had exploded into chaos. He was on the run, pursued by unknown but very dangerous forces. That situation wasn't new to him, but it never got any easier to live with.

After leaving the scene of carnage at Grant's place, he'd made his way back to Soho and his hotel. He'd made sure he hadn't been followed on the way back, but he knew Grant wouldn't have been so careful. He'd shown very little spy craft during the time Dan had been watching him. He'd followed him to the nightclub relatively easily, after which Grant drank enough to extinguish any skills he did have.

Whoever killed Grant might have been waiting around his apartment for hours for him to come back, but more than likely they had followed him back from the nightclub. That meant they will have been aware of Dan and probably got a look at him. There had been further face time with the thugs downstairs.

Lying back on his hotel bed fully clothed, he twisted the top off the bottle of London Pride ale he'd bought at the all-night store next to his hotel. He took a long swig, the bubbles refreshing his throat and a warm stream of relaxation flowing through his body. He'd bought the booze to calm down after the frenzied night he'd endured.

Then he put the bottle down. *That's not a good idea*, he told himself. He needed to keep his wits about him. He needed a plan.

He stood up and went to the bathroom to pour the beer away. He turned off the creaking tap and sat down on the bed. He held his phone in his hands for a few seconds, then called McBride. With no weapons on him and no expectation of help from the US government, Dan needed to talk to McBride. But his old mentor didn't answer.

Dan knew he needed at least a little sleep so he turned out the light. As he tried to sleep, he came to the worrying conclusion that Jeff was his best – only – hope in London. After a short and fitful sleep, he gave up and passed the time watching a cooking competition on TV and wished his definition of a stressful situation was the same as the contestants'.

Early morning, he checked out. Before he did anything else, he needed weapons. A Sig Sauer P 226 was highly desirable. A kukri knife was essential. One name sprang to his mind immediately.

Spikey Dobson, ex-SAS and 22nd Regiment in Northern Ireland. He'd served in the Falklands, the Balkans, and countless deserts. Now in his sixties, he kept a stash of decommissioned weapons in his cluttered flat. A stash that even gang members in his sketchy area of South East London would be astounded by.

To protect the old boy and himself, Dan had to make absolutely sure he wasn't being followed. He took a bus towards South East London, getting off a good distance from where he needed to be. That would give him plenty of time to lose anyone tailing him.

In the backstreets of deprived council estates, he doubled back on himself and deliberately got lost in a place where most people would be terrified to lose their way. He walked past houses with boarded up windows and graffiti covering the doors, as the sound of a screaming argument echoed from some home nearby. He stopped periodically to feign tying his laces, an opportunity to have a quick check around for a tail.

Entering the estate where Ferguson House was located, the tower block in which Spikey was one of hundreds of residents, he was approached by a boy, younger than ten, who was topless and spat aggressively at Dan's feet as he passed him. *Ballsy little fuck*, Dan thought to himself. He wondered how Spikey had ended up in this kind of place.

He looked up at the tower block. Almost unbelievably, it had only got worse since he was last here. He remembered Spikey's flat number from his previous visit. Forty-three. He buzzed it.

"Yeah?" the answer finally came.

"Spikey. It's Dan. From way back."

"Dan who?"

"I just slotted a couple of Spetsnaz guys down here who were looking for you." Spetsnaz meant Russian special forces. Dan had talked about them with Spikey before, and he hoped it might jog his memory. After a pause, a throaty, cackling laugh came back down the line.

"Well, fuck me sideways," Spikey said. "I'll buzz you in."

Dan went upstairs, and Spikey opened the door. He looked a little frailer than before, but he was still heftier than most men his age and his white vest revealed there was muscle definition on his arms.

Spikey turned and went in without greeting Dan.

"Can't say I expected to see you again anytime soon," he said to Dan as they entered the living room.

"I like to see old friends when I'm in town," Dan replied.

"Yeah? Were they all busy?"

Dan grinned as he moved a pile of newspapers to make space on a torn-up sofa.

"How are you, good?" Dan asked him.

"Good as gold, Danny boy," Spikey said, suppressing a cough. "You're looking well. You Americans always looked the part, I'll give you that."

"Yeah. Well, you Brits always did the business when it came down to it. Luckily war's not about looks," Dan said.

Spikey grinned as he fixed his eyes on the TV.

"So, what d'you need? Don't tell me you only came here for reminiscing."

"A Sig Sauer P226 would be ideal."

"Sorry, matey. Best I can do is Colt M1911. I know most of you Delta guys like 'em."

"It'll certainly do," Dan said. "How much?"

"For a repeat customer? I'll do 100 notes with extra ammo thrown in."

It wasn't exactly 'mate's rates', but Dan reckoned the old boy could do with the money.

"Okay. Any chance you got a kukri knife?"

"I've got plenty of highly sharpened shit. But a kukri I do not."

"Shame," Dan said.

"You fussy about what you stick in someone?" Spikey asked.

"Kinda am, actually."

Spikey thought for a moment. Then he got up, found a pen and notepad, and wrote down an address.

"This guy'll take care of you," he said to Dan.

"Is he reliable?"

"You can trust him as much as you can trust me," Spikey said.

"I'll take that as reassurance," Dan replied.

After saying his goodbyes with Spikey, Dan made his way back into central London, avoiding being followed. The address Spikey had given him was in Soho, two blocks from the hotel he'd left that morning. *Would be, wouldn't it*, Dan thought to himself.

Spikey's contact was a Nepalese guy who owned a shop in Soho. He found the address and walked into the overfilled shop. He waited until there were no customers in the shop.

"Are you Samir?" he asked the man behind the counter, who fitted the description given by Spikey – a circle of thick black hair around a fully bald crown, and almost certainly wearing a smart business shirt with no tie.

"Who's   asking?"
"My name's Dan. Spikey sent me."

Samir pushed his lips upwards and nodded slowly.

"He say anything?" Samir asked.

"Told me you'd have a question for me."

"Right. What is *kaida*?"

"The style and tradition of the Gurkha people. Kaida is culture." Dan replied. His palms then met at his chest, and he bowed his head. "*Namaste*."

Samir Thapa responded with the same greeting.

"Let me show you through the back," Samir said. He lifted a counter bar for Dan, and he stepped behind it. Samir parted a bead curtain and disappeared through it. Dan glanced around, and did a quick 360 sit rep, then followed.

They were transported from a London shop to a Nepalese living room. Low sofas were placed on a wood floor with warm, intricately decorated rugs.

"You any idea what the hell you were talking about just then?" Samir asked Dan. "Or just letting me know you're the real deal?"

"Actually, I have a connection with Nepal," Dan told him.

"Really?" Samir asked, as he shuffled around pulling a box from the back of furniture.

"Yeah. We have military service in common too," Dan said. "I believe you're 1st Royal Gurkha Rifles?

"Indeed so," Samir said. "A veteran of the British Army."

Samir opened the box to reveal a beautifully presented collection of kukri knives. It made Dan smile a little.

"You knew what I wanted?" he asked Samir.

"Well, Spikey doesn't send people down here for milk. And this is all I have, currently."

"It's all I need," Dan said, picking one out and twirling the 11 inch blade expertly in his hands. "Superb."

"That's not your first time with a kukri," Samir said, watching carefully.

"My parents were UN aid workers in a Nepalese village," Dan explained. "In the mountains, beautiful place."

"Well, well," Samir said.

"I used to spend time with the Gurkhas as a kid. Hell of a friendship group. I used to run up the mountain path with them with the Doko bag on my head."

"That'll toughen you up," Samir agreed. "Nothing beats low oxygen workouts." He offered Dan some tea.

"Thanks,   I'd   better   be   quick   though."
They shared a quick cup of tea and chatted a little more about
Nepal. Dan handed over the asking price for the kukri.

You can never be sure of anyone, he thought to himself as he left,
but he seems like a decent guy to me. He decided to drop in for a
more leisurely cup of tea when – if – this whole thing was over.

*****

Dan wanted to try McBride again. He remembered going to a
coffee shop in Soho that had a single table upstairs in a private
little area away from the main seating. He went back there to call
McBride. This time, he answered.

"Where the hell have you been?" Dan asked him without
pleasantries.
"Nice to talk to you, too. I've been on a plane."

Dan explained the situation in London. McBride was aware of
some parts of it but not others.

"You need to get out of London, now," McBride told Dan. "You
could hide out in the sticks somewhere in the UK. But France or
elsewhere in Europe would be better."

"Yeah,"   Dan   agreed.
"Just   don't   use   your   passport.   Or   an   airport."
"I know that," Dan said, bluntly. Then, "I mean. Thanks." He
ended the call.

He had the Grant dossier Jeff had given him, and while he was still
in the privacy of the coffee shop's upper level, he checked what
was in there on Tatyana Mirov. Grant had been seen meeting her
at an address in Edmonton in North London. That had to be his
next port of call.

In North London, Dan sat outside a Turkish cafe sipping black coffee and waiting. He waited for an hour. Rush hour arrived, and more and more traffic whizzed past him on the North Circular Road. He ordered another coffee and waited some more. Finally, Tatyana emerged from an unremarkable redbrick house. He let her get a few steps ahead before standing.

He followed her southwest, keeping on the other side of the street and making sure there were always a few other pedestrians between them.

After a mile or so, they entered an area where several shops had Russian signs outside. Dan was highly familiar with the Cyrillic script. He was also aware Tottenham had always had a large Russian population. It even had an area that was once known as Little Russia.

As Tatyana walked into a shop, Dan stood at a nearby bus stop. He watched her through the window. This was the closest he'd been to her, and he noticed that she was incredibly beautiful. Her black hair fell past high, pronounced cheekbones and almost down to her waist. She was unmistakably Slavic. She talked with a man in the shop for a few minutes then walked out.

Dan looked down the street as if checking to see if a bus was coming. Waiting at the bus stop had been his ruse, but somehow Tatyana put her eyes on him as soon as she left the shop, even though he was across the street. *My fault for being so damn attractive*, Dan thought, hoping a little joke in his head would calm him down and help him think straight. But it was too late. She was walking toward him, and if he moved away from the bus stop now it would seem odd. She glided past him, her striking brown eyes looking straight into his. She had the drop on him.

CHAPTER 20

When Tatyana was out of sight, Dan turned and walked away from the bus stop. He couldn't follow her now that he'd been rumbled. He started walking, steaming down the street at fast pace. He was angry at himself for getting spotted, and he was pressuring himself to decide what to do next. He didn't even have a place to stay, and he had stored his backpack in a locker in Kings Cross Station.

He started walking back toward central London. It was six miles from Tottenham, but that was nothing to him. He thought the walk might clear his head. As he approached the tree line of Finsbury Park, he heard the screeching of tires behind him.

He didn't wait to see who it was. He jumped into the trees along the pavement and went to ground. The Colt was in his hands and pointing straight at the burly, wide chested men who popped out of the black SUV.

They looked around for him. About time to end this bullshit and get some answers. Gun arm elbow ramrod straight, he slowly stood. One of the men saw him and patted his friend on the back. Both raised their hands as Dan stepped toward them.

"I'll count to five before you lose a kneecap." He stared to count. The men looked at each other, hands still raised. One of them spoke. His voice was calm, unhurried, despite their posture of surrender. These men had buzz cuts, hard faces, flat eyes that had seen combat. They were ex-military. Both of them had their eyes fixed on Dan now.

"Our boss wants to see you."

"Who is he?"

"If you come with us you can find out."

"Call him and tell him to come here."

The bigger guy up front showed yellow teeth. "*She* doesn't work like that, Mr. Roy."

Dan lowered his gun, but didn't alter his aim.

"Who is she?"

"Enough talk," the man said, his tone hardening. "Either come with us or go. But we will come after you again."

Dan thought for a few seconds. Clearly, they didn't want him dead. And he was armed.

"I keep my weapons," Dan said. "No negotiation on that."

The two men glanced at each other and the smaller guy nodded.

The big man approached Dan, holding a black hood. Dan shook his head. He had used a hood like that many times over the heads of insurgents in Iraq and the Stan.

"Do that when we're in the car." He indicated with the Colt. "Move."

The men looked pissed off. But they had no choice. One of them opened the door, and Dan glanced inside. The back seat was empty. He slid inside and one of the guys ran around to the other door. The driver turned the ignition and the car took off.

Dan had the muzzle of the Colt lodged firmly against the side of the guy to his left. He snarled at him, but Dan smirked in silence.

"Now," said the other guy, holding out the hood. Dan nodded and the black cloth slid over his eyes, obscuring his vision.

One of the guys muttered in Russian. Dan could only make out the swear words, but at least now he knew where they were from.

114

After a drive that he guessed was almost an hour, the car stopped. Two iron-hard pairs of hands took him by the arms and led him stumbling up a small flight of stairs. He was shoved into a chair. The hood was removed, and standing in front of him was Tatyana. The scent of expensive perfume had replaced the cigarette stench on the hood.

Tatyana slipped off a plush fur coat to reveal a sheer, low V-neck dress that displayed the perfect pale skin of her cleavage. With this look and her hourglass figure, Dan noted she was the archetypal seductress used for a honey-pot sting. The kind carried out by the KGB. He could see why Grant had fallen for her.

"Dan Roy," Tatyana said, drawing out her vowels. "Ex-special forces, savior of the US embassy. Catcher of buses." The right side of her mouth curled into a smile.

Dan stared at her calmly. "How do you know about me?" he asked her.

Tatyana ignored him, took a step closer and leaned down toward his face. Dan had the gun loose in his hand, finger resting lightly on the trigger.

"Are you going to shoot me with your big gun, Mr Big Man?" The smell of perfume was as powerful as the cloud of sexual haze that surrounded Dan. He didn't look away from her.

"You could've just called, Tatyana. Sent me a message. After all, you know more about me, it seems, than I know about you."

She straightened, and Dan lost his enticing view of her deep cleavage. He swallowed and let out a breath. Tatyana rotated her mesmerizing hips as she moved to the middle of the room, then twirled around to face Dan.

"You're going to meet somebody for me. A Mr Kennedy. He has a friend who needs your help."

"And why should I do that?"

"It's that, or stay here for an evening of torture."

"You're gonna pump even more of that perfume in here?"

Tatyana gave him a wry smile. She was standing in front of an enormous arched window fitted with stained glass. A grand piano sat in the corner of the white-on-white room. This was a far cry from the humble house in Edmonton. Given the distance and direction of the drive, and the grandeur of the home, Dan figured this was Knightsbridge.

"What does this Kennedy want me to do?" he asked Tatyana.

"He's just a fixer. You'll find out when you get there."

Dan turned his head to look at the men, who had bundled him into the car, standing behind him. They were huge, both wearing three-piece suits and leather gloves. He figured he didn't have much choice, and he was intrigued to know what Kennedy – or rather his client – wanted.

"Fine," he told Tatyana.

The heavies put the hood back on and bundled him back into the car. Secretly, he missed the perfume smell.

They were in the car for a long time. At least 90 minutes. Finally, they pulled to a stop. The suits took him out of the car, removed his hood, then got back in and drove off. The smell of cow shit hit his nostrils immediately. He looked to his left and saw a crumbling farmhouse. There was nothing but fields all around. There were two guards standing at the entrance to the farmhouse. Dan approached them.

"Here to see Kennedy," he said. He looked the guards up and down. Definitely not ex-military. They looked more like burly farmhands-turned-bouncers. Much less competent than the men who had just brought him here. The lack of decent security was odd.

"In you go," one of them said.

Dan walked straight into a kitchen. The walls were exposed stone, and above him were wood beams filled with woodworm holes. The room was freezing. Sitting at the end of an oak table was a skinny man, probably in his fifties. He had a sallow, almost grey complexion and was dressed in a pinstripe suit. He held a briefcase in front of him on the table.

"Sit down, Mr Roy," he said weakly in a middle-England accent. He seemed like a low-level civil servant. Dan sat down.

"What's the deal?" Dan asked.

"If you'd kindly wait for my employer, Mr Roy."

Dan went over the cooker, switched on the gas and burned through the plastic zip ties on his hand. Kennedy looked concerned but said nothing.

Dan was about to demand to know what the hell was going on when the lights went out. Total darkness. Dan knew it was no accident. A trap. He made his way outside as a van pulled up. Four men, all wearing night vision goggles, came piling out.

Dan was fully tooled up with weapons for the first time in a while. He pulled out the Colt and ran, firing as he went. He put a bullet into the necks of two of the men. His disadvantage was reduced in seconds. He slid behind the van on the opposite side to the two remaining men. They were shouting in panic.

He could see their feet through the bottom of the van and fired another round into the ankle of one of them, who screamed and hit the deck. The other pair of legs disappeared.

A gun was firing wildly, some rounds hitting the van. Dan pressed his body hard against the van and slowly stepped in the direction of the firing. He knew that once he rounded the front of the van, it would be a simple question of who was quickest on the draw. Dan turned the corner and was surprised to see nobody standing there. He looked down to the ground as the injured man was turning his gun toward him. Dan instantly straightened his arms out in front of him and fired twice into the man's chest.

He now knew that one fully able assailant still remained. He turned around as the final man pointed his gun at him. He brought the butt of the gun over his head and hard into Dan's face. For some reason, he couldn't use his weapon as intended, and he was improvising. The blow had rattled Dan's brain, but he shook it off and slammed an upper cut into the attacker's stomach. The air flew out of his body, and he double over in pain, giving Dan time to pull out his kukri and thrust it into man's neck. Bones crunched as it passed through, before Dan slit his throat expertly, holding the knife steady in his fist.

With all four men dead, Dan caught his breath. Kennedy must have remained in the house, presumably terrified. He searched the men's pockets and found burner phones on two of them. He went inside the house to find Kennedy cowering behind the kitchen counter on the ground floor. Dan hauled him up by the collar. Fear had widened Kennedy's eyes. Dan thrust him against the wall, and put the tip of the kukri against his neck.

"Talk," he said.

"I'm just a go-between," Kennedy squeaked. Dan increased the pressure on the knife and Kennedy whimpered.

"Who contacted you? The Russians?"

Kennedy shook his head.

"Then who? Describe him to me."

"Average height. Older than you. Swarthy."

"Accent?"

"I don't know. But English isn't his first language."

"Arab?"

"Maybe. Looked middle eastern."

Dan released his grip on Kennedy who stumbled backwards then slid down the wall.

One of the burner phones began to beep inside his pocket. Dan took it out and stared at it for a few seconds. The steel casing was cuffed, rough. No Call ID on the screen. Dan knew what would happen if he answered. He would provide proof that he was alive. *To hell with it.*

Dan answered and held it to his ear.

"What's happening there?" a man's voice asked.

"Your men are dead," Dan answered coldly. He waited, listening to the breathing on the other end.

"Dan Roy," the voice shook. He said an oath in Arabic Dan didn't understand. There was a pause and Dan waited.

"The time has come," the man said, obvious emotion in his voice.

"Time for you to stop wasting mine and tell me what you want?"

"Remember Waleed?" the man said. "Do you?"

An uneasiness prickled inside Dan's mind. He frowned. "Rashid?"

"Yes, this is Waleed's cousin, Rashid. I'm coming for you, Dan Roy. And hell's coming with me."

CHAPTER 21

Dan had no intention of staying around the farmhouse after a firefight. They seemed to be miles from anywhere, but somebody could have heard and called the police. Worse still, Rashid could be sending more men.

"How did you get here?" he asked Kennedy.

"My car. It's about half a mile away," Kennedy whimpered.

"Show me," Dan told him.

Dan walked behind Kennedy, the muzzle of his weapons lodged against the fixer's back. When they got to his car, Dan searched Kennedy for the keys and got them from his pant pocket.

Then he made Kenndy kneel, and put the gun against the back of his head.

"Please," the man whimpered. "Please."

"Give me one good reason."

"I brought you to the car, I'm helping you escape."

Dan muttered an oath. In reality, he wasn't going to kill Kennedy. Killing unarmed, defenseless men, even if they were douchebags, wasn't his style. Even if he was sorely tempted, and his finger rested lightly on the trigger.

Dan removed the gun from Kennedy's head. "Get up."

The fixer scrambled to his feet. Dan said, "Go back and tell Rashid I know about his plans. They're not going to work. Can you at least do that?"

Kennedy gulped. "Ye–yes."

Dan kept his gun trained on Kennedy while he got into the car, turned the ignition with one hand, and then drove off.

Dan took the car as far as he could while it was still countryside, then ditched it on the edge of the road when he saw the signs for central London. He started running. He'd managed to finally get hold of Jeff using one of the burner phones and took the subway, or tube, to the meeting point.

Jeff had told him to head to a jazz club in Pimlico. They had to meet somewhere Jeff could wait without hanging around on street corners late at night. By the time Dan arrived, it looked closed. He was deciding what to do next as Jeff strolled out. He nudged his head to the right indicating Dan should follow him. Dan followed a distance behind, and a few blocks away watched Jeff unlock the door of a house. Dan waited five minutes then followed him inside.

The safe house was sparsely decorated. The kitchen had little besides a buzzing fridge and a small table with a plastic tablecloth on it.

"I'm starving," Dan said.

"Should I call room service?" Jeff asked. He opened a cupboard, pulling out a stale loaf of bread and a bottle of 10-year-old Laphroaig whiskey.

"I can see where the budget goes in this place," Dan said. Jeff poured them both a drink.

"I've just had rather an unpleasant chat with one of your countrymen," Jeff said.

"Yeah?" Dan asked, pulling a chunk off the bread.

"Martin Shaw. Head of CIA London. Unofficially, of course." Jeff raised his eyebrows.

Dan asked, "He asked you about Grant Pearson?"

"Exactly. Have a five-minute chat at a party then get interrogated about it. That's how this game works."

Dan gave up on the bread and picked up the whiskey.

"They're desperate," Jeff continued. "They don't like the accusation that Grant was a traitor."

"They'll also be as interested as I am to know who killed him at his apartment," Dan said.

"Precisely," Jeff agreed. "Even if he was a double agent, there's no way the Russians would take out a CIA spy in London and leave that kind of mess behind. They'd be reluctant to do it cleanly, even. We don't kill theirs, they don't kill ours."

"You're saying spies have honor?" Dan asked him.

"Some," Jeff replied, draining his whiskey and looking at the bottom of the glass.

"Whoever it was had resources," Dan said. "Russian-level resources. But none of their honor."

Jeff nodded in agreement. "One more?" he said, waving the whisky bottle.

"I'd better not," Dan said. "I need a clear head for the morning."

"Then I suggest you stop letting people hit you on it," Jeff replied, looking at Dan's bloodied nose.

The next morning, Dan sat at the same table. He was reading the folder on Grant again. Jeff, who had slept in a chair at the table, was making coffee.

"The name Carlos keeps cropping up in here," Dan said. "Who is he?"

"That's the nickname of a Russian embassy official," Jeff said without turning around. "Real name is Gennady. A senior cultural attaché, which, as we know, is Russian speak for spy." He sat down and put two weak cups of coffee on the table. "Irish?" he said, picking up the whiskey bottle. Dan shook his head.

"Business meeting with Gennady later today," he told Jeff.

Dan stepped out of the safe house into sunlight. He was headed to London's West End where Gennady resided. Jeff had arranged for two agents to be sent with him as back up. They arrived at an elegant townhouse with colorful plants on hanging baskets outside.

"Just hang around the street and make sure nobody comes in," Dan said to the agents who both frowned at him for giving them direct orders. "I won't need you inside. It's just a little chat."

He'd spotted a window open on the floor below street level, obscured from the view of the street by bushes. Nevertheless, he checked the street was clear before climbing in.

He climbed through the window and dropped to the floor. A woman with permed brown hair and hoop earrings shrieked. Her hands, covered by cleaning gloves, flew into the air as she started to fall. Dan instinctively went to grab her. Both hands were holding her as he felt the muzzle of a gun on his neck.

"Hands on head," a man's voice said. Dan lowered the cleaner to the ground and put his hands on his head. He cursed himself. He'd let his guard down because Gennady wasn't formal FSB, then he'd let himself be distracted by the cleaner's hysterics.

"Who are you?" the voice asked. Dan didn't reply. "

"Who sent you?" still no reply.

Then, Gennady appeared, holding a cup of tea. He smiled at Dan.

"I know who this is," he said. "A dead man walking."

Gennady had pale skin and a large protruding vein on the side of his forehead. His short hair was parted in the center. His face hardened as he spoke to Dan again.

"When you were on your little country break you met the brother of the man standing behind you now. And killed him." Dan could hear the deep breathing of a heavy-set man in his ear.

"I'm going to let Egor decide what to do about that," Gennady said.

The muzzle was pressed hard into Dan's head as Egor took him out of the room and shoved him through a thin corridor. They entered a stylish games room with wood-paneled walls. A billiards table was in the middle, and several chairs with tall backs and ornate wood frames were positioned around it. Egor removed Dan's knife and gun and pushed him into one of the chairs, still pointing his weapon. Dan's hands were bound behind his back. Egor shut the heavy door, then left.

Dan worried about what kind of contraptions he was going to come back with. He had to take action. He got to his feet and went over to the billiards table. One of the pockets was full of balls. He was able to rest his butt on the side of the table and dip his hands inside the pocket.

He picked out one of the two balls in there.

The time for subtlety had gone. If his hands were not free, he couldn't defend himself. There was a glass cabinet on the floor, and with all the swing he could muster in his bound hands, he flung it towards the cabinet. The glass shattered. Dan grabbed a shard of glass. He rolled it up toward the tie on his hands and moved it back and forth until it broke. Footsteps sounded outside the door.

Egor lunged at Dan, who threw a roundhouse punch at him with his right hand, holding the shard of glass. He was aiming for the neck but missed and sliced Egor's cheek. Egor screamed as the other man smashed a billiard ball into the side of Dan's head. He squeezed his eyes closed tight with the pain before opening them to see the man about to land another blow. Dan slipped him skillfully and moved behind him before thrusting the shard of glass towards his neck. This time, he landed perfectly, the gushing blood confirming he'd hit his target.

Egor was back on his feet, his eyes bulging with the anger of being cut by a man who had recently killed his brother. He picked up a heavy chair and threw it in Dan's direction. As Dan covered himself, he felt a billiard cue hit his rib cage with appalling force. He was disabled by the pain. His head then flew back as Egor held a cue to his neck and pinned him on the billiards table.

Egor turned red, then purple as he forced all of his weight onto the cue and Dan's throat. No amount of training can remove the panic of suffocation. Egor was so strong it could take him only seconds to break Dan's windpipe. Fear and lack of oxygen overtook his mind. He felt an alien sense of helplessness as he looked into Egor's crazed and bloodshot eyes above him. He grabbed the cue with both hands and pushed upwards with all his strength, snapping it in the middle.

The broken ends pressed into the skin near his throat, but the pressure had been removed. Egor was taken aback by the sudden release of pressure and was figuring out what had happened as Dan rammed one of the broken ends straight into his eyeball. Then he yanked it out with a squelch. He moved behind Egor and held the cue across his throat, pulling as hard as he could. Sweat poured from him as he resisted the big Russian's struggle. He clenched his teeth, pulling and pulling until finally Egor stopped moving.

Dan dropped the cue and breathed heavily. He searched Egor and found a pocket knife on him. Then he made his way upstairs.

Making no sound, Dan crept through the house to where he could hear the noise of a TV. Two floors up, he peered around a doorframe and saw Gennady relaxing on a sofa, his feet stretched out on to a futon. He was chuckling at the TV.

Dan moved stealthily behind him and held the knife to his throat. Gennady gasped.

"Still walking," Dan said. He checked Gennady for weapons. He had none. Dan picked the Russian up and walked him to the kitchen, where he found a zip tie and tied Gennady's hands before sitting him in a chair.

"Grant Pearson," Dan said. Gennady tightened his lips and shook his head nonchalantly.

"What do you know about him?" Dan asked.

"What was the name again?" Gennady said. Dan switched on the ceramic hob of the cooker. Gennady eyed it, nervously. Dan took him by the scruff of the neck and yanked him, chair and all, towards the cooker.

"Everything you know about Grant Pearson," Dan growled.

"Fuck you."

Dan grabbed Gennady's head and shoved it onto the searing hob. The smell of burning flesh filled the room as Gennady wailed.

"Okay!" he pleaded. "I'll tell you!"

CHAPTER 22

The Scorpion was walking along the River Thames, silently telling the pain in her leg it was nothing while trying to figure out her next move. She moved along the walking path next to the river which was deserted on a rainy night. She kept close to the bushes at the side and listened for anyone behind her. She allowed herself to hope that none of Delgado's associates were in the area right now.

While she was deep in thought, the phone in her pocket buzzed. The phone she'd taken from Delgado. She answered it and waited. The slow, calm voice that had sent a chill through her in the hospital spoke again.

"I didn't expect you to come quietly," the man said. "But you will do what we want. There's no way out of it."

"And what makes you think that?" she replied.

"If you refuse we'll stop at nothing to hunt you down. Believe me, it won't take long."

"Listen," she told him firmly. "The fact that you keep calling me means you need me for something. So, there's no point pretending I'm any good to you dead. And if you think it's easy to kill me, you're in for a shock."

The man let out a short laugh.

"Your reputation is deserved, Scorpion," he said. "You've got guts."

"Just tell me what you want."

"We need to meet."

"Not going to happen. If you're as good as you say you are, you can come find me."

"Guts or no guts, you need to stop pushing your luck and agree to a meeting. You don't even want to know what you're getting yourself into by refusing."

"I'll tell you what I know," Natasha replied. "From your voice, I can tell you're American. Fifties. You don't smoke and your accent is polished, East Coast. Probably a DC type. Maybe run a private security company. But you're not in the USA."

"Oh, really?" the man said. "Then where am I?"

"You're outside, maybe in a park. I can hear faint traffic. Someone just jogged past you, I heard the crunching of gravel. Most importantly, I just heard church bells ring. No ordinary church bells. These are ten bells ringing in harmony. Goes on for a long time, that's why I heard it. It's time for the evening mass. You are in the 4th arrondissement of a European capital, next to Pont Neuf on the river Seine. Those bells are from the Notre Dame Cathedral. Have you been inside? It's beautiful."

This time, the man was silent.

"So while you have no idea where I am right now," the Scorpion continued, "I know almost exactly where you are. And I'm coming to find you. On my terms."

Back at her safe house – a meagre apartment in Battersea – Natasha put all her stuff in a duffel bag. She didn't have much. A kukri knife she had received from Dan Roy, three passports, glasses, scissors, hair dye and wig for disguise, and two Makarov pistols. She had an arsenal stashed in a locker at Kings Cross station, and she would go there later to store her guns and knife before she flew out to Paris.

Outside, she called Borislov from a payphone.

"What is Cyclone?" she asked him directly.

"I have no idea," Borislov replied.

"You sure?"

"I'm telling you. I don't know. What are you talking about?" Natasha decided not to embellish and told him exactly what Marutov had told her.

"What did you find out at the house?" Borislov asked her.

"Nothing."

"That's not like you," he said. "We need that job finished. Do not screw it up again."

Natasha hung up. She was going to go back to Marutov's house but not because Borislov was getting testy with her.

There was no time to get another car. She took a black cab as far as Weybridge town center. She didn't want to be tied to the area of the mansion, so she walked the rest of the way, making sure she wasn't followed. Taking on guards seemed almost inevitable, but she felt confident even partially recovered. And it felt great to have her belt on again. She approached the mansion with adrenaline coursing through her, ready for a fight.

From the edge of the grounds, she looked at the entrance. There were no guards. Even stranger, the back door appeared to be open. No lights were on anywhere. The place looked deserted.

She feared it was a trap. But she couldn't leave this place with nothing again. The ideal outcome would be to find out everything Marutov knew, then kill him. Not easy.

She made her way along the darkened edge of the mansion grounds, just as before. But this time, strangely, it seemed unnecessary. She thought for a moment and headed straight for the open door. No need to make life harder for herself.

She made her way through the house, cautious despite being unchallenged. Up the grand staircase, she saw the entrance to the room Marutov had been in before. This time, there were no guards. She stepped as silently as she could, the house offering no noise to cover her own.

The door at the top of the stairs was open. She put her hand on a needle and approached the entrance, then pinned herself to the door. On the floor of the small section of the room she could see a trickle of blood making its way toward the door. She heard the troubled breathing of somebody injured.

She peered round the door. Marutov was lying face down, his mouth open. She checked the room for other people. Clear. If Marutov was tricking her, he had gone to some lengths. He was topless and had terrible wounds on this back. It looked like he'd been tortured. She made her way slowly towards him.

"Where are your family?" she asked him. His left eye rolled toward her, but nothing else moved.

"I don't want them involved," she said. "Where are they?"

"I don't know," Marutov croaked. "Find them."

"I don't want to find them," she said. "They need to stay in another   room."
"Not here," Marutov said, barely audible. "Find them. Find Black Beauty."

"Wait," Natasha said. "What's…"

He didn't hear her final sentence. His eyes closed. He was gone.

CHAPTER 23

CIA HQ

Virginia

Susan Harris was sitting in her office at the George Bush Center for Intelligence in Langley. The spacious office was immaculate, everything in its right place. Nothing was lying on the graceful wooden desk that didn't need to be there at that moment. The office was far more orderly than Susan's current situation.

She was on the phone to the White House Chief of Staff, James R. Hague. It was not an easy conversation. The Chief of Staff was the closest person to the president, and the president wanted answers. She ran her hand through her hair, scratching her scalp with tension.

"A CIA agent has been killed. Not only killed, but shot to bits," Hague said, telling Harris what she was already well aware of. "Yet, the CIA knows nothing about it, and neither do the Brits."

Susan allowed him to continue.

"I'm going to do you the favor of assuming you really know nothing," he said. "Which is bad, but not as bad as keeping something from us."

"I assure you, we're keeping nothing from you," she replied. "And I assure you we're doing everything we can to get a lid on this before the press gets hold of it." "I assure you we're doing everything we can..." Hague said. "Sounds like press release talk to me. The president assumes you're always doing everything you can. The only alternative to that is taking it easy."

"We'll get results," Susan said, trying to speak as plainly as possible. She needed to keep it cool, and knew that Hague was being as asshole on purpose. He wanted to see her blow up. She wouldn't give him that satisfaction. For her, Hague was a sideshow. She couldn't let him distract her.

"Like we always do. Please, tell the President that."

The call ended.

Susan paced her office, her head down and her forefinger resting across her top lip. She needed some air. She left the building and headed into the woods behind the CIA Espionage Museum. Ever since 9/11, the CIA had taken a lot of flak about not acting on the latest intel. But that was easy to say and virtually impossible to do. Acting on every intel meant the CIA had to be a hundred times its size, and it was widely regarded as bloated already.

It stung when an internal matter like this was spiraling out of hand. No terrorist bomb had detonated in a major American city. This was the death of a CIA agent, for which there should be a viable explanation.

But she was worried about a different reason. Gant Pearson had been one of the four people in Operation Nectar Flower. The somewhat ludicrous name belied its importance. The CIA conducted its own due diligence into the members of the government it deemed important. Operation Nectar Flower had a long precedent, and was a secret CIA ritual. One that only a few were privy to. Susan needed to know if Grant had spoken to anyone about the Operation. If he had, this shit storm was just beginning.

She took out her phone and called McBride.

Two hours later, she was sitting on a secluded bench, looking out over the Potomac River. McBride approached and sat down beside her. She wasted no time it getting to the point.

"Dan Roy," she said.

"Dan Roy," he replied impassively, clasping his hands together on his lap.

"Why did he follow Grant?"

"I don't know," McBride told her. "I passed on the message that my friend wanted to see him. Jeff Pearce."

"And?"

"Wanted to talk about a possible double agent. Grant. Beyond that, I'm not sure of everything that went down in London. I wasn't there."

"Come on," Susan said, turning to look at him for the first time. "I need more than that."

"Grant was in a lot of trouble," McBride told her. "Got himself captured in Yemen. Rashid Al-Falaj, who handed him over to the Russians. In London, he told Dan everything."

"Jesus," Susan said, an angry growl in the direction of the river.

"He's better off dead, truth be told. No more leaks," McBride told her.

"But if Grant was a Russian asset, why kill him?" Susan asked. "And why kill him like *that*?"

"You'd be better asking them," McBride said. "Even if they lie, it's good to know what lies they want you to believe."

"I already went straight to the top of the SVR," Susan said. "They swore they know nothing."

"That's all?"

"Yeah. I don't believe them, but that's all we're getting."

They both stared into the distance, the stone needle of the Washington Monument towering in the background.

"Is Dan a liability in your view?" McBride asked after a time. "He knows a lot of things you'd prefer were kept buried. Deep."

"I'm not going to fire a shower of bullets into his London apartment, if that's what you're worried about."

"I'll tell you why I'm worried. He knows plenty about Intercept, and you want Intercept kept secret. That's a simple equation. And now, people will be trying to make him talk."

"I'm not the only one who'll suffer if Intercept is made public," Susan hissed. "I'm not the only one with plenty to lose."

"I've got little to lose" McBride said. "You've got reputation and career. I've had my career already. You'll spend what's left of yours in front of senate special committees."

Susan turned to him. "And what do you think I'm gonna say under oath, McBride? That you, me, and a handful of others decided to form a black ops group made up of ex-special forces, gave it a bullshit office in the State Department, and gave them authority to act out our orders? You think the senate committee won't want all the names?"

The powerful coterie of bureaucrats, politicians, and generals, no more than ten of them, who had formed Intercept seventeen years ago in the aftermath of 9/11 were watching proceedings closely, Susan knew. McBride was trying to protect his boy, but to hell with it.

What they had at stake was more important. She sensed a softness in McBride she hadn't detected before. It seemed he genuinely cared for Dan. Sometimes, these Army types could be real gooey with stuff like this. But comradery wouldn't win the new Cold War, which Susan knew had started again. The war on terror was present sure, but the old beast from the 1970's was back, and this time it could be more dangerous. She remembered those days well, when she was a junior analyst in the Far East.

No, now was not the time to be soft. Intercept, and other organizations like it, needed more protection than ever.

McBride said, "Just tell me you'll leave Dan out of this for now. He has a right to do what he's doing. Let him find out what he's involved in. He's not just gonna go back to walking in the Blue Ridge Mountains."

"I'm not making any promises," Susan said. "The best way he can protect himself is to get his answers sooner rather than later."

McBride stood. He paused momentarily, then walked away. Susan watched him moving with his back erect. McBride had shown had literally begged her to leave Dan alone. If Intercept turned its claws on Dan, there was no way he could escape. McBride's plea had shown the soft spot the old man had for Dan Roy.

Doesn't matter what you've done before, she thought to herself. *Weakness always looks weak.*

CHAPTER 24

The Scorpion arrived in Paris on a bright, blustery morning. She exited Gare du Nord train station onto bustling Place Napoléon III. She had no time to admire the magnificent 19th century station building with its statues and stone columns. Only briefly, she turned her head back toward the station to check she wasn't being followed.

She crossed the street and made her way south past cafes with tables squeezed into every available inch of space outside them. Walking through the 2nd arrondissement, she chose quieter side streets. They had fewer pedestrians and so were easier to assess. Any face she saw more than once on these quiet cobbled streets was a sign of trouble.

She headed through grand covered arcades with glass ceilings and high-end boutique stores of the *Place Vendome* before arriving at the right bank of the Seine. She stood beside the striking metal-and-glass pyramid outside the Louvre Museum, this time having chosen a busy spot to lose herself in a crowd. Tourists strolling and taking selfies were good camouflage if anyone was trying to keep an eye on her. She made it to the apartment on Boulevard Saint-Germain, just across the river, where she would be staying. A quick check told her the one bed apartment wasn't bugged, and it had a fire escape in case she needed it, as well as a rooftop from where she could easily jump to the next terraced building.

She wanted to get to the park she'd figured the Cyclone caller had been at the day before. In the green space beside Notre-Dame Cathedral, she sat down on a bench next to a beggar, who was bearded and in a filthy green khaki jacket. She handed him 10 euros.

"*Merci,*" he said quietly.

"Do you spend a lot of time here?" she asked him in French.

"Yes, every day."

"So, you see who comes and goes?"

"Nothing else to do. Just watching people."

"Do you remember an old man here yesterday, talking on the phone? Probably smartly dressed. Probably alone."

"*Oui,*" the beggar replied. "There was only one man like that here yesterday. Talked on the phone for a while then a car came to pick him up."

"What kind of car?"

"SUV. Big. Black."

"Number?"

"Can't remember."

She handed him another 10 euros, thinking back briefly to her own penniless days back in Russia. As she headed back across the river, the burner phone in her pocket buzzed. She answered.

"You'll want to come to the Latin Quarter," said an unmistakable voice. Cyclone's relentless cold caller.

"I told you," the Scorpion replied. "When I find you, it will be on my terms."

"You can spend a week looking," the man replied. "Or you can find me right now and find out what you need to know about Marutov. And trust me, you need to know." Hairs prickled on the back of the Scorpion's neck.

"Why not tell me right now?" she asked him.

137

"Because that's not my offer. My offer is we meet and then I tell you." He paused, then added, "Listen to me. You work alone. I have teams of the most highly-skilled security experts in the world. You could meet me on your terms, but you will still leave on my terms. If you leave at all. Or we could meet today for a civilized chat."

The Scorpion realized that however and whenever she met this man, he would be ready and waiting for her. "Address?" she said. He gave her an address on Boulevard Saint-Michel and immediately hung up.

It was only a short walk from where she was to the Latin Quarter. She moved there quickly, past university students serenely carrying books and takeout coffee into the Sorbonne. Finding the apartment building, she chose the relevant number from the dirty row of buttons. The door buzzed open.

She entered a dusty corridor with paint peeling off the walls. Three flights up, she found the apartment she had been directed to. She knocked on the door. Slowly, it was opened by a man with black and messy curly hair, his eyes ringed with red lines. She knew a junky when she saw one. He was muscular and wearing a filthy vest. This was not what she was expecting.

"I was told to come here," she said.

"Sure," the man said, opening the door fully to let her in. She walked inside, adrenaline filling her body in anticipation. The man walked over to a table which he hurriedly cleared leaving scattered white powder behind. The room stank of a mixture of sweat, weed, and piss.

"You don't look like our usual customers," he said, smiling and revealing a missing tooth. "What do you need?"

"Coke," she said, improvising while she gauged what was going on. "Weed, too, if you've got it."

138

She felt a searing pain erupt at the back of her head as a blow came crashing down. She fell to one knee, then stood immediately, turning to see a huge, shaven-headed man carrying a broken bottle. He came at her with the broken end, thrusting it as she dipped to the right. She came back to land a crushing punch on the side of his head. He stumbled, and she turned back toward the table. The man in the vest was pointing a gun straight at her forehead. She put her hands in the air.

"Weapons," he said. "Whatever you're carrying on the floor."

"Okay," she said, slowly reaching for her belt. The shaven-headed man had recovered from the blow and was now looking at her like he wanted to kill her in the most painful way possible.

She moved her hands down toward her waist. She put her hand on a needle and flung it across the room, straightening her arm and opening her fingers as the weapon flew at incredible speed and pierced the man with the gun between the eyes. He fell backwards, a round from the gun exploding into the ceiling.

She turned back to the big man but she was too late. He put all his weight into an uppercut landed under her chin, lifting her whole body into the air. He pulled at her belt, releasing it and sending it skidding across the floor under a sofa. He landed a crushing headbutt on her nose. She felt her legs buckle. She jabbed a thumb in the man's eye, giving her just enough time to land another right hand on his face. He came back with a left hook. It was now an all-out fistfight.

He staggered the Scorpion with three quick right hands to her face, the hardest punches she had ever felt. She fell back into the table then to the ground. The man put his knees on her chest, hammering punches onto her face and chest while she fought back.

From the corner of her eye, she saw a heavy glass tube on the floor beside her. A bong. She stretched her hand until her fingertips could just roll it towards her, then grabbed it and smashed into the man's head. She slashed his face with the glass, sending blood squirting over her, then slid from under him. She stood up over the kneeling man and landed right hand punches on him, one after the other until all her strength was gone. Finally, he was dead, his face so bloodied it was unrecognizable.

She grabbed her belt from under the sofa and headed for the door. As she reached for the handle, the door was kicked open. A team of police streamed in, fully kitted in flak jackets and helmets, their guns at the ready. She was overwhelmed as they pinned her to the floor, unable to move. As she lay there with her face pressed hard to the ground, she realized the evidence against her in that room meant she could spend the rest of her life in prison.

*   *   *   *

The Scorpion was sitting on a wooden bench in a bare cell. She was leaning forward, her hands clasped together in front of her, cursing herself for letting herself get arrested. Suddenly, she stood. She went over to the thick metal door and kicked it as hard as she could. When that got no response, she kicked it again.

An officer came running down the hall.

"Hey!" he yelled. "You need to calm down."

"I want my phone call,"

"Soon, soon," the officer said, waving his hand dismissively. The Scorpion looked into his eyes through the grill on the door and fixed him with a stare once taught to her by a martial arts master. He'd taught her how to imagine a distant mountain far away behind a person's head. To look through them like they didn't even exist. Like they're nothing and their life means nothing to you. It worked.

He opened the door of her cell and led her down the corridor toward the phone.

"One person," the officer said. "You get a single call, that's it."

That was fine because there was only one name in her mind. Dan Roy.

CHAPTER 25

Colonel Vladimir Borislov crossed Lubyanka Square in a hurry. He was an old stalwart of the KGB, but he was getting frustrated with the lack of promotion and the way the SVR had gotten stuck in its ways. The insiders in the Kremlin were too scared to make bold moves. It was time for him to make moves of his own.

He had emerged from the Lubyanka Building, the headquarters of the FSB, which could have been a public library or city hall with its imposing Baroque Revival architecture. But somehow the building spoke of something more sinister behind its yellow-brick facade. Opposite, the Central Children's Store – one of the biggest toy stores in the world – stood as a reminder of life's stark contrasts.

Borislov stepped into a waiting Zil limousine. It proceeded away from the square down clean, stately boulevards and out of central Moscow. They were heading for a very different kind of place.

After 30 minutes, the car arrived at a square lined with warehouses. Most of them had dusted and broken windows after years of disuse. Zil limousines – and men like Borislov – were not seen in places like this. Borislov took a brief look at the square before ducking into the doorway of an abandoned warehouse.

He made his way through a dark, cramped tunnel, with exposed pipes above and moisture running down the red-brick walls. Emerging into a large room, he laid eyes on a strange scene. Some of the world's most powerful and dangerous people sitting in flawless tailored suits amid the bleak surroundings of a decaying

Soviet-era warehouse. Crystal whiskey tumblers and decanters were placed on the long table in front of each of them.

"You'll excuse the choice of venue, I'm sure," said the middle-aged man at the head of the table, speaking in a slow, calm voice. He then stood, rested his outstretched fingers on the table and leaned toward the people gathered before him.

"We are Cyclone," he said. "The organization that will blow a storm of change through the world. Western civilization is crumbling. It is plain to see. They are financially and morally bankrupt. Their tax revenues are spent on useless wars they cannot win. They talk of democracy but implant a corporate stooge in the White House who bends to the will of billionaires that make money cheating taxes."

The man then stood up straight, raising his right hand into the air with his forefinger aloft. His speech was now a performance.

"With Brexit, the old cracks are appearing again in the map of Europe," he continued. "When did Europe last see a hundred years of peace? It never has. Is it so surprising these idiot English politicians caused Brexit? Can you really sidestep the lessons of history?"

Now pompous and self-indulgent, his voice echoed off the warehouse walls and around the huge room.

"I promise you, in a decade or two war will break out in Europe. And when it does, we will already have sown the seeds of disharmony and chaos."

Everyone around the table had their eyes fixed on him, some looking on with admiration and fascination, others with the competitive contempt the powerful can't put aside.

"We will be in position to push the old order out and take control," he stated. "It is us, the guardians of Cyclone, who will write the new history books. Because we will be the victors. Let the weaklings who run their shabby, corrupt democratic states be cast aside by the tides of war. Let new blood cleanse the streets of destiny."

He then paused and lowered his voice back to calmness. He knew the dynamics any good performance needs.

"Yes, many of us will die, but their deaths will not be in vain. Because when the new world order is imposed, they will be remembered like the immortal leaders of the great socialist revolution."

He paused once more, then said: "To that end, operation Black Beauty is the first step. Comrade Borislov, how are we progressing?"

Borislov, who hadn't touched his whiskey tumbler, took a sip of vodka from a hip flask he'd pulled from his jacket.

"There's been a slight hiccup in England," Borislov said. "But it was rectified. Marutov is dead."

"What about your agent? The Scorpion?"

"I denied the existence of Cyclone. But it seems someone from here spoke to her on the phone."

"Yes. That was me," the man at the head of the table said. "I wanted to see how good she was. We shall see her in Paris. We have a hold over her she cannot break."

Borislov nodded in agreement. "She will fulfill the final step of Black Beauty."

"Indeed," the meeting leader said, still standing. "She will be our crescendo, our finale, our climax. The star of Black Beauty's glorious final act."

CHAPTER 26

Dan had been through innumerable burner phones in his life. Memorized God knows how many numbers. But there was one phone he always kept with him, a number kept secret to all but a select few people. Natasha was one of those few.

Sitting at the kitchen table in the safehouse Jeff had provided, the phone rang in his pocket. He pulled it out and looked at the screen. The number was withheld. He answered. The voice on the on the other end immediately made his pulse quicken. His fingers clutched the receiver so tight he could crush it. It couldn't be. But it was. The voice still held a promise for him, a seductive light that was like a glow inside his heart.

"Hello?" It was Natasha, the Scorpion, his arch rival, fellow assassin, the woman who knew him inside out. The woman he could communicate with without speaking. Dan shook his head, wondering if this was a dream.

"Are you there?" Her voice was low, husky, and she knew why she hadn't said his name. Just in case he was dead and the phone was in someone else's hand.

He thought quickly. It had been a year since the job in Sardinia. He hadn't heard from her in all this time. Memories of her luscious, ripe body sprang to mind. He shook his head, closed his eyes, filing the visions away. Why was she calling him now? She must be in trouble. If she just wanted to see him, she would drop in unannounced. He would wake up in the middle of the night to find her straddling his chest, a sharp needle pointed at his chin. Then, maybe, she would lean over, and his lips would meet hers.

That's the kind of woman she was.

But this felt different. Her tone was more wary.

He put her out of her misery.

"Yes, it's me. Dan. Is that you, Natasha?"

The sigh that came down the line told him a lot. She was bottling up a lot of unsaid stress.

"What is it?" Dan asked. "You can talk."

"I'm in Paris, held by the DGIS. I got one call."

His mind was racing as he rapidly tried to calculate what was going on. The Scorpion had been his enemy and a fierce one. But they had later shared a bond of passion that couldn't be ignored. Passion and respect.

But Dan sensed danger. He always told himself to trust no one, and that meant *no one*. Even someone with whom he shared an attraction that was hard to fight.

Scorpion might not even be the one who was dragging him into this. Maybe she was in a situation, and she was being blackmailed. He remembered again about Jeff saying he was a wanted man. Did the Scorpion know something about it as well?

"I need a lawyer," she said.

Of course. Someone was listening, maybe on a wiretap, and the call was being recorded. He imagined her leaning against the wall, knuckles white as she clutched the phone.

He needed to get more out of her. Not for the first time he wished they had a code set up, like all agencies did across the world. They didn't so he had to improvise.

After a pause he spoke slowly. "What. Is. The. Weather. Like. In. Paris?"

To anyone listening, it would sound odd. It would sound like a code or a trick question. But that was okay. He wasn't giving anything away. And he figured the Scorpion would know exactly what he meant by it.

146

She waited before replying, which he liked. She was thinking about it. She spoke back just as slowly. "Weather. Is. Fine. No. Need. For. Umbrella."

Dan relaxed. Scorpion spoke again but in a normal voice. "But I need help to get across the river."

He nodded and knew she would know what he was thinking. So, it didn't seem like a trap, but she did need help.

There was a lot he didn't understand. What the hell was she doing in Paris? This had to be an operation gone wrong. An operation he knew nothing about. What he did know was his situation in London was getting stickier by the day. He was in the middle of something big enough for a CIA agent to be killed for. And the Russians were involved, which the Scorpion, being a *russkaya debushka,* or Russian woman, could help out with.

A short break in Paris might be just what the doctor ordered.

See the sights. Burn down the Eiffel Tower.

"Sit tight," Dan said. He hung up. He knew he had to go to Paris. Paranoia told him not to, but instinct told him it was the right thing to do.

He contacted Jeff and asked him to get back to the safehouse as fast as he could. An hour later, Jeff walked through the door. He shook off his raincoat and hung on the back of a chair before sitting down at the table.

"What have we got?" he asked Dan.

"Plenty," Dan told him. "I've got plenty to tell you, but I need something from you too."

"I believe I've conducted that sort of business once or twice before," Jeff said, sarcastically.

"I talked with Gennady," Dan said. "Let's say we had a robust discussion. He told me there's an operation called Black Beauty."

"I'm listening," Jeff said.

"He didn't know much about it," Dan continued. "And believe me, he would have told me if he did. He only said that it's highly secretive. Not even Kremlin's top brass knows about it, just a select few men in the SVR."

"How big are we talking?" Jeff asked.

"Hard to say until we know more about it. But if Gennady is even half right then this is something that can't be ignored." Dan looked down at the floor, covered in large slate tiles. "I don't know how Grant is connected to this, but somehow, I know he is."

"Well," Jeff said, leaning back in his chair. "I'll get people on that immediately. Good work, my friend. Now, what can I do for you?"

"I need help getting to Paris," Dan said. "Get me across the Channel, and I'll do the rest."

Jeff gazed at the wall, thinking for a moment.

"I've got to tell you, I think it will be quicker without our help."

"How so?" Dan asked.

"By the time we get everything set up. A boat. Agents. You'd be better off doing it like the people who do it every day."

"And who's that?"

"People smugglers."

Dan looked at him, holding his gaze. "Is that the best you've got?" he asked.

"It's a well-trodden path," Jeff said. "If terrified refugees can do it, then you definitely can. Get to Dover, get in a truck. Wait until the truck drives onto a ferry and off the other side."

"Sounds simple," Dan said, insincerely.

"People swim the English Channel, Dan. It's not like you're a stowaway headed for the New World. 90-minute crossing."

"I can tell, you *have* done this sort of thing before," Dan said, standing. "Getting something for nothing." Jeff held out his open palms and smiled lightly.

"Can you at least get me to Dover?" Dan asked. "Clearly a boat's too much for you. How about a car?"

"I'll get you a car," Jeff said. "Couple of agents as well if you want it."

"After those guys left me to deal with Gennady and his friends while they waited outside? The car will do."

Dan figured Jeff was under orders not to give him too much help. More resources assigned to a foreign agent meant more eyebrows raised. He knew how bureaucracy worked, and he had no time for it. Jeff had provided him with the safe house at least, that was good enough.

"Just how robust was your discussion with Gennady?" Jeff asked, raising an eyebrow.

"He's alive," Dan said. "But I don't know how long the SVR will leave him walking around as a loose end. He's their problem now." He levelled a look at Jeff. "You can't help me cross the Channel, but do you have a contact in Paris?"

Jeff pursed his lips and looked away for a while. Then he nodded. "Between you and me, right?"

"Sure."

"His name is Claude. Just that." Jeff handed Dan a scrap of paper with a phone number and the words 'I can't make our rehearsal tonight' scribbled on it. "That's your password. I'll let him know you're coming."

*****

149

Dan made the 90-minute drive to Dover on England's south coast and ditched the car in the long-stay parking lot where Jeff had told him to leave it. That was the easy part. He didn't have a lot of time, but he wanted to get a sense of what the migrant crossing situation was before he went in head first. He looked up and down the street. Fifty meters away was a whitewashed pub with a sign saying, 'King's Arms.' He headed toward it.

The pub was mostly empty. It had was a lounge area with a roaring fire, but nobody sitting in it to enjoy it except a black Labrador lying on the worn carpet. The barman, a big guy with a shaved head, was chatting to two middle-aged men sitting at the bar. Dan strode up to them. This was not the time to order a diet coke.

"Pint of Guinness, sir," Dan said to the barman who served him without speaking then went back to talking to his regulars.

"Wow. That's superb," Dan said, holding up the pint of black ale. "You obviously take care of your beer. It's obvious when pubs don't bother."

The barman and two customers gave him hostile looks. They clearly thought they were talking about something important that shouldn't be interrupted.

"You must have nonstop immigrants coming over the channel and landing here, no?" Dan said to the group, ignoring their hostility. Suddenly, they perked up.

"Bloody right, mate," one of the regulars said. "It's relentless. What are we supposed to do with them all?"

"I wouldn't mind if they were real refugees," the other regular joined in. "But most of 'em are only coming here for the money."

"There's a whole bunch of 'em camping up near the castle," the barman said. "All that effort just to camp outside Dover. It's freezin'."

"Well they're not gonna come in here with your prices are they, Ken?" one of the regulars said to the barman, and all three of them laughed. Dan downed his pint of Guinness.

"Actually, that tasted like piss in the end," he said to the barman, handing him the glass. He walked out.

Dover Castle, one of the largest and best preserved medieval castles in England, sits on a hill above the town. Dan was making his way toward it. He could see the fire coming from what he thought must be the migrant camp the men in the pub had referred to. As he approached the fire, the faces of several men turned toward him. They were checking to see if he was a threat, but they had the slow, jaded movements of people who'd spent too long in tough conditions.

He approached the group and said, "Cold night." His own disheveled appearance suggested to them he was most likely a charity worker who also spent a lot of time in tough conditions. He handed out biscuits and cigarettes. Not a classic combination, but that's what he'd decided might cheer them up a little and get them talking.

"What's the best way to get to Calais?" he asked. "With no passport."

A couple of them turned to look at him in surprise.

"Most people don't go that way," he said. "Most of us come the other way."

"Well, I need to go to France."

"If you take a boat you could die," said one man with had a scarf wrapped around as much of his face as it would cover. "Lorry's not easy, but it's safer."

"Why's it not easy?" Dan asked.

"First, you got to get in," another man said. "Then you got to get past the checks. Dogs, x-ray machines. They even have heartbeat monitors."

"Most of that's on the other side, though, and half the time they don't use it," the first man said. "My advice to you? Soon as those doors open, run."

"That's good advice," Dan said.

"And take a knife," a third man added. "Easier to cut your way into those lorries than break the lock." Dan handed them the rest of the biscuits and cigarettes. He made his way toward the port. He'd decided to go that night.

He spent half an hour watching the pattern of traffic boarding ferries bound for France. Then he moved. He headed to a grass verge than ran along the side of the road where the lorries approached. He pushed himself down hard into the grass and mud. He waited until the traffic started to back up, leaving a good line of stationary trucks. Then he leopard crawled down the grass bank toward the red lorry that had unwittingly drawn the short straw.

Approaching the lorry in a low crouch, he pulled out his kukri. Without hesitation he cut into the tarp at the side of the truck, opening a gash big enough to squeeze through, but as small as possible so it wouldn't be noticed.

He rolled into the truck and lay on his back in the dark. His eyes adjusted, and he looked around the space. He was surrounded by crates with the names of charities stamped on the side. Makes sense, he thought. Most migrants are on the other side. They want to come this way, while the handouts go the other way.

The truck's engine revved and the vehicle started moving. His senses were heightened as he listened to the sound of dogs barking in the distance. He lay on his back for what seemed like hours. He knew when the truck had pulled onto the ferry because the engine was shut off and every clank echoed so much it seemed right next to him. He was sure the door would open at any moment. Finally, the engine roared to life, and they were moving again. He closed his eyes and squeezed them tight. He was almost there. Suddenly, the bolt on the lorry door began creaking, then snapped open. Light flooded into the lorry as the deafening sound of a dog's bark exploded into his ears.

CHAPTER 27

Rashid Al-Falaj made his way slowly down the majestic imperial staircase. His home, a Grade I listed Regency mansion in London's exclusive Sloane Square, was a white stone retreat behind pointed black railings. He crossed the marble floor of the mansion's entrance hall to the drawing room and lowered himself onto a green velvet sofa.

He flicked a speck of dust off his black cashmere suit before straightening his emerald cufflinks. Behind him, the wall was filled with photos of himself and his family meeting the world's business and political elites, shaking hands, and smiling. His family was made rich in the business of providing the heavy machinery needed in oil rigs. Their business stretched far beyond the Arab world to all corners of the globe. Like his cousin, Waleed, had done before Dan Roy crossed his path, Rashid used the business as a cover for terrorist activities.

A scrawny figure stepped off the street and into the luxurious mansion escorted by a butler. Kennedy was enjoying none of the luxury surrounding him. Rashid stood from the sofa. He followed Kennedy and the butler into the kitchen. The butler left them alone, closing the door.

Kennedy was invited to sit at a chair at the dining table. Rashid sat at the head of the table. Kennedy pushed his greasy hair across his forehead as Rashid stared at him.

"It should have been Dan Roy who was brought to me," Rashid said, finally. "Not you."

With his calm tone, shining, healthy skin and perfectly parted hair, Rashid was the picture of tranquility.

"Yes, sir," Kennedy said, shakily.

"But here you are," Rashid said.

"Yes, sir. I'm sorry."

"I'm offering you the opportunity to explain yourself. You're just agreeing with me."

"I can't explain, sir," Kennedy said, shuffling in his chair. "I have no excuse."

"Off course you have no excuse," Rashid said, squeezing his intertwined fingers tight together. "Just tell me what happened. What do you remember?"

"I just heard it all from inside," Kennedy said. "It was all happening outside."

"Roy was supposed to be inside with you."

"Yes, sir."

Rashid's eyes widened as he looked into Kennedy's.

"So, you let Roy go outside. What else went wrong, in your opinion?"

"I don't know, sir. I should have made sure he was inside at the right time."

"Anything else?"

"Maybe more men. If there were more…"

"So there was an error in the planning?"
"No, sir. Just... Maybe…."

"Maybe what?"

Kennedy was sweating so much his shirt collar was damp, sticking to his neck. His eyes were wide, and he licked his lips like his mouth was too dry to speak.

"Well, Roy said he... He knew what your plan was."

Rashid stood and walked over to Kennedy who shrank back in his chair. "Carry on. What else?"

"That's it. He didn't say anything more."

"You sure?"

Kennedy gulped. "If I did I'd be telling you, believe me."

Rashid walked over to a side table and slammed his fist onto it, making a vase in the center tip over and spill water across the silk tablecloth.

"You are a fixer!" he bellowed at Kennedy. "What exactly did you fix? You're a waste of oxygen. A maggot." Rashid straightened his tie. He took out his phone and typed out a message. Then he looked at Kennedy again.

"Make me a cup of tea," Rashid said. Kennedy hesitated.

One of Rashid's men stepped forward. "The kitchen is this way."

Kennedy looked wildly from the man back to his master.

"*Fix* me a cup of tea, Mr Fixer," Rashid said, pointing to the kitchen.

Kennedy walked over, followed by the man. Rashid watched from the room. Kennedy went to the kettle and filled it with water. He fumbled around in jars, looking for what he needed. The man came up behind him and put a plastic bag over Kennedy's head. Kennedy fought; his mouth opened in a silent scream. The man wrestled Kennedy to the floor and held the plastic bag in place until the lungs stopped moving. No sound and no blood. The tall man then slung the lifeless body over his shoulder and carried it out of the room without a word to Rashid.

Sitting calmly at the table, Rashid pulled out his phone again. He dialed and held it to his ear, gazing out of the window at a rosebush until an answer came.

"Where is Roy?" Rashid asked.

"I don't know," Borislov's answer came back. "But I know where he's going."

"Why don't you enlighten me?"

"Paris. DGIS HQ. Scorpion is being held there. And she called Roy for help."

"Well..." said Rashid, impressed. "You got someone on the inside?"

"Of course, I've got someone on the inside," Borislov answered. "I've got sources in much more impressive places than that."

Rashid hung up without saying anything else. Then he dialed a new number.

"Have it ready in an hour," he said. "Paris." He was headed to a private airfield and a plane with its nose pointed towards France.

CHAPTER 28

Dan raised his arms and legs above his body as he lay on his back, trying to protect his vital areas from the dog's vicious attack. It was thrusting its head towards him with teeth bared, trying to get hold of flesh. Its fangs were pulling at his clothes. Thankfully, he always wore thick and sturdy clothing. But it wouldn't be long before the dog was able to sink its teeth in.

The dog, a big German Shepherd, took a step back before coming in for another attack. Dan seized the moment and landed a fierce kick on its jaw. It let out a high-pitched yelp. But it wasn't enough to deter the dog. It came back even more determined. It dived over Dan's outstretched left leg and sank its teeth into his right thigh. He yelled in agony.

He was trying to get to his kukri, but it was caught underneath him. He pulled back his left hand and slammed it into the dog's ribs as hard as he could. He felt bones shatter beneath his fist. He'd remembered that dog's ribs break easily. He had no idea where he'd once learned that, but it might have saved his life. The dog rolled onto its side, yowling in pain.

Dan jumped to his feet and headed for the back of the truck. He was ready to take on anything. He leapt out of the truck, feeling a hand on his left shoulder. He swung an elbow at it. The hand lost its grip, and Dan ran. He sprinted as fast as he could, not once looking behind him to see who was shouting.

Seeing a large wall in front of him, he scaled it without hesitation. He landed on a muddy path next to a small stream. He sprinted along the path until he saw a thick group of bushes and headed straight through them. He emerged on the other side in a field and crouched down behind the bushes. After catching his breath, he moved in a crouched position through the field until he saw some thicker vegetation. He climbed right into the middle of it, branches scratching his hands and face, and laid down. Then, he waited.

He waited until it got dark, then he made his way through the farmland south of Calais. As he was walking, a voice whispered to him in the dark.

"Hey!"

Dan turned and saw a man in a heavy jacket and a kufi cap, a blanket around his shoulders.

"The cops are clearing the camps down that way. Not been seen round here tonight. You're better off here."

The man was clearly a migrant. Dan just didn't know if it was a good idea to be in a group. But he needed food. Water, at least. He'd be willing to pay them. He stepped toward the man and they walked the short distance to a small camp.

The camp had one tent provided by a charity, but it was badly torn. The other shelters were pathetic structures cobbled together from whatever materials had been scavenged. The man walked off. The migrants warned each other about what camps might be cleared but had little more help to offer.

"You got any food?" Dan called after him. The man turned around.
"Does it look like it?" he said, his palms upturned and his arms outstretched.

"Water?" Dan asked.

The man went into a shelter and rummaged around before emerging with a container of water. Dan drank from it eagerly. The man was watching him closely.

"Where you from?" he asked.

"Here and there," Dan said. The man looked at Dan askance.

"What are you doing here?"

The guy spoke good enough English. Dan examined him closely. He wasn't Middle Eastern. More likely from the Maghreb, the part of North Africa France used to colonize once – Algeria, Tunisia and Morocco. Where the *Le Afrique Blanc*, as the French called them, or the pale skinned Africans, came from.

Behind a weather beaten craggy face the man had a pair of intelligent dark eyes. He could be an undercover cop, working for the DGIS, keeping an eye on illegal immigrants. But even if he was, Dan could use his help without giving much away.

"Hiding," Dan replied. "Thanks for helping me. Things look pretty bad for you here. You've got enough to worry about."

"It's worse since they cleared The Jungle," the man told him. Dan knew that was the name for the huge migrant camp that had been in Calais. "That place was hell, but at least people knew where to bring food and water for us. Now we just camp wherever we can until the cops come and destroy it again."

"Where are you from?" Dan asked him. "Algeria. I'm Adham Amari." Adham held out a filthy hand. Dan shook it and introduced himself.

"I was a journalist," Adham said. "Was too critical of the wrong people so they tried to kill me. Almost did, too."

The two of them talked beside a small fire for a while before Dan fell into an exhausted sleep. In the morning, he borrowed some rusty scissors from someone in the camp and cut his hair. He also trimmed the beard that had grown since he'd last had time to take care of himself.

"What's the next big town south?" he asked Adham, who had walked up from that direction several weeks earlier.

"Saint-Omer, I think. About 40k southeast."

That's a steady morning's run, Dan thought to himself, *but I'll be too exposed*. His phone battery was dead, so he borrowed Adham's phone to find out the time of the next bus to Paris. Then he waited until the last minute before heading into town. Before he left, he took Adham's number.

"Thanks for everything," he said to Adham. "I'll make it up to you one day."

He headed into Calais and found the bus station four minutes before the bus was due to leave. He bought a ticket with cash, stepped onto the bus, and headed for a seat at the back. He pulled his jacket over his face and slept.

When he awoke, he was in Paris. He cleaned himself up as well as he could in the bus station bathroom, then he went to find a payphone. He picked up the cigarette-burned phone and called the number Jeff had given him.

"Oui?" a male voice on the other end said.

"I can't make our rehearsal tonight," Dan replied. It was the code Jeff had given him.

"Are you Claude?"

"Oui. Who are you?"

Dan said his name and gave his location.

"You'll need a car," Claude told him, switching to English. "Hire one and pay cash. Use FastRent in the 2nd arrondissement. When you get here, wait outside at the back of the building. On the cobbled path by the banks of the Seine."

Dan did as he was told. An hour later, he was close to DGIS HQ, staking out the building. He was watching everyone who went in and came out. He was watching anyone who went near the place. Then, he saw something odd. He noticed someone doing the exact same thing as him. Watching.

CHAPTER 29

The Scorpion was leaning out of the window already, twisting so she was facing the SUV hurtling toward them. She squeezed off three rounds, and Dan knew without looking she would be aiming for the tires.

"Watch out," he shouted. "Left."

He hung a sharp turn left as she hung on. The Citroen bumped along the charming cobbled street, a hallmark of Parisian street life, but right then, Dan thought, gritting his teeth, annoying as hell, because it made his head bump against the car's roof.

His eyes widened. His head bumping was suddenly the least of his problems. Because right in front of him was a street full of cafes. White tablecloth from tables laid out on the pavement fluttered in the breeze. Well-dressed men and women were gathering around the tables, holding aloft glasses of wine and chatting. The street was narrow, wide enough for a small car, and several cars were already parked, effectively blocking Dan's way.

"Oh, shit!" Dan said.

The Scorpion sat down beside him and said something similar in Russian.

The SUV turned its headlights on. It was blinding. Dan shielded his eyes and pressed on the gas. The Citroen's engine growled as it thrust forward. Dan saw the people at the cafe closest to him look up, and their faces changed when they realized the Citroen was headed straight for them.

"Move!" Dan screamed as he floored the pedal. He hit the side of a table as he swerved to miss a human, and crashed into a metal pole holding a parasol. The parasol folded on the car as Dan kept barging through, hitting chairs and tables. A bottle of wine flew at the windscreen, smashed and red wine colored the screen red.

Dan twisted the steering wheel left and right, desperately trying to avoid as much as he could. Screams and shouts filled the air, glass splintered on the ground and people dived for cover.

Then he was out on a main road and narrowly missed hitting a car as he hurtled on. Horns beeped, windows lowered, and drivers shook their fists.

Beads of sweat dripped down Dan's neck. "See what you made me do?" he asked the Scorpion.

She ignored him, twisted in the seat to face the rear. "They're still coming at us."

Dan glanced at the rear view. "Don't worry," he said. "They won't shoot now."

His words were drowned as the sound of sirens filled the air. Both of them groaned audibly.

"Who's in the SUV?" Scorpion asked.

Dan shook his head as he swerved around a station wagon. "I don't know. But they followed me. Which isn't good news."

They were coming up to an intersection. Dan gritted his teeth and jumped the red lights. Traffic was crossing sideways ahead of him. He wrenched the wheel to either side until it felt like it might come off in his hands. He narrowly missed one car, then another smashed into his tail gate. The bigger crash happened behind him as two cars banged into one another head on. Dan kept driving and suddenly he was in a much bigger, four lane avenue. Up ahead, a massive arch rose to the sky, lit up by a thousand lights.

"You're on the Champs-Élysées," Scorpion unformed him matter-of-fact. "And there I was thinking I wouldn't get a chance to see the Arc de Triomphe."

Without comment, Dan dodged traffic and drove for the Arc. He knew twelve roads joined this massive intersection, and with any luck, he could give the approaching police cars the slip.

Claude had given him the address of a safe house in Saint Denis, a less desirable suburb just outside the capital. He had no idea of how safe it would be now. It wasn't every day a captive escaped the clutches of the DGIS. Paris will be on high alert.

The sound of a bullet hitting the metal work brought him back to his senses.

"I'm on it," Scorpion shouted. She leaned out the window and aimed, but Dan could see a was car between them and the SUV.

"Get back in," Dan shouted. "You can't shoot and not attract attention."

He sped up and took the ramp when he saw the sign for Saint Denis. A dark, quiet bypass loomed ahead. Dan drove into it and turned the car off. Minutes later, he saw the black SUV drive past, then the flashing lights of the chasing police cars.

They got out, leaving the car in the lay by. Dan grabbed Scorpion's hand, only to find it hard and unyielding. When he looked at her face, her eyes held a curious light, her mouth slightly open. He tried his best not to focus on her sexy lips and failed miserably. He coughed and squeezed his eyes shut.

"Best to look like tourists, right?" Dan asked.

Her hand became softer, the muscles relaxing. He hadn't forgotten how pliable, warm her skin was. How, despite all her years in the business of killing men, she had a feminine touch that warmed him inside and made the blood flow to his loins. Her mere touch still jolted his senses like a spark of electricity to a raw nerve.

Oh man, this is harder than getting shot at.

She gripped his hand and he found himself staring down at their entwined hands. When he spoke, his voice was hoarse. "Let's go."

They found a cab two miles from the Arc and got dropped a mile outside their address in Saint Denis. The cab drove off, and they found themselves alone on a street with tall apartment complexes that reminded Dan of housing projects in New York, and the council estates he had seen in London. Graffiti adorned the walls, an upturned rubbish bin stood a few yards away, and a burnt car was propped up on bricks because the tires were gone. Lights were on in the forest of nondescript apartment complexes.

All of them looked like they needed new paint and a makeover. Housing for the poor and marginalized in society. Funny, Dan thought, how they were situated so far from the glittering splendor of Paris. At least in NYC and London, the projects rubbed shoulders with the wealthier parts of the city. Dan liked that. Everyone knew the score. Social classes would always exist, but the feeling that they all belonged in the same society was important. In France, it seemed to be different. There was no place in the city proper for these massive concrete villages.

"Guess we just arrived in the *banlieues*," Scorpion said.

Dan had heard that name before. Literally, it meant suburb in French. But colloquially, it stood for where the poor in France lived, and in this area many were of North African descent. The huge immigrant population who were not fully integrated in French society and whose life, and location, seemed to be on the outside, looking in.

164

This was where, periodically, the French riots took place. Dan spread his hands. "The address is right. Our place is around the corner."

He had bought a map from a tourist shop and used it to navigate to the right building. It was at the corner of one estate, next to an iron grill fence, overlooking the train station. The building was a single floor, family home, one of several in a block.

"You sure this is safe?" Scorpion asked.

Dan shrugged. "Well, it's all we have. Don't turn the lights on and keep an eye out for the trains. That's our best escape route."

Dan opened the door with the key Claude had given him. The door opened with a screech. Dan stood outside and turned his Maglite on. Inside, it was sparse but neat and clean. Two bedrooms, a lounge with TV, kitchen, and diner. The kitchen was well stocked, down to bottles of white wine in the fridge.

Scorpion was bending over, fridge door open. Dan was again having a hard time not looking at the shape of her butt, but the Maglite seemed frozen in his hand, pointed directly at her.

She pulled out a bottle of wine. "Courtesy of the French government?"

"Not for me, thanks," Dan said.

She put the bottle back and shut the fridge door. "I was joking."

She came closer. Dan switched the Maglite off. Streetlights came in from the window, and their eyes grew used to the dark. She came closer still, and Dan could feel the heat of her body. His back hit the kitchen counter.

She reached out a hand and with one finger traced the outline of his jaw. Dan closed his eyes as her palm caressed his face. The warmth of her touch was strangely comforting, relaxing.

"Thank you for coming," she whispered. She leaned into him. Dan didn't stop her. She put her head against his shoulder, and a

165

soundless sigh escaped his lips as his jaw clenched and brows furrowed together.

Natasha and him had always been a harbor in the tempest to each other. Like wildly tossed ships at sea, their chaotic lives were mired in uncertainty and violence. It was the only life he knew. She was the only one who understood because she was just like him.

And they also understood how one day they might get an order to kill each other.

Dan knew he couldn't do it. If that was weakness, then so be it. He had never knowingly killed a woman, and one he had feelings for? No way.

But Natasha he wasn't so sure of. Her childhood had been hard, cruel even. It had shaped her into what she was. If it came to killing him, she might just do it.

He couldn't explain why he found that attractive.

Her finger was tracing lightly over his lips. He could feel himself harden, and the light gasp from her meant she had, too. Dan put a hand on her shoulder and separated himself gently.

"Not now. We need to talk."

She sighed, and it took Dan every ounce of willpower to stand apart from her.

Dan asked, "Do you know of someone called Gennady in the Russian Embassy in London?"

"No. Why?"

"He used to meet with Grant Pearson, the CIA agent who was killed in front of me. Gennady tried to get heavy with me too."

Dan walked into the darkened living room, and she followed. They sat down on the floor, shielded by the sofas around them, but able to see out the windows.

Dan asked, "Do you know of something called Black Beauty?"

CHAPTER 30

Melania Stone was having a long day. She had just come back from vacation, and the list of emails she had not replied to seemed to have gotten longer since she arrived this morning. Her division was South Europe. It had something to do with her choosing Italian language to major in and then living in the Rome campus of her university. But mostly, because she liked the food and culture. Developing assets in Italy sounded a lot better than doing it in Baghdad.

Today, it seemed like a bad idea. A CIA agent had been killed in London. The ripples of enquiry had spread all over Europe, and Italy, especially south Italy with its highly porous borders and proximity to North Africa. She had to contact all her assets in Italy one by one, seeing if they knew anything. It was painstaking, and she was exhausted.

The clock ticked the twentieth hour of the day. Melania ploughed on, pulling up reports from local south Italian newspapers to scan for anything unusual. One thing did bother her. Just a year ago, she had busted a big criminal gang in Sardinia. Dan Roy, a shadowy agent whose real identity she was never sure of, had helped her a lot in the operation. She wondered where and how he was. Part of her could also not help but wonder if Dan would know anything about the death of this CIA agent.

There was a knock on her door, and before she could tear her eyes off the screen, the handle turned and a blonde head leaned in. It was the big boss, Susan Harris. Melania sat upright in her chair, then half rose.

"Ma'am—"

Susan swept in gracefully, her six feet three frame almost hitting the top of the door frame. She waved at Melania. "Sit down, please. And stop calling me Ma'am. Makes me sound old. Can't afford it, at my age." She chuckled.

Melania tried not to gape. To have the supreme head of the CIA, or the President, as agents called her behind her back, was a big deal. But to have her drop in unannounced and shoot the breeze like they were old friends was even more bizarre.

Melania had never seen her leader this up close. She wondered if Susan had a hairdresser and stylist somewhere in her office. Despite the hour, the highlights in her hair seemed newly done, and her light blue pant suit didn't have a single crease in it. The color complemented the blue in her eyes, which was untouched by the mirth in her voice. Susan had flat, cold eyes that could outstare any man.

"So, how are you doing?" Susan asked.

"I, oh, guess I'm fine," Melania said. She rearranged a stack of papers on the table.

She looked up to find Susan's blue eyes fixed on her.

"Did you get the report on the death of Grant Pearson?" Susan asked.

A sense of unease tickled in the back of Melania's mind. The report on Grant's death had been sketchy to say the least. It described how he had been killed inside his apartment by a long-range snipers rifle, and the MI6 were looking into it. Apart from that, however, there was hardly any information.

The fact that this happened in London was cause enough for worry. Add the minimalist report to that, and the fact that Susan Harris herself was sitting in her office asking her about it – Melania was getting the distinct feeling her long day was about to get worse.

London was a friendly zone. The CIA had never admitted they had a large London office, but that fooled no one. Almost a third of the employees in the newly opened Battersea Square offices were CIA. One of the reasons for the new London offices was unease about the owners of the grand old offices in Grosvenor Square – the Kuwait Sovereign Wealth Fund. Embassy offices were rife with harmless individuals who turned out to be spies. And as owners, the Kuwaiti Fund could send an inspector at any time to visit the premises.

The CIA had been a major backer to re-site the US Embassy in London. And it had been at the goading of the MI6, who were also concerned about security issues. None of this ever hit the headlines. But it was well known within the agency.

Therefore, Melania couldn't understand why Six, as MI6 was known, hadn't gotten the straight dope on this as yet. After all, if one their agents was killed in New York the FBI would be all over it.

"Penny for your thoughts," Susan said.

Melania shrugged, trying to act casual. But she was too beat to act. Tiredness had a way of bringing out the real self.

"It's a big deal, right? I'm surprised we don't know more at this stage." She bit her lip, wondering if she'd said too much.

Susan didn't seem bothered. Instead, a light smile hovered at the corner of her lips.

"What's your take on the proceedings?"

"I don't know enough about it to have an opinion."

"You just got back from vacation, I get that. And technically, London isn't your zone."

"Right." *Why the hell did you ask then?* She couldn't help thinking to herself.

Susan's eyes wandered to the books stacked on her shelf. A few in Italian and Spanish, mostly on Italian history. The blues moved back to settle on Melania.

"You must be wondering why I'm here," Susan said.

"It did cross my mind," Melania smirked.

Susan leaned forward, clasping her hands together. "What I'm about to ask you is totally confidential. Got that?"

"Yes ma—I mean Susan."

"Okay." Susan paused for a moment before speaking. "Last year, you were in charge of Operation Condor in Sardinia."

The unease was like a black cloud at the back of Melania's mind now. It unfurled and moved, darkening her mindscape.

"Yes, I was," she said.

"Then you will remember a man called Dan Roy."

The rain clouds burst, drenching her mind with alarm. She kept her face impassive. "Yes, I do."

Susan was observing her. It was unnerving, having to look back at her eyes, but Melania forced herself to. Her job was always a game, a dance, and the worst dances were those she had to perform with her own colleagues. But she needed to do this until the music came to an end.

"Do you stay in touch with him?" Susan asked, spacing the words out slightly, watching her reaction.

Melania didn't answer immediately. But not too late either. "No, I don't."

"I see."

"What's this about? Does Dan Roy I have anything to do with what happened to Grant?"

Again, Susan took her time in answering. She sat up straight her, then landed back in her chair.

"I'm trusting you with this information, Melania." Susan raised her eyebrows and Melania noted the silence.

Susan said, "Dan Roy was following Grant Pearson in London. We don't know why he was there. He is known to work for Consular Operations which is a part of the state department.

Melania nodded. "Yes, I remember that." She also knew that Consular Operations was a bullshit office that existed only in name. It was a front for Intercept agents. From the sardonic expression on Susan's face she guessed Susan knew this as well.

"I think it is time for us to be honest with each other," Suzanne said. Melania said nothing and waited.

"We don't know at this stage exactly what happened. But Dan was in London because an MI6 agent wanted to speak to him." Suzanne went on to tell Melania what Dan had been doing in London.

Melania listened, the knot of worry in her mind getting tighter by the second. She tried to figure out what Susan wasn't telling her, but it was foolhardy at this stage. She was better off concentrating on what she did now.

"So, just to recap," Melania said. "At this stage, we don't know who killed Grant, and we don't know where Dan is."

Susan nodded. "That's right."

Melania spread her hands. "So what do you want from me?"

"I want you to contact Dan Roy," Susan said.

Melania stared at her boss for a few seconds, and then said, "But I haven't spoken to him since last year. What makes you think he will respond to me?"

"It's worth a try. No one else we know has worked with him recently. In fact, we are not even sure what he has been up to for the last year." Susan shrugged, and her lips downturned. "This guy likes to live under the radar."

Melania pursed her lips and waited. She knew now that Susan knew a lot more than she was letting on. Dan had opened up to Melania about his background, and she knew that it was top-secret, highly classified.

"I'll see what I can do," Melania said. "I must have his number somewhere, although I last used it over a year ago."

"It's the best anyone can do at this stage. If you could do this it would be a great help. For a fallen comrade." Susan added with emphasis.

She had to drop that in, didn't she, Melania thought to herself.

Susan smiled and stood. Melania felt obliged to stand as well. They shook hands again, then Susan turned and left.

Melania sat down to think after the door shut. A storm settled on her mind, lightning flashes sparking into the distant corners.

Memories were suddenly exposed by the light, memories that she had kept hidden for more than a year. On her last trip to Sardinia, she had found out things about herself she never thought were possible.

And Dan Roy had been central to those findings.

She put her elbows on the desk, and her head sank down into her hands. Her forehead hurt, and she was desperately in need of a coffee. No, scrap that, what she needed was a strong gin and tonic.

She stood and packed her things. She put the laptop in her tote handbag and some paper files into a backpack. She checked her phone for any messages then left the office. The parking lot was almost empty when she emerged.

Her Audi A5 accelerated smoothly as she drove out of McLean and took the highway to Bethesda where she lived in a two-bedroom apartment. She had the option of living in Maclean, but the cost was the same, but the latter was quieter, leafier.

She arrived back home in less than half an hour. Muggles, her tomcat, was mewling for food when she opened the door. She stroked his black head, then gave him some food. Then she fixed herself dinner and poured a drink. She put the lights on, opened up a laptop by the table next to the window, and took a sip of her gin and tonic.

That's when she noticed the car parked opposite her apartment. Of course, there was nothing unusual about cars parked on a residential street. But none of them had a broad-shouldered man sitting in the driver seat. The man was sitting motionless. She couldn't see his hands or make out his face, but she could tell he was looking up at her window. A cold fist of fear circled around her guts.

She scrambled off the chair and turned off the light.

She closed the blinds. The man was still sitting quietly. The car was a black Escalade, a vehicle commonly used by the agency.

Melania went to the safe in her bedroom, punched in the combination, and took out a Glock 17. She slipped the magazine out, checked it, then slapped it back in. She put the weapon in a shoulder holster. She got changed into dark colored gym tights and sneakers, and put a light, black coat on top. She locked the door behind her, and went down the stairs.

174

Once outside, she didn't give the man a second glance. Her ball cap was pulled low over her face. She detected movement as she passed the car, but didn't look back. She walked briskly to the end of the road then took a left toward the bus station located at the end. She didn't have to wait long. She didn't miss the man in a long, black overcoat and dark glasses walk up to the bus station slowly. The same guy from the car.

Only one other person was waiting for the bus. Melania tried her best not to stare at the man who was following her. He took out a newspaper and pretended to read it. When the bus arrived, she got on and so did he.

CHAPTER 31

1600 Pennsylvania Avenue NW

Washington DC

From the North facade, the Executive Residence is the central and most visible part of the White House. It is where the First Family has lived since 1800.

The Executive Residence primarily occupies four floors: the Ground Floor, the State or First Floor, the Second Floor, and the Third Floor.

The First family's Dining Room is on the first floor, adjacent to the State Dining Room. Bertram Ryan, the President, looked at his wife, Janice, as he took a sip of the orange juice next to his plate of roast chicken and vegetables.

In the distance, he could hear the muffled vibrations of Marine One, the President's helicopter, landing on the East Lawn.

The Family Dining Room underwent its first significant renovation since the Kennedy years in 2015. First Lady Michelle Obama had the room painted a light grey, and the decor, furniture, rug, and artwork now reflect a Mid-20th century modern look.

Janice, his wife of 19 years, liked the decor, and although Bertram had an issue with it, preferring the classical wall papers himself, he had little choice but to go along with it. After all, he was hardly ever in this room. And when he was present, Janice and their two children took up most of his attention. The children were at college and wouldn't be back until the winter holidays. Bertram missed them, and like many men his age felt a pang of guilt when he thought about how much he had ignored the children when they were young. All for his career, of course. Now the children were out of his hands, and it was strange that even in his busy schedule thoughts of them as small children came to his mind. His relationship with them was still strong, thanks to Janice.

Janice Ryan was fifteen years younger than her husband, which made her forty. She was his second wife, and he never regretted marrying her. She had been a staffer in the House of Congress and knew the slimy capital city like the back of her hand. She had managed to keep her reputation intact despite the advances of several senators and congressmen, all lured by her stunning looks. At forty, Janice managed to look almost ten years younger. Her blonde locks and dark eyes had turned many a man's head, and Bertram still considered himself lucky to have her.

Besides, she was a dynamo between the sheets. Whatever little time Bertram has to have sex, he enjoyed it to the fullest. Both of them still took a voracious interest in each other's bodies, and he was always pleased to see how hard she worked to stay in shape.

"More veggies?" Janice asked. "It's good for you, Bertie."

"And hardly any calories, I know." He winked at her, eyeing the heaped vegetables on her plate. "Just wish they tasted like steak."

Janice waggled a finger at him. "You had that last night at the Hungarian dinner party. And quite a lot of red wine, I might add."

"Only two glasses," Bertram said, smiling at the defensive tone in his voice.

A butler came up to pour some tea for them, and a maid walked in with a pot of gravy. They were dining alone, but had guests often, including foreign state dignitaries they knew well, like the UK Prime Minister.

Bertram asked, "Are you sure you want to do this?"

Janice took the gravy and thanked the butler. "It's important to make an appearance. You said so yourself."

A woman's jail outside Jersey City, NJ, had seen a female inmate die, and the event caused a riot inside the jail. The forced suppression of the revolt became headlines, and the town folk surrounded the jail, protesting and waving placards. Other groups across the country joined them, and the protest movement was now in full swing, TV broadcasters having a field day.

Things grew so bad the army was mobilized in the town. The government was criticized for its lack of response, hence the President's planned visit. Janice was aware of the events unfolding through her involvement in women's rights groups.

She made sure these groups were not political. Although her own political beliefs remained firmly in the center, similar to her husband's central Republican stance. It was not becoming of the First Lady to be active in politics or to choose sides.

Bertram knew very well his wife was keen to drop her charity and fundraising work and dabble in politics again, but it wouldn't work out well for either of them. But his wife's interest was endearing. She had the guts and panache to do it, he knew that.

"I did ask you to come," Bertram said, pouring gravy over his chicken. "But I don't want you to feel pressured."

"I'm fine. I want to do this." Her tone was firm, but also flat. Bertram picked up on it.

She looked at him. "I'm also coming to Moscow with you. For the G20 Summit in two weeks time."

He couldn't hide his surprise. After her cyst removal, he had thought she wouldn't agree to come. But Janice had been different since she came back from her mother's house. Margaret was dying, Bertram knew that. Maybe it was affecting his wife more than he realized.

He put his knife and fork down. "Darlin', I know you're having a hard time dealing with Margaret's condition."

"I'm fine." The words came out harsh, louder than expected.

Bertram frowned. "Janice, are you okay?"

Janice pressed the sides of her forehead, leaning on her hand. Bertram rose and walked down the table. He squeezed her shoulders.

"Honey, I'm sorry."

Janice sat up straight. "I'll be all right." She smiled at her husband, a weak, wan effort. "Honestly."

"Are you sure? You don't have to do this."

"I want to, Bertie. I need to take my mind off things. Besides, always wanted to see the Red Square."

Bertram stared at her for a while, like he was trying to open the closed doors of her mind and look inside. Then he walked back to his seat and sat down.

Janice said, "But I am going to Paris first, okay? That's been in the planner for a while."

Bertram nodded. "That's fine. But sure you can manage Moscow a week after Paris?"

"Yes," she grinned at him. "Might as well travel the world while I have the chance."

Bertram said, "Has the Press Office been over what you're going to say today?"

"Sure have. I got the stats on new women prisons opened last year, and how suicide rates in all prisons are at a historic low."

"Only because we kill the really bad ones," Bertram said and regretted it immediately when his wife frowned.

"I think I'll give a better interview," Janice said dryly.

"No interviews," Bertram said quickly. "Cory knows, right?"

Cory Brent was the White House Press Office Liaison Officer who travelled with the First family.

"Relax, Bertie, I'm joking. You're the only one holding the talk. I know that."

There was a knock on the main door, and a butler poked his head in. "It's Randall, sir," the butler said.

Bertram wiped his lips with a napkin. "Show him in."

Randall Rann, the head of the Secret Service, was ushered in. In his late forties, he was a handsome, tall figure in his black suit. He coughed into his hands, lingering by the doorway.

"Apologies for disturbing your lunch, Mr. President."

Bertram waved him closer. "No, we're almost done. Is our ride ready?"

"Marine One is, Sir," Randall confirmed. The Secret Service were responsible for the President's safekeeping, but Marine One, the President's personal helicopter, was normally checked over by the

Marines assigned to the White House. In this instance, as the First Lady was travelling as well, extra checks were in place.

Janice was dressed and ready to go. She took a sip of her coffee and nodded at her husband. "Let's do this."

*****

Randall Rann's phone beeped as his shoes clicked down the stairs of the East Wing. Not his work phone. Eagerly, he pulled out his iPhone, and his face split into a grin. He stopped on the landing, checking to make sure he was alone. From the long, stained glass window, he could see the deep-blue helicopter waiting at the end of the lawn.

"Hello?" Randall said, trying to hide the smile in his voice.

"Hey sexy," a woman's voice purred.

Randall exhaled. He swiveled on the balls of his feet. "I told you not to call when I'm working," he said, injecting authority into his voice. He knew she liked that. Liked the fact that he was big and tough, willing to take a bullet for his job. She'd made that very clear last week when they met for the third date. How she liked him being the alpha man, liked him taking control. The way she knelt, looking up at him with his cock in her mouth.

"Shall I hang up then?" she asked, sounding downbeat.

"No," Randall said too quickly. He cleared his throat. "I mean, it's okay. I'm busy, but told the guys what to do."

"You're the leader of such an important team," she gushed. "Keeping the President safe."

"It's just a job," Randall said, trying to sound modest. Then he thought, what the hell. She likes it when he's in control. "But you're right. It's more than a job, it's a calling."

181

"Oh, yeah," she said. Her voice dropped two octaves and became husky. "I find that so sexy."

Randall closed his eyes and licked his lips. His mouth was dry. He was one year out of a divorce that had cleaned him out. He'd given Helen the house, half his savings, the bitch even took the Tesla. Damn fucking expensive lawyer she hired treated him like trash. So what if Randall liked to drink a bit? Who didn't in this day and age? Hell, the pressures of his job drove him to have a few after work.

Randall was lonely. He was hitting bars, looking for women. Not hookers. Respectable, clean women, those who would pass security checks. And Skylar was all of those. A divorcee as well, similar age to him, no children. Randall looked up her ex-husband. Rich businessman. His loss was Randall's gain.

"I want you," Skylar breathed down the phone.

Randall's cock was embarrassingly hard. He looked around him wildly, then scampered down the stairs, trying to hide his hard on. He smiled at one of the Admin ladies, then ran inside a restroom. Thankfully, it was empty.

"What's going on?" Skylar asked.

"I've got to go. About to leave."

"I need to see you."

Randall gripped his forehead. Mixing business and pleasure was not allowed in his job. But he wanted this woman. It had been so long, and she was so good to him. So obedient, so...

"Randy? Honey?"

He liked, no loved, when she called him Randy. Which right now, he was. Randy as hell.

Fuck it. What harm could it do? All he wanted was some human comfort. And it would only be after the job, and he'd make sure he could leave at any time.

He'd given his life for the job. And what did he get back?

Government salary and his wife fucking some asshole from her office.

He wasn't doing anything wrong. He was the boss, damn it. All leaders needed to blow off steam.

"I have to go to Jersey City, NJ," he said. "You can't tell anyone else this. If you do I'm gonna be pissed off."

She breathed heavily down the phone. "What will you do to me, Randy baby?"

His mouth opened when Skylar continued, "I want you to tie me up. Shall I get some handcuffs?"

"Up to you," Randall said in a strangled whisper. "Just remember those red lace panties."

CHAPTER 32

Hammond was a small town close to Jersey City's industrial parks. Stainforth Prison was outside the Town's borders, but most of the prison guards came from Hammond.

The White House entourage was staying in Jersey City. The central Westin hotel had been taken over by the White House staff and the Secret Service men, including the President. Due to the President's schedule, this had to be an evening visit. The President was due in Atlantic City early morning to address their Chamber of Commerce, so it made no sense to travel overnight back to DC.

It was 10pm, and on a third-floor bedroom of the hotel Randall was fast asleep. Skylar was naked and raised herself up on elbow to look at him. It had taken him a while to fall asleep, but she knew he would. Men had a habit of dozing off after the event, and she had also shaken the contents of a small sachet containing GHB or gamma hydroxy butyrate, a potent central nervous system depressing drug, into his vodka and orange when they met. GHB was also known as the date rape drug.

While Randall snored with his mouth open, Skylar got busy. She got up, dressed and packed all her clothes. She opened her backpack and took out a black zipped bag. She checked its contents carefully, ensuring batteries were inserted into the objects.

She got hold of Randall's pants and searched them. She had his ID card already, but in the inside pocket of his coat she found what she was looking for – the black key card that opened the door to the Presidential Suite on the top floor.

Skylar went out of the room and into the elevator, backpack over her shoulders. At the top floor, she didn't step out of the elevators though. She'd made a mistake. Secret Service agents would be guarding the doors. She pressed the buttons for the lower floor and got out of the elevators quickly, then dashed for the fire escape. Once she reached the top, she encountered what she had feared – in addition to the main doors of the top floor, there was an agent at the fire escape door as well.

Damn. She had to improvise, but Skylar was good at improvising.

She took the elevator to the reception lobby, then the stairs to the service level in the basement. She slipped inside the laundry room, then ducked beneath the counters. The room was huge, and luckily for her, not too busy right now. At the far end, she saw a housemaid folding bedsheets into a mobile basket. Skylar checked her watch – 11.15pm. Randall would begin to stir in half an hour, maximum. She had to be out of the hotel by then. It didn't leave her with much time. She pulled down a pillowcase, and used her knife to cut it into a strip.

Silent as a ghost, she padded up to the uniformed housemaid. She was the right shape and size for Skylar. The housemaid was humming a tune to herself and didn't clock anything until a hand clamped over her mouth and banged her head against the counter. Skylar didn't use excessive force. She just wanted to stun the poor girl not kill her.

She tied the maid up, but not before removing the uniform.

"Hello?"

A man's voice made her freeze. It came from her left, across three aisles of clothing counters. The laundry was piled six layers high. But regardless, the owner of the voice would see Skylar soon.

"Charlene?" The footsteps came closer.

185

Skylar had moved around the corner, half dressed, dragging the semi naked body of the maid with her. She took her knife out and waited, heart knocking against her ribs. This was the last thing she wanted. But if it came to it, she wouldn't hesitate. She knelt on one knee, knife cocked in her fist.

"Charlene?" the man raised her voice. His steps came closer.

Skylar muttered an oath under her breath.

The steps turned and then faded. Skylar leaned her head out a fraction to look. A bell boy was walking away. She made sure he had left before she got dressed as fast as she could in the maid's uniform.

She went up in the service elevator and pushed the large wheeled basket into the top floor. A Secret Service agent came up to her. She smiled and waited. He checked inside the basket, which contained nothing but sheets and cleaning materials in the drawers outside. Satisfied, the agent waved her on. He spoke on the radio to alert the other agents. When Skylar got to the door, one agent held it open for her. She slipped inside, and the agent followed.

Damn.

She made a show of cleaning around the spacious lounge and noticed the agent following her movements with his eyes. She dusted, hoovered lightly, then went into the bedroom.

The agent didn't follow. The door was ajar, and the room was large enough that she could hide in one corner. Deep inside the basket she had hidden the contents of her backpack. All three objects were small enough to look like a shirt button. They were the color of the wall of the bedroom – lavender.

Skylar made sure the agent couldn't see her. Then she quickly dragged a chair over to a wall and stood on it. She could reach high enough to plant the round remote camera to one side of a picture frame, hidden from casual view. It had a wide-angle lens that allowed a 180-degree view.

She went inside the bathroom and attached another camera next to the soap container in the shower.

There was a knock on the door.

"Are you almost done in here?" the agent outside asked.

"Yes," Skylar said, emerging from the bathroom. "All done. Thank you."

*****

Skylar was in a cab, riding out to the park and ride parking lot where she had left her Honda Civic. She turned on her phone and clicked on the app that controlled the remote cameras. A 180-degree view of the Presidential Suite bedroom and then the bathroom sprang to view. The room had no lights on, but the cameras worked on the same principles as night vision goggles, they collected ambient light, including infra-red, and made an image visible. The rooms were empty as both the President and the First Lady were out at dinner.

Skylar got into her Honda at the parking lot, then called her contact. She reverted to Russian. Skylar's real name was Nasirova, and she was from Dagestan.

The woman who picked up the phone had blonde hair and deep blue eyes. It was the same woman who had killed every person inside the clinic in Geneva.

"Black Beauty has eyes," Nasirova said, "Do you copy?"

"Yes," said the woman.

187

CHAPTER 33

The President and First Lady didn't get back to the five-star hotel until late at night. Randall escorted them from the lobby into the elevators. As the elevators ascended, Bertram took a close look at Randall.

"Are you okay?" the President asked his Chief of the Secret Service.

Randall didn't answer. He had his back to the First couple, and his head was turned down. Randall was staring at his feet.

"Randall!" Bertram raised his voice.

The man jumped and turned around to face Bertram. His hair was disheveled, like he had tried to hastily pat it into place, and his suit seemed crumpled. His eyes were hollows in their sockets.

Bertram eyed him warily. "You seem strung out, Randall." Instinctively, his arm tightened around Janice's waist, drawing her closer. "Is everything okay?"

"Sorry, Mr. President. Yeah, everything's fine." Randall smiled and tried to look normal.

"Looks like you could do with some sleep." Bertram yawned. "Mind you, so could I."

Randall smiled and cleared his throat. "Your room is cleaned and ready, sir." He nodded politely at Janice, then turned his back to them quickly.

"You sure everything is okay though, right? Has the Press Office been in touch?"

Randall turned again, stiffly. "No, sir. No news. All under control."

Bertram relaxed and sighed. Janice rubbed his arm as the elevator dinged, and they stepped out on the top floor. The agents on duty moved toward them, looking alert.

Once the door of the Presidential suite was shut, Bertram fixed himself a drink at the bar while Janice went to get ready for bed. She went into the bedroom and closed the door. She undressed, then in her underwear, padded over to the bathroom. She took off her underwear and slipped into a bathrobe. The shower came on, and as the hot power jet cascaded over her skin, Janice closed her eyes, enjoying the sensation.

*****

4,700 miles away, a computer screen blinked to life inside a dark office in Lubyanka Square, Moscow.

Borislov and Anna Ramitrova were leaning over the screen. Janice's naked body was visible in the shower. On another screen, the bedroom was shown. The door opened, and Bertram came in. He sipped from the drink in his hand, then sat down on the bed and took his socks off.

Borislov pointed at the dragon tattoo on the left of Janice's abdomen and more on her upper thighs. "Well, well," he smirked. "Who knew the First Lady was, as the Americans call it, a *badass*."

They continued to watch as Janice finished her shower and stepped outside. The bedroom was large, one side was taken up by a walk-in wardrobe. Janice vanished inside it. She emerged with her bathrobe on and stood in front of Bertram. He put his drink down and slipped his hand inside her robe. The robe fell off, and she stood stark naked in front of him, while he was fully dressed. She pushed his shoulders, and he fell backwards on the bed.

"Now," said Borislov, eyes fixed on the screen but addressing Anna. "Watch very closely."

CHAPTER 34

Saint-Denis

Outside Paris

Dan was leaning against the side of a sofa, streetlight falling across his legs, striped by the window blinds. The lights inside were still off.

Scorpion was facing him, and Dan could see her posture become rigid when he mentioned Black Beauty.

"Who told you about that?" Scorpion asked.

Her face was half lit, the other half lost in darkness. He wondered how apt that was, how their lives were lost in the play between shadow and brightness, between truth and lies. How much he wanted to be close to her, and how distant she got every time he tried. That wasn't her fault, or maybe it was. He didn't know, and she wouldn't tell him. He sometimes wished he had a normal life, but that was like an Eskimo wishing for a life in the desert. It would never happen.

"Someone I know," he said shortly.

She kicked his leg. "Stop it. Tell me."

He grinned in the darkness, aware that despite the lack of light she would still be able to see him. Or know what he was doing.

He became serious. "A man called Gennady in the Russky Embassy in London. That was the reason Grant Pearson was coming to meet him."

"You lost me. What reason?" Her English was perfect, without accent, but when she was alone with him, the thick, guttural Russian tongue became pronounced. Dan found that funny.

He laughed, and he could tell she was getting pissed off. He put his palms up.

"Right, I'll tell you. Grant was caught in Yemen by Rashid's men. When he realized who Rashid was, he told him about me killing Waleed, Rashid's cousin. So, Rashid spared his life. In return, Grant became a double agent."

"So Gennady was working Grant? For what?"

"For this operation called Black Beauty. But here's the funny thing, although Gennady was getting information regarding the CIA's classified stuff, Gennady didn't know exactly what they were for. He was just feeding them upstairs."

"To the FSB?"

"I don't know to who. His role was to act as a funnel. He only knew the name of the operation, not what the mission was."

Scorpion nodded. "He was a break in the chain. That's normal for security reasons. You sure he told you the truth?"

Dan shrugged. "Unless he wanted his eyes cut out, yeah."

"Your turn," Dan said. "You acted all shook up when I mentioned Black Beauty. Why?"

Scorpion told her about Marutov, then became silent for a while. Her chin dropped to her chest.

Dan asked, "What is it?"

"It's what Marutov mentioned the first time. Those who are closest to me are the ones I should fear the most. I wonder what he meant." She lifted her eyes to stare at Dan.

"Well, I didn't know Marutov, so don't ask me. Why were you sent to kill him? I mean, why you and not another contractor?"

Scorpion didn't reply immediately. After a while, she told him. "Many years ago, Ali Marutov killed my husband. On our wedding day."

Dan gaped at her. Then he shook his head. "Jeez, that sucks. I mean, I'm sorry. No one should have to–" he stopped suddenly. "When was this?"

"A long time ago. I was much younger. Innocent. Just graduated from the Red Chamber. Only done two jobs."

They sat in silence for a while, each lost in silent musings. Dan said, "You didn't really answer my question."

"What do you mean?"

"I mean, why did your handler want Marutov killed?"

She caught on. "I don't know," she said slowly. "But there must be a reason."

"Could the reason be what he told you as he died? Black Beauty?"

Scorpion nodded, her eyes fixed on Dan's. Suddenly, Dan was restless. He didn't believe in coincidences. He stood and looked out the window blinds. The streets were empty. He didn't see any new cars.

"Why did you call me?" Dan asked, his voice rough.

She stood too, her stance coiled, ready. Her feet were spread slightly apart, and she was balanced on the balls of her feet. The posture didn't escape Dan's notice. But he was ready too.

They were about two yards apart, facing each other. Dan knew she had a weapon on her, taken from the guard at the prison. She still had some rounds left. But he would be quicker on the draw. Or maybe they would shoot at the same time.

"Don't do this," Scorpion said, softly.

"I don't like being played," Dan said.

"I'm not playing you!" she hissed. "I've just busted out from a DGIS prison, damn it. Half of Paris is looking for me. Why would I do that if I was trying to kill you?"

She stopped, breathing heavily. Dan couldn't see her face at all any more, her head was swallowed by the darkness. But what she said made sense. But something still bothered him.

"Why did you come to Paris anyway?"

"Because this guy kept calling and threatening me. The man from Cyclone. I couldn't kill Marutov, and for whatever reason, they knew about it. Now they're chasing me."

"Maybe they think Marutov told you more than you should know."

Dan could see from the way Scorpion's shoulders dropped his comment made sense to her.

She flopped down on a sofa. "Shit, you're right. Never thought about that."

Dan moved closer to her. "And that's why you were sent on that job. Because Marutov knew about Black Beauty. Hence he had to be killed."

Scorpion was nodding. Dan asked, "Who was your handler for the job?"

She told him. Dan asked if Borislov knew about Cyclone or Black Beauty, and she shook her head.

"But he could be lying," Scorpion said. "How did this Cyclone guy get my number? Had to be through him."

"Exactly. I imagine Borislov knows more than he's letting on."

They looked at each other. Dan felt more relaxed now. If the Scorpion, Natasha, did want to kill him she didn't have to cook up this whole story and get arrested. In fact, he was hating himself for

194

doubting her. Looking over his shoulder, like he had done all his life. It was ingrained in him not to trust anyone.

But he was still uneasy. Aloud he said, "We need to find out what Black Beauty is."

Scorpion nodded. "While I'm here, I might as well track down this old man."

"And I have the license plate of the SUV that chased after us. My contact should be able to give me an address," Dan said. "Get some sleep. I'll do first watch. Relieve me in three hours."

She stood, standing so close to him they were almost touching. Dan didn't move back.

Her voice was silky, soft like the darkness surrounding them. "I can think of another way of relieving you."

CHAPTER 35

Pulses of photons danced on Dan's closed eyelids. It warmed his eyes, and made a yellow red glow. He was awake, and out of habit, his hand slid down to his waist, to his weapon. His eyes were open as his fingers curled around the butt of the Colt.

He was on the floor of the lounge room downstairs. His neck hurt from resting on the floor. He got up quickly. Sounds of traffic and voices came from outside. He listened closely, but the house was silent. He went to the staircase and looked up. He was staring at the barrel of a hand gun pointed at him from above. He flinched, ducked, as the figure above did the same.

"Shit," Scorpion said from above. "You scared me."

She came down the staircase. Dan shook his head at her. "I scared you? You were the one pointing a gun at me."

"I heard a sound. Decided to check. Coffee?" Her shapely derriere swung its way across his field of vision. God, he wanted to reach out and grab a handful. It was getting harder to restrain himself.

Good job she's got a gun on her.

"Yeah," he said aloud. He stared out the window. The massive apartment complexes were coming to life. A bunch of kids were playing soccer with goals drawn on the wall by chalk. Women with headscarves moved on the sidewalk. Closer to him, an old woman stepped out of a bungalow. Dan figured these one-story buildings were designed for older residents. In which case, it made a good hiding place.

He washed and came downstairs to the invigorating smell of coffee. He called Claude, who picked up on the first ring. He said something in French Dan didn't get, but it sure sounded like he was swearing.

"What the hell are you playing at?" Claude fumed. "Did you have to rip up the streets around Vendome?"

"We were trying to escape, unless that escaped your notice," Dan said in a steady voice.

"What is it with you Americans, huh? Can't you do anything quietly? Everything has to be loud and brash."

Dan grinned despite himself. "Nothing wrong with a bit of va-va voom, Claude."

The Frenchman again said something in his own language that Dan didn't catch.

Dan asked, "Another car chased us last night. Not the police. A black SUV. Can you get me a name and location? *S'il vous plait?*"

Dan gave him the license plate, and Claude called back in five minutes.

"The car is registered to a factory in Champigny Sur-Marne. It's a small town southeast of Paris."

"What does the factory make?" asked Dan. "And what is it called?"

"It's called Horizon. And it makes drill pipes."

Dan frowned. "Drill pipes used in oil rigs?"

"I guess so."

"Then it could belong to the Al-falaj family. They have oil rig machinery factories all over the world," Dan said. "Thanks for this. Have you got the address?"

He hung up, wrote the address down, and thought for a while. If the car that had chased him last night was Rashid's, how did they know Dan was here?

He called Claude back. When the Frenchman answered, Dan said, "I figure you have a leak to the Russians, who in turn might be telling the Arabs." Dan told Claude about Rashid, and why the man was after Dan.

"Wouldn't surprise me we if have a mole to the Russians," Claude said. "This country is full of socialists."

"Watch your back," Dan said before he hung up.

Scorpion had cooked some bacon and eggs in the kitchen, and Dan realized suddenly how hungry he was. As he ate, he filled her in.

"I can't prove it, but I bet you it was Rashid who chased us last night. We were lucky to escape."

"So, what will you do?" she asked.

"Find out what he's doing here."

"Want me to come with you?"

"No. Best if I do this alone, and also you need to keep your face hidden right now." Dan could see she didn't like that. But both of them knew it was the right decision.

*****

An hour later, Dan had driven a car down the congested highways of south Paris to Champigny Sur Marne. The place was a sleepy village, the streets deserted. An industrial park was outside the village, and Dan's GPS was pointing in that direction. Horizon turned out to be even further out than the industrial park. One single tarmac road led to the factory, something Dan didn't like. If he drove down that road he might as well call in advance to let them know he was coming.

He ditched the car by going off-road into the woods. He didn't have his kukri, but he had the 8-inch blade hunter knife, and he hacked at branches until he had enough to hide the car from casual observers driving past.

Then he took off through the woods, the factory about two miles to his right behind some fields. He had on his hiking boots, his old ones from the Army store in Fort Bragg, North Carolina. It wasn't a cold day, and the sun was out. While it was nice walking over the farm fields, he wasn't too keen on the good visibility. He was the only moving object for miles around, which meant he would stick out like a sore thumb to anyone keeping watch.

As he got closer to the factory, he could see why they had chosen the place. The land surrounding it was flat. The strip of the tarmac was on a bank, and behind him he could hear the roar of traffic on the highway.

Luckily, there was a bank of trees to the rear of factory. The compound walls were more than two meters high with barbed wire on top. As he got closer, Dan could see two guards at the gates. Both were armed with what seemed like AK-47's hanging from their shoulders. But both were smoking, trigger fingers nowhere near where they should be. Their poor training was also apparent in their casual posture, the way they slouched around, looking bored.

Dan went to ground. The soil was soft, and it clung to his clothes. He observed for a while. Then bent low at the waist, covered as much ground as he could at a brisk run. Then he went to ground again, lifting his head cautiously to see if he had been spotted. The roar of a vehicle made him close his eyes again. The car passed him by about fifty meters away on the road. He watched it stop in front of the guards who flagged it down. It was a pick -up truck, and the back was covered in a tarp.

The driver had a quick chat with the guards, then the truck was waved in. Dan got a visual of a wide courtyard when the gates opened. Men were unloading machinery from cars, most of them were armed.

While the guards were closing the gates, Dan got up and ran forward again. He made good distance, and by the time the guards had resumed their position Dan was less than twenty meters away. One of the guards was the same size and shape as him. But his muscle had gone to fat, and his belly hung low over his belt.

Dan wasn't concerned about these two. He had to make sure there wasn't more guards patrolling the perimeter. He waited for a while, but saw no one.

He couldn't hear any cars, and it was very quiet, save the buzzing of bees and the sharp cry of an eagle high in the air. Dan shuffled closer. He was hidden in the undergrowth now, and the men were almost within reach.

The big guy was slouching against the wall. His friend said something to him, and he laughed. He threw his cigarette away and moved off the wall. He trudged toward Dan, who shrank back against the undergrowth. The man kept coming, and Dan had to roll to his side to seek shelter behind a tree trunk. He was covered in mud now, face protected by having his arms crossed in front.

He heard the sound of a zipper being lowered, and the man urinating. Dan clenched his jaws. The man was pissing against the tree trunk. Dan took his knife out and waited. The stream lessened, then almost died. Dan leapt out to one side and before the startled man could register anything, he grabbed him by the collar and slammed his face against the tree. The man was shocked, but he tried to resist. Dan got behind him, held his neck, and slammed his large fist to the side of his neck, hearing it crunch. The man fell like he'd been poleaxed.

Dan crouched and whirled around. The other guy was around the corner, as this man had walked to the side. Dan took the weapon, and the black, flat peaked farmers hat the man wore. He had a light blue jacket on, and Dan put that on as well. He walked back quickly, flattening himself against the wall. The smaller guy was nowhere to be seen. Dan scurried over to the gates. There was a side entrance carved into the tall gates for men to move without opening the gates fully.

Dan unlocked the latch, then stepped inside.

CHAPTER 36

The Scorpion didn't like the safe house. For one, she could see the punks on the street corner. Kids came up to them, paid money, grabbed a packet in their hands, and went away. Any minute now, she expected a police car to roll in to bust the drug dealers.

Second, it bugged her that she had come here on a mission and had failed. She needed to find the man in the park next to Notre Dame. She didn't need Dan's help. Her thoughts turned to the night before. Nothing happened, but if Dan had made a move, she would have gladly given in to her desires. She knew he felt it as well.

She breathed out, closed her eyes. Thoughts of his body, the hard stack of his muscles made her want to clench her thighs together. She hadn't seen him in over a year and had missed him every day.

And yet, she was more afraid of what could happen between them than of what did not.

She couldn't live like this, pulled in two directions, torn between desire and despair. There seemed to be no in-between for her, no middle ground, only the extremes. The middle ground was for normal people, the ones who did the nine-to-five, took their children to and from school, and died slow, ponderous deaths after a long, uneventful life. What would she give for a few days of that life? Not to live like this – always on the run.

She drank the rest of her coffee, wondering if she had too much of the brown stuff. Her mind was overactive. She field stripped her weapon, then reassembled it. By the end, her mind was made up. She had to go back to the drug den in the Latin Quarter. By the time she came back, Dan would also return from his recon, and they could swap notes.

If she was still alive.

*****

The 5th arrondissement of Paris, or Latin Quarter, is a hive of shops, a rabbit warren of streets filled with cafe's, underground jazz bars, and ancient bookshops. The Pantheon looms over the neighborhood, and Scorpion was one of many hooded figures as she cut through the side of the massive building, then crossed an old cloister house that dated back to just after the roman times. This area on the Left Bank, filled with hipsters, intellectuals, and long-haired arty types, was undeniably Paris's coolest neighborhood, what the Greenwich Village was to New York during the 1960's, and Haight-Ashbury was to San Francisco.

But the poverty and filth associated with those cities wasn't present here. In fact, Scorpion had not expected any trouble, which is why the first time she was attacked she was surprised.

It was the only reason her attackers were still alive.

She would not make the same mistake again.

She stopped outside the bookstore opposite the tobacco shop. Latin Quarter was also home to Paris's largest mosque, the aptly named *Grande Mosque de Paris.* Many Algerians were about, and so was the shopkeeper, whose curly hair and sandy skin reminded her of North Africans she had seen before.

She observed for a while, then cut around to the back. The side street was quieter, and when no one was looking, she climbed the wall. The apartments were above the shop, going up three floors. The apartment she wanted was on the first floor. But she was going through the front like last time.

She was in the courtyard, and ignoring the well laid out garden, went swiftly up the steps of the back door. It opened just as she reached for it. An Algerian man looked up at her in surprise. His eyes widened, and his left hand moved to his waist. She slammed her foot into his chest, a high kick that sent the man sprawling backwards. A big flower vase crashed on his head from one of the shelves above, and the man stopped moving.

The gun was in her hand, scanning for others. The shopkeeper emerged, and promptly put his hands up.

Scorpion kept the gun aimed at the man's chest. "The men in the apartment above. The dealers. Where are they?"

"I don't know, mademoiselle."

She crossed the space between them so fast he didn't have time to blink. The butt of the gun smashed on his head, then she grabbed his neck and pushed him against the wall. She kicked his legs out, and he collapsed on the floor. The gun's muzzle ground against the spine on his neck.

"Last chance. You were here last time, so don't lie."

"Okay, okay! They're... They're gone."

"What do you mean gone?"

"They were sent here. Now they–"

"Sent by who?"

He didn't answer. She slammed her knee down on his hand. He yelped in pain as his fingers were crushed.

"Who?" She asked.

"This... This old man. Came in a black car, American make."

"Carry on."

"He gave us money to capture you. We were meant to take you to him."

"Where?"

The man whimpered. With the butt of the gun, she hit him behind the ear, and he yelped again.

"I'll break each one of your fingers for every second you delay telling me."

"They'll kill me," the man said in a strangled voice.

"And I won't? Trust me, I'll take much longer to kill you than they will."

He kept silent, and she got the ominous feeling he was buying time. Like he knew reinforcements were on their way. She took out her knife. She cut a straight line behind his ear, holding him down as he screamed and kicked.

"I'll cut your whole ear off, right? Then I'll start on the other ear."

"Okay, okay, okay!" the man screamed. "I'll tell you where it is." He whimpered out an address, and she memorized it. Then she got up and spat on him.

"If I find you were lying to me, a chopped off ear will be the least of your worries."

She took his cell phone, then hit him twice with her weapon, rendering him unconscious.

CHAPTER 37

Rue de l'Abbaye is one of the most charming streets in Paris. It is on the left bank, and the Seine flows close by, but the street is so named because in medieval times the street was the entrance to the Abbatial Palace. The Palace is now restored to its pink walled glory, and the ancient buildings around it have also been renovated. The old residences now house modern abodes that are among the most expensive in the capital of fashion.

Scorpion kept a close eye on the people milling around, and the cafes, boutique art galleries, and shops that were open. She passed by the Palace and entered a small enclosed area called the Place de Furstenberg. She was in a square, and she could hear the distant sound of someone playing the saxophone. A breeze from the river swept in, humid and heavy, and lovers clasped hands tightly as they strolled on the cobbled streets. The smell of lilac flowers moistened the air as dew does to early morning.

If she wasn't on a mission, Scorpion would have felt almost romantic.

In fact, she thought as she hunted for the address on the Rue de Furstenberg, if she could live anywhere in the world it would be in this delightful, secluded square.

Scorpion wasn't a romantic soul, but when in Rome we are all Romans. Now she was a Parisian for sure, from the smell of coffee, to the wafts of saxophone in this medieval square, to the heady, dense sense of being submerged in another world.

She wished Dan Roy was with her. The man she was once ordered to kill, and who once tried to kill her.

Strange how love and death coexisted in the same relationship.

Maybe that was how all her relationships made sense, a vortex of violence and emotion.

She moved slowly past the white tables full of stylish bohemians, her eyes sharp and alert because she knew in the softest of places lay the hardest of human hearts. Her gaze missed nothing – from the Gauloise cigarette packet a man lit a smoke from, to the amethyst necklace a young woman touched as she sipped her coffee. It was all in the details, the lifeblood that painted a thousand brush strokes on the canvas of her sharp mind, the picture that spoke a thousand words.

She sauntered along, not forgetting to cast her eyes on the roofs of the charming buildings, the long sash windows so distinctive but opaque in the afternoon sunlight.

She wouldn't know if someone was observing her from behind those windows.

She approached the terraced apartment. The tall, black door was shut, and the numbers of the apartments, with calling buttons, stood on the side wall.

She didn't want to alarm the other occupants of the building. There wasn't much to do but act discreet until someone turned up to open the door. She pretended to examine art through the window of a nearby gallery. Soon, an old lady appeared and entered the building, dragging her shopping cart behind her. Scorpion slipped in behind, offering to help the old lady. After a smile and Merci, she was inside the white marble stoned lobby.

The old lady with a scarf wrapped around her head and a shabby overcoat turned to Scorpion. "Do you live here?"

She saw no point in lying. Old ladies were very observant and often a fount of knowledge. She said, "No, just visiting the residents of Apartment 1214."

The old woman frowned. "Often empty, that one. But last month a new guy moved in. Always has another man that follows him around."

"Like a bodyguard?" Scorpion asked.

"Maybe."

"*Merci.*"

Scorpion was glad for her mediocre French. She ignored the suspicious looks the woman gave her as the elevator door closed. She didn't go up the broad wraparound stairs. She went to the end of hallway, where a locked door showed a well-kept garden through the glass panels. She tried the windows next to it. They were locked, but with her knife she was able scrape off the putty surrounding the glass. She looked behind, expecting someone to walk in through the main door. She worked fast. The sash windows were old and so were the single glazed glass panels. She got two free and that was enough, with some calisthenics, for her to squeeze her body through.

The garden was lovely with weeping willow trees on either side and a dry fountain in the middle. It was also empty.

She transferred her attention to the building, noting the eaves that stuck out at every floor. Each apartment had a small balcony and grille, waist railings. The windows had ledges that protruded. She hopped on the nearest ledge, and her moccasin clad feet found enough of a toe hold on the sides to climb. She got a hand to the iron railing of the second-floor apartment, but her foot slipped. She cursed, dangling from one hand before managing to pull herself up to grab the railing with both hands.

The exertion made her gasp and sweat coursed down her face. As her face came level with the balcony floor, she could see the doors half open. A pair of shoes were visible, belonging to a body that was half reclining on a chair. The feet weren't moving.

She couldn't remain hanging like this for long, the tension on her hands and elbows was killing off the blood supply. Her fingers were turning numb. Even if the feet were to move, she would be in a better position on her own feet. She raised herself with a huge effort, then climbed over the balcony. She slid to one side, gasping. The feet still hadn't moved, and she could hear snoring. Something told her this was the guard. She moved closer and peered in.

It was the bald guy from the apartment in the Latin Quarter, the one who had almost killed her.

His mouth was open, and he was fast asleep, reclining in a large armchair.

She padded silently past him, into the bedroom that faced the square. The door was shut, and she could hear more snoring inside. There was a bathroom and kitchen opposite the bedroom, both were empty. She checked the front door, making sure it was locked and the chain was on.

She picked up a cushion from the sofa. It was large and thick, ideal for her purposes. She took her weapon out, the gun she had taken from the guard in the DGIS prison. It was a 9mm Glock 17, a gun she was very familiar with. She didn't have a suppressor, but the flat retort from the weapon would be dulled by the cushion. With any luck, it wouldn't wake up the man sleeping in the bedroom.

The Glock was cocked and ready. In one smooth motion, she pressed the cushion over the man's face, hard as she could, and the muzzle of the Glock followed over it. One round was enough. His head slammed back against the armchair. The bullet ejected from the upholstery, embedding itself on the wooden floor.

She didn't wait to see that. She was at the bedroom door, turning the handle with her right hand while the left aimed the weapon at the figure on the bed.

He was just sitting up, one arm reaching for the bedside drawer.

"Don't," Scorpion said. "It's not worth it."

The man on the bed froze. He wasn't as old as she had imagined. Maybe he did smoke, and the raspy voice made him sound older. His hair was salt and pepper, face square jawed, eyes dark and glittery. He was in his mid-fifties, she guessed.

"Your man is dead. The door is locked. Put both hands up where I can see them."

He raised both hands. Keeping her eyes, and gun, on him, she reached forward and flung away the bedsheets. He was wearing pajamas.

"Anything under the pillow?" she asked.

"No." He cleared his throat. "You must be Scorpion." A slight smile hovered on the corner of his lips. "Can I put my glasses on?"

Her eyes fell on the bedside table. There was a book, and a pair of glasses on top. "Very slowly," she said. "I don't care about the noise. I will shoot."

"I know that. Your reputation precedes you. Is Nikolai dead?"

She nodded. His expression didn't change. He put the glasses on, then raised his eyebrows as he looked at her. The smile remained, and the corners of his eyes crinkled in genuine mirth.

She didn't like that. "What's so funny?"

He shook his head. "You must excuse me. There's nothing funny about this. But it's good to see my instincts were right."

"What do you mean?"

"You passed every test. For every obstacle you found a recourse. You even turn opponents into allies, and that is the hallmark of a true leader."

She frowned, her sense on high alert. This guy knew a lot about her. And what he was saying bothered her a lot.

All of this was a test? "Explain yourself."

"I, we, wanted to see what you were capable of. So we sent you on a mission, knowing you might not succeed as Marutov's family would be present. You don't kill women or children."

The sense of unease was rising to a steady hum inside her skull. "Borislov sent me on the mission."

He shook his head. "No. Borislov was under instructions to deny our involvement."

So, Borislov had been lying after all.

"Who the hell are you?"

"I told you," he replied in an easy voice. "We are Cyclone. A global group with the power to do as we please. We can change governments, start wars or end them."

"If you're that powerful why do you need me?"

"Because you are one of the best. And you've just proven that."

He shifted, and her weapon shifted with him. His arms were lowered, and his hands were folded on his lap. He was very relaxed, and she didn't like that. Not at all.

"And who are you?"

"A mere servant of Cyclone."

"Bullshit. You call the shots. You decide who to hire. Which means you're high up in some government hierarchy somewhere." She could tell this man wielded power, the type of influence that only came with age and leadership.

"You keep saying Cyclone can do whatever it wants, well, that doesn't happen without knowing the political power brokers. Given that you're American, I bet you're high up on the feeding chain in Washington DC. Maybe you have an office in Capitol Hill with Senator or Congressman before your name on the door."

For the first time, she saw his easy smile falter. But he regained it quickly.

"You're a very perceptive young lady. I hate to disappoint you, but you're wrong."

"The DA's office? You're a lawyer–"

He put his hands up, and she surprised herself by stopping. The smile had left his face entirely now.

"We could waste a lot of time doing this," his voice hardened a touch. "And we wouldn't get anywhere. If you're here, pointing a gun at me, I guess what you really want to know is what we want from you."

She nodded, not hiding her curiosity.

"Killing Marutov was the first step. He knew about Black Beauty, and I guess he told you about it as well."

She didn't say anything. He nodded. "I can see that is correct. To be honest with you, there were many errors in this operation. We hired that fool of a CIA agent, Grant Pearson. He was too emotional, too weak. He did provide useful information, but it came at a cost. He had to be neutralized."

He continued. "The Arabs helped obviously, mainly by providing Grant. But they, too, are headstrong. We need someone to clear this up. That's where you come in."

"And if I say no?"

The smile returned on his face. "I don't think you'll do that."

"What makes you think that?" The hum of anxiety was a dull roar, engulfing her thoughts. She didn't want to go there, but this man was dragging her.

He said, "I can see you're wondering the same thing as me."

The butt of the Glock was moist in her hand. She wanted to change hands but didn't want to give him the pleasure of seeing how rattled she was. But she had a horrible feeling he knew already.

He sighed, like he was about to say something momentous but then refrained.

"What am I wondering, then?" she asked, somehow managing to keep the shake out of her voice.

He uttered the words she had been dreading.

CHAPTER 38

"Melania Stone. CIA Agent, South Europe Directorate. 39 years old, lives in Bethesda. No children but has a new boyfriend. Ring a bell?"

Scorpion felt like she had been punched in the gut. Her lungs were hollow, airless cavities. Her brain was ice, words lost inside a deep arctic blue crevice of shock. But she managed to keep her face neutral.

"Nope. Have no idea what you're talking about."

He sighed. "She's your sister, Natasha." He used her name for the first time. "Your dear, beloved older sister."

Scorpion shrugged. "You've got me mistaken for someone else. I have no relations. No family. In my line of work, it's dangerous. You know that."

He smiled tolerantly. "Of course, I do. And that's why all assassins have false identities. Hardly anyone knows the real Natasha Karmen, right?"

"What makes you think that's who I am? You fell for the same bluff everyone else does. Congratulations."

He raised his eyebrows. "So you don't care if Melania Stone is tortured then brutally killed? My men are animals, they will really go to town on her. You want that?"

Her heart was thudding so loudly against her ribs she thought they'd break. So would her heart. She shrugged again.

"Like I said, the name means nothing to me. You want to do this, go right ahead."

"Fine." He reached for the phone on the bedside table and lifted the receiver. He pressed a button, then held the receiver against his ear.

Blood was pounding against Scorpion's ears, a rushing tide of sound that threatened to splinter her ear drums.

The man spoke into the phone. "George? Yeah, it's me. Kill Melania–"

"Wait," she said loudly, stepping forward. Her weapon was up, jaws clenched so tight her teeth were grinding together. "Let's talk about this."

"You sure?"

She nodded.

"George? Forget it for now. I'll be in touch." He smiled at her after he put the phone back in its cradle. "So. You do remember your sister after all." It was a statement, not a question.

She said nothing, her mind a storm of conflicting thoughts.

He continued like nothing had happened. "Melania is being followed by a team of Cyclone operatives as we speak. At my word, she will be captured and then tortured until she dies a very slow, painful death."

Melania. The sister she had lost in Russia, and then found later after a search of twenty years. She still wore the red hair tie they had used as children. Melania was all the more precious to her because of all the years she had missed. Nothing would ever tear them apart again.

Nausea rose in her throat like a geyser. She couldn't help it. Her mouth opened, and she retched on the floor. Nothing came out but a thin trickle of saliva.

The Glock almost slipped out of her hand. She leaned forward, then slipped down to the floor.

"The two of you are still close. I can see that." His voice was softer, almost endearing.

A guttural, low cry came from her throat, like a wounded animal. She wiped her mouth, raised herself and advanced on him, weapon pointed at his chest. Her finger caressed the trigger.

"My men have orders to move on Melania if they don't hear back from me in an hour. Killing me will only make your predicament worse."

"Fuck you."

"I understand you are angry. Believe me, if there was any other option we would have exercised it." He spread his hands. "But there wasn't."

Scorpion's chest heaved, rage and frustration boiling inside her like a kettle about to burst its top. She had to put the emotions to one side. Now, more than any other time, she needed a clear head. Emotions were always dangerous, but now they could kill Melania, or her. Which was ironic because she always killed with a cold heart, not thinking twice about it.

Her whole world was turned upside down.

"How did you find out about her?"

"I told you, there is very little we don't know."

She shook her head, trying in vain to clear the mist inside. "Touch one strand of her hair, and you get nothing from me."

"Understood. But also understand this: if you don't do exactly as we say she's dead meat."

"I will be in touch with Melania all the time," she said. "I'll call her as soon as I leave this place. If anything happens to her, I'm coming after you. Don't think you can hide from me. I have contacts in USA, too. I can find out who you are then expose you. Which might be worse than death for you."

He raised his eyebrows. "Are you threatening me now?"

Scorpion spoke softly, "You must have family too, right? Live on the East Coast, not far from DC, nice little suburbia." She cocked her head to one side. "Your children might be in college. Maybe you have a boy in Yale, wants to go to law school, follow his dad's footsteps."

"You'll never know."

"I don't want to do this. I don't go after families. But you're after my only flesh and blood."

"So, do as we say, and she will be left alone. You have my word on that."

Scorpion shook her head. This whole thing was unreal, like she was having an out of body experience. And yet, she had feared this more than she feared death. After Melania and her had come together last year, her life had new meaning. She had never thought it possible, but it was. Like a cactus that grows in the desert, her desolate heart had dreamt of a little life, some greenery.

She would die so Melania would live. No question about it.

She focused back on the man.

"What happens after the job is done?"

"We go our separate ways. Never see each other again."

She shook her head. "No. You will cut a deal with me. If you use Melania as a lever again, I will tell the media about Cyclone and about you."

He shrugged. "Then she dies."

"And you get the full glare of the media. No one wins." She frowned, wiped the weapon down, and put it in her pocket, hand still gripping the butt, eyes still watchful.

"Tell me. What are you after? What do you want?"

A strange light gleamed in his relaxed eyes. "Really? Look around you. What is happening in the world today? We talk of democracy, of having a say in who ends up as our leader. But we don't. The people at the top are corporate stooges. Put there by their cronies. They fight useless wars to make money. Wreck the economy for their own gains. Who holds them responsible? You call that a democracy? I call it a den of thieves."

"That's your opinion. Others will have a different one. Besides, who says you're not a thief? You're holding a gun to my sister's head, forcing me to do something I don't want to."

"Better than holding a gun to the whole economy's head, right? Or the whole country? How much tax revenue have these useless wars wasted? Let me tell you. More than $6 trillion. That sum will grow by the time interest is paid off because wars are fought with borrowed money. To put it into perspective, the entire US GDP is $19.4 trillion. Think of what we could do with that money."

Scorpion smiled bitterly. "For someone who's an opponent of war, you sure love violence. Here you are, using it to get where you want. Which brings us back to the question. What do you want me to do?"

He rubbed his palms together, then raised them to his face and inhaled.

"You will be told when the time is right. For now, you must do as ordered. This has been years in the making. Now it is time for the grand finale."

CHAPTER 39

Once inside the gates, Dan slouched to one side, walking slowly. His shoulders were drooped,

back bent slightly to give the appearance of a lazy man. The flat peak farmer's cap, almost like a beret, was pulled low over his face. But his eyes missed nothing.

France didn't have any oilfields. Very little natural gas and none in this region.

Why did an oil rig company need to have a factory here?

Men were whipping tarp covers off the back of pickup trucks and helping each other to unload what looked like generators and farming machinery. The stuff was carried over to the factory at the end of the compound. On either side there was a bank of single-story huts with corrugated iron roofs.

Most of the huts appeared empty from a distance, their windows blacked out, doors shut. Closer to the factory, from where men in overalls kept going in and out, there was an office, where Dan spied a man in a suit. The man looked Middle Eastern, and he was joined by a white guy who was considerably paler than the well-tanned, swarthy working men. Dan leaned against a hut, then dropped to his knees, pretending to tie his shoelaces. He observed the two men closely. The Arab guy was explaining things, gesturing with his open hands. The pale skinned guy nodded, listening closely.

Dan pulled his phone out, his own cell that he normally kept turned off. He powered it up and clicked on an email McBride had sent him. It contained photos of the Al-Falaj family, and Dan found one of Rashid. He had suspected this. The man, who was now walking around, was very similar to the photo. Dan had to get closer to get a better view, but he knew it already.

Rashid Al-Falaj, the man out to kill him, was standing across the compound.

If Dan could get rid of him... the thought came and went quickly. It was foolhardy to try that now, surrounded by Rashid's men. He didn't have backup or transport. This was a recon mission, nothing more. And he hoped it would stay that way.

He fired off a quick email to McBride, warning him that Rashid had a factory in France. It could of course have a perfectly legitimate reason. Maybe they were branching out into farm machinery. But it wouldn't hurt to look closer.

Dan snuck a look at the gates. The other guard hadn't come inside yet. If he was looking for his friend and raised the alarm when he found him, Dan was in trouble. He needed to be out of here before that happened.

He slung the AK-47 over his back after checking the magazine. It was full. He went to the back of the hut. As he had suspected, there was a little space along their back that led all the way to the top where the factory was situated. Some trees leaned over the barbed wire at the top of the fence, and Dan took some time to make sure the wire wasn't electrocuted. He didn't see any signs. Those trees would be his means of escape later on, as long as he didn't get fried on the wire.

He moved swiftly, silently, eyes roving for any figures coming towards the huts. He slowed his pace as he got closer to the factory. Men were speaking loudly over the hum of machines. He picked up French words, most of which he didn't understand. But he also heard plenty of Arabic, some of which he did know. As he came closer to the main compound, down the side of the last hut, what surprised him the most was the quiet muttering of two men standing close by and smoking. Dan had slowed his pace, back stooped again and slouching. The men were speaking in Russian, a language he did know.

One of the men nodded at Dan, who nodded back, then moved on swiftly. Grant Pearson was meeting with the Russians, Dan knew that. And Tatyana, the alluring siren in London who was almost certainly an SVR agent, had drawn him into the trap where Rashid had almost killed him. Dan didn't know exactly how the Arabs were in the mix. But he needed to find out and fast.

He moved past a few trucks, then the office came into view. Dan looked around but not for too long. Everyone seemed busy, taking material inside the factory. The office door was shut, but he could see movement through the windows.

Dan moved to one side, down to the nearest hut, a row of them mirroring the ones opposite. He vanished between two of them, and the backed up to the rear of the office. More trees reared over the fences.

A few yards to his left, men swarmed on the compound. To his right, the fence rose up to the barbed wire and leaves. He would have to be quick to avoid being noticed. Luckily for him, the sounds from the factory masked the sounds his approach and the small twigs he stepped on.

But it also hid the footsteps that approached behind him. A sharp voice rang out, stopping him in his tracks.

"Qu'est-ce que tu fais?" *What are you doing?*

Dan didn't miss a beat. He turned quickly, smiling. He saw two guys less than a couple of yards away. They hadn't drawn their weapons but were eyeing him with frank suspicion.

Dan utilized the little French he did know.

He shrugged casually. "C'est tres bien!" *It's all good.*

The men were frowning heavily, and one of them stepped backwards, looking to the side. If he shouted or raised the alarm Dan was finished. He hurled himself at them like a rocket. A football tackle, grabbing the man closest to him by the waist, slamming them both against the wall. Before one could utter a strangled cry, Dan was up, his large hand closing around the face of the man standing up, pushing his head against the wall with savage force. The man below Dan hit him in the waist, and Dan pressed his knee on the man's neck.

The other guy was dazed from his head bashing, and one massive punch to the chin knocked his head back again, and he slumped to the floor. Dan was pressing down with his knee, which was wide, heavy, and like a boulder on the neck of the guy below him. He was being strangled. Dan moved his knee momentarily, then double punched him, rocking his face from side to side. The guy stilled.

Dan stood up, panting. Sweat was cascading down his face. It had taken less than twenty seconds, and as far as he could see no alarm had been raised. But he was in trouble. Any minute, he will be discovered.

Knife in hand, he hurried to the back window of the office. He went to ground and put his ears to the wooden wall. He could hear sounds as the wooden walls of the office building weren't very sturdy. Muffled voices, at least two men. He couldn't make out any of the words or the language. He looked at the window. It was slightly open, and he raised his head until it was level with the lower ledge. With his fingers, he gave the lower panel of the window a slight, gentle push. It budged. He pushed further. He couldn't see anything apart from the wooden rafters on the ceiling.

But the voices became clearer. The men, one of whom must be Rashid, were speaking in English.

Dan looked behind him quickly. Still clear. He paid attention to the voices.

"Black Beauty…. final stage in…" Dan recognized the accent and the voice. The same person had told him he was a dead man over the phone. It was Rashid.

"Yes, that's right." The other guy said. His accent was heavy, Eastern European or Russian.

"…teach these imperialists a lesson–"

He strained to hear as the other guy spoke. "Elections…Ohio, capital…–"

Rashid's voice said, "No, never been… Midwest, no operations there. But could enquire. You sure about this?" His voice was louder and carried more to Dan's ear. The other guy's voice was softer.

Dan couldn't raise his head, but he could imagine why. Rashid must be facing the window.

It became very quiet in the room for a while, save the rustling of paper and the drone of machinery from the factory. Unease filled Dan's limbs.

Then he heard a chair being scraped across the floor and stiffened.

Rashid asked, "Did you leave the window open?"

CHAPTER 40

Dan could hear Rashid getting up and approaching the window. He was trapped. He couldn't rush out into the compound, and the fence wall didn't allow him to run backwards. He crawled back as quickly as he could, then around the side of the office.

He could hear the window open wider and imagined Rashid craning his neck out, looking. Behind him, Dan could see men loitering. Any second now, one of them would look in his direction. Then he heard the office door open. Was Rashid coming outside?

Dan ran forward, behind one of the huts. He could just put the tip of his boot on the window ledge. There was a pipe running down the wall, next to the window. He gripped the pipe and climbed up on the slender window ledge. Voices were louder on the ground. The corrugated iron of the roof was rusty and denied him an easy hold. The iron cut into his palms, but he had little choice. He bore the pain and rolled onto the roof. Gingerly, he stood. Moss covered the sloping roof, and although it took his weight, the groan was audible.

The gap between the roof and the wall was no more than three yards. Dan took two steps back, then flung himself at the top of the fence. He aimed for the thick branch of a tree that was leaning over. His finger gripped the sturdy branch, and it bent lower. He managed to get his foot on the parapet of the fence, He couldn't avoid the barbed wire as it tangled into his trousers. He shook his legs free, then grabbed the branch and climbed, praying it would take his weight.

It creaked and bent lower but held.

He was exposed, vulnerable. He glanced down and saw a suited man standing below, hands on his waist. It was Rashid. How he had not looked up and seen him, Dan didn't know.

And he wasn't about to waste any time finding out.

Dan climbed up into the tree, feeling dizzy with gratitude for the massive plant. He scaled down and jumped onto the ground.

It was then he heard a shout from inside. A man was speaking rapidly in French, and then a familiar voice started bellowing out orders. It was Rashid. Dan reckoned they had found the guard he had knocked out earlier.

He took off like a hare, aware a search party would be out within minutes.

Dan reached the hidden car without incident. He spent a while lying in the undergrowth, still as a statue. They could've found the car and were waiting for him to turn up. He watched a pickup truck speed down the road. Two men sitting in the back and another two up-front. It was followed by a black SUV. Dan recognized this vehicle, this one had chased them from the DGIS prison near the left bank. He could still see the bullet marks on the side. Both cars swept past him.

He waited for another minute, then got up and removed the foliage that was hiding his small Fiat Punto. He drove it out from the copse of trees it was secluded in, then drove down the road, following the cars because there was no other road in this stretch of the country. The sun was leaning to the west, firing up the horizon with a riot of purple, gold and pink. Dan couldn't wait for darkness to fall.

****

The arrondissements of Paris are organized in outward spreading circles. So the first arrondissement is at the center, aptly named the Premier, or Louvre arrondissement. And the 2nd arrondissement was between the first and third, and so it spread all the way to the 13th, or Gobelin arrondissement at the southeast edge of the city.

Paris, as any Frenchman will proudly tell you, is the most well-planned city in the world.

While Dan was headed to the 13e where Claude lived traffic was a nightmare. He had to see Claude to find out what was going on.

How did Rashid know where Dan would be? Someone had tracked Dan from the minute he landed in France.

He checked the burner phone once to make sure Scorpion hadn't called or been in touch. He hoped she was still in the safe house, but if not was staying safe.

He parked two streets away from the address, left the AK47 in the trunk, and then walked. It was evening now, and lights were glowing in the windows of 19th century townhouses. Dan reflected how much it felt like walking around one of older districts of NYC, close to central park.

He waited for a while at the end of the road, sitting on a park bench. Apart from a couple families, and two women who rode their bikes home from work, he saw nothing suspicious.

He approached the building. Claude lived on the ground floor apartment. It had its own door, and a door beside it, leading to the stairs for the apartments upstairs.

Claude's door was open. Dan's hand slid inside his pocket, fingers curling around the butt of his gun. It was dark inside, but he was lit up by the streetlight above.

If there was someone inside, he would've spotted Dan already.

Dan took the gun out, flicked safety off. He kicked the door open, tumbling down on the floor, and rolling inside.

He lay quietly. Nothing happened. He hadn't expected gunfire, not with civilians outside. But it could be a suppressed weapon and a well-aimed shot. No shots came. Dan listened to the silence for a while, feeling it settle, and not liking it. Too quiet.

His hands felt up the wall and found a light switch.

The sudden glare of the ceiling lamp was blinding. He got up and scanning with his weapon moved from the hallway into the living room.

A man was lying on the floor, face down. Blood pooled beneath him, staining the blue carpet a darker shade. Dan leant by the side of the fallen man and put two fingers at the carotid. No pulse. The body was cold.

Claude had been dead for a few hours.

CHAPTER 41

Dan took a quick photo of Claude's face and sent it to Jeff for verification. Staying low, he switched all the lights off. He cupped a hand over the mouth of the Maglite and checked out the rest of the apartment. It was small but comfortable, befitting a government employee. The lounge led to two bedrooms, kitchen, and bathroom. All were empty. This being the ground floor apartment, there was also a postage stamp sized garden. A security light came on when Dan stepped outside, which made him retreat quickly into the shadows. The garden was surrounded by a brick fence, separating it from the other gardens.

Dan went back to the front living room where the body lay. Now that the room was dark again, he parted the curtains slightly to inspect the street. His eyes dwelled on the cars. All were empty. One pedestrian walked past, a commuter on his way home. Dan checked the front door. No signs of a break-in. Claude, if that's who the dead guy was, had let this person in. He was killed by someone he knew.

Dan's phone beeped. It was Jeff.

"Is it Claude?" Dan asked, referring to the dead man.

"I can't believe it," Jeff said. "He was one of my best men."

"Someone was onto him. They knew he was passing information over to you. Which means everything is compromised. Including the safe house and Scorpion."

Dan swore under his breath. "I gotta go. I need to find her. Damn it, Jeff, I rescued her, then maybe lead her straight into a trap."

"If it was then why didn't they kill you last night?"

Dan paused for a second. Jeff did have a point. But the risk of assuming the safe house was as its name suggested was now a huge risk.

"Maybe they took their time or got it out of Jeff just now. Which means I have to go."

"Okay, check in with me soon. But don't worry. I'm sure the Scorpion can take care of herself. Where have you been all day?"

Dan put his headphones on and went out of the house, shutting the door. Jeff was still on the line. Dan spoke as he walked back to the car, explaining to Jeff about Rashid's factory in Champigny Sur Marne.

"Rashid's mole in the DGIS listened to Scorpion's call to me," Dan said. "That means they have someone at a high level. Otherwise they wouldn't have access to phone data. That in turn, means Rashid must be using his Russian contacts. Powerful as he is, I doubt an Arab will have a mole in the DGIS."

"Agreed, there's an SVR agent in every European secret service, including ours, I'm sure." Jeff snorted in derisory laughter. "You better watch your back, Dan. What's the plan now?"

"I'll let you know," Dan said and hung up. He got back in the car and pointed it to the northeast toward Saint Denis. Traffic on the ring roads of A1, one of the main arteries cutting from north to south across Paris, was heavy. Dan fumed at the delay and rang the Scorpion several times without success.

A cold serpent of fear slithered across his spine.

Had he led the Scorpion to her death?

*****

It took him half an hour to get to Saint-Denis and another ten minutes to the block of apartments behind which the one-story bungalows were situated. Dan parked four blocks away. He still

229

had an extra mag left for the Colt, and he hadn't fired a single round all day. He had to leave the AK-47 in the trunk.

Evening had fallen, and youngsters were out in the corners of the banlieue. A fast food shop was open next to what looked like the French version of a strip mall. There was a drug store, a gas station, and a food mart.

A group of kids were playing soccer in the courtyard of the strip mall. Cars were parked around them, and on the pavement. Dan figured the courtyard was a parking lot as well, but the soccer players had claimed it as their own.

Some of the older kids sat on the brick walls, shouting and whistling at their friends. Some of them turned their heads as Dan walked past, maybe recognizing him as a stranger. He heard some voices call out to him in French, but he didn't understand a word.

The row of bungalows was visible, and lights glowed in several of them, elderly people shuffled around, visible through open windows, and blue lights of TV's gleamed. The house Dan wanted was the last one, it's back to the fence that led to the train station. Three bungalows were dark, silent. The safe house was one of them. Dan hid himself in the awning of a garage and observed. After ten minutes, in which time he called Scorpion several times, he detected no movement.

He could sneak in through the back. He could deal with the goons inside, no problem. But his weapon didn't have a silencer. If he shot, the sound would carry and someone would surely call the cops. If the cops arrived before Dan could leave he was in trouble.

He wondered where Scorpion was. His heart lurched when he imagined her inside, attacked and–no. He couldn't think like that. She couldn't be dead. He dealt with death all the time. And the Scorpion had been sent to kill him more than once.

But he couldn't bear to think of her as gone. The sharpness of the raw emotion took him by surprise. He wasn't used to strong feelings. No, that was a lie. He was human like anyone else and to deny himself that normality was wrong. He had to admit he didn't allow himself any human warmth because in his line of work it was a weakness. *Not that he didn't have feelings at all.*

And strangely it was Scorpion, Natasha, who had evoked them in him, like a mask she had removed from his face and seen the real him. It was strange because she wore the same mask herself. Hid her true self from the outside world. Not just her face or identity.

But when you hide yourself from everyone else, do you ultimately become the shadow you pretend to be?

Maybe that's what all assassins became, Dan mused as he stared at the darkened window of the safe house. Whatever it was, he now saw it as a mask he wore, and the woman who made him realize this might be lying dead inside that house.

Rage glinted inside him, and his jaws flexed. He couldn't afford anger right now, he needed a level head.

He dug his hands inside his pocket and came up with a bundle of euro notes. Enough to serve his purpose.

Briskly, he walked back to the boys playing soccer. They were in their mid to late teens. Dan walked into the middle of their makeshift pitch in the parking lot. The game stopped and amidst a chorus of plaintive cries a circle of kids formed around Dan. The taller boys stood at the back, watching him carefully.

All of them were either black or Algerian.

Dan held up a bundle of notes. "Who speaks English?"

"Me!"

"Me!"

Many voices chattered at the same time. Dan ignored the smaller boys at the front and focused on two tall black kids, perhaps sixteen to eighteen years old, whose eyes were now lit up with interest.

"Who can hit a football the hardest?" Dan asked.

Several heads turned towards the boys at the back. One of them addressed Dan in perfect English.

"What do you want?"

Dan moved, and the crowd parted to let him get closer to the boy who spoke.

"What's your name?"

"Bappe," the boy said. He was a few inches shorter than Dan, and he looked Dan up and down with frank curiosity. "Who are you?"

"A friend," Dan said, "who has a request."

"Depends what it is, and how much you are offering."

"You speak very good English."

"And you speak rubbish French. From the way you dress you must be American." Bappe shifted on his feet and laughter broke out among the crowd. "Being patronizing must come natural to you. We don't have time to waste. Why don't you spit it out and then get the hell out of here?"

Dan shrugged. He realized Bappe was acting tough, showing off to the kids around him.

"I need to break a window. In five minutes. Can you do it for me?"

"That's easy. Mr. American. How much are you offering?"

"Fifty euros."

"Make it one hundred and you have a deal."

"Deal."

Bappe whistled and someone threw him a soccer ball. "Show me the window, and I'll do it."

"You sure it's gonna break?"

Bappe frowned. "You guys worry too much. Relax, man. I know what I'm doing."

Dan grinned. "Another thing. I want you guys to set off some firecrackers at the same time the window breaks. Can you do that?"

Bappe snapped his fingers and several hands went up. "Easy," the teenager said, his eyes not leaving Dan's. "As long as you double the money."

"No problem. Can we synchronize our watches?"

When the watches were in sync, Dan showed Bappe the house, several other curious kids following as they walked down.

"You have to be quiet, right? Don't get too close, don't let them see you."

Bappe snorted. "I've scored thirty-yard free kicks, man. Who do you think you're talking to? This is easy."

"Good," Dan said. He glanced at his watch. "In five."

Bappe called out as Dan walked off. "Hey, you can come again, Mr. American."

CHAPTER 42

Dan moved quickly. He cut swiftly down the side of the bungalows, silent as a panther. He got to the fence, then turned right to the bottom edge of the row. He went past the gardens where the retired people sunned themselves during the day. There was a faint chill in the air and all of them were indoors, thankfully. Dan went to ground when he was diagonally opposite the safe house. The garden was wild, unkempt. That was good for him. He scurried and hid behind an overgrown plant. From here he could see inside the lounge where the night before Scorpion and him were chatting.

He hoped Bappe would deliver on his word. He checked his watch. Two minutes left. When he looked up, he saw a shadow move on the staircase next to the lounge. His fists clenched. Someone was inside. Another figure moved in the darkness. Dan watched as the person opened the back door and moved into the garden. The light didn't come on this time. A red glow appeared, and the man smoked casually. Dan stayed low, his eyes on the smoker. He shifted slightly to his left, then again. Too much movement attracted the eyes, even in darkness. But a smoker often looks at his red cherry, and it spoils his night vision.

Dan stayed behind bushes and rolled away until he was out of man's field of vision. Thirty seconds left for the fireworks to start. Dan stayed close to the fence but broke cover. Staying low, he reached the house, flattening himself against the wall. The smoker was around the corner; Dan could hear him.

Ten seconds.

The crash came, a tinkling sound from the front of the house. Bappe had delivered. At the same time the fireworks started, their chattering sounding like machine gun fire.

Dan turned swiftly. The smoker tossed the butt away and was about to vanish through the door when Dan reached out and grabbed his collar. The knife rose high and slashed into the man's throat at the angle of the clavicle, instantly puncturing the top of the right lung. Dan pressed the eight-inch knife down to its hilt and held the dying man as he thrashed and fought against. He put the twitching body down when it was in its death throes and extracted his knife.

He crept inside. The firecrackers were still going off. Two figures were hunched over the front window, staring outside, their backs to Dan. The football hadn't broken the window, only cracked it. In the distance, through the window, Dan could see the small figures of some of the kids.

Dan thought about checking upstairs first. He was in trouble if someone snuck down and got the drop on him.

But he had to deal with these guys first.

The man closest to Dan turned when he sensed Dan behind him. The gun arm came up, but Dan grabbed it and pointed it to the ceiling. The gun fired, the sound loud but merging with the crackers. Dan stabbed the man in the face and neck, a flurry of quick, sharp movements that practically gouged the eye's out and snapped his trachea.

The other guy fired but hit his buddy whose body was Dan's cover. The gun came loose in Dan's hand, and he flung the man backwards, and they both tumbled to the floor. Dan was still standing and had the better aim. The guy with the gun was trapped behind his friend, and as he tried to lift himself Dan shot him twice. He shot the knifed one as well, then took cover immediately.

The fireworks had stopped, and the last two shots were louder. The sudden silence was total, almost unnerving. Dan stayed still. Both the men on the floor were still, dead. So was the guy in the garden.

Any upstairs. Dan waited for two minutes. No sound at all.

He crept out, scanning with his gun, paying attention to his peripheral vision. He cleared the kitchen, then went up the stairs, testing each step for creaks. Some couldn't be avoided. This was the most dangerous part, where he had no shelter from gunfire above him.

CHAPTER 43

The Scorpion stared back at the middle-aged man with mounting fury.

"I need to speak to my sister first."

The man shrugged. "Do you have a phone, or do you wish to use mine?"

She gave him a look, then took out her phone. Keeping her eyes on him, she moved backwards. Melania's phone rang out. Scorpion tried again, but there was no response. She wanted to leave a message but would have to do it later.

"She's fine for now," the man said. "Whether she stays that way is up to you."

"What do you want me to do?"

"For now, head down to Marseilles."

Scorpion frowned. "Why Marseilles?" The southernmost city in France had a massive port close to the border with Spain. It was also a hub of crime and drug trafficking.

"Do as I say. When you get there, go to the port. Find the office for Maersk Shipping. Next to the office you'll see a bank of phone booths. The third phone booth will be ringing if you're there in"— he checked his watch—"ten hours. The flight time is 90 minutes."

"And then?"

"You get further orders when you're in Marseilles."

"I need more than that."

He shrugged. "Take it or leave it."

Scorpion breathed deeply. She was in a tight corner, and she knew it.

The man said, "I need to get something out of the drawer."

She pointed her weapon at him. "Very slowly."

He nodded, then opened the bedside table drawer and took out of a white envelope. He tossed it at her feet.

"Plane tickets. From Charles De Gaulle to Marseilles Provence Airport. Head straight to the port when you land."

She didn't bend to pick it up or move the gun away. "Why are you doing this? I mean, you won't get away with it. You know that, right?"

"You wouldn't understand. What you have to do is just one part of a gigantic game of chess. Yes, your role is critical, but it is just one move."

Scorpion thought for a while. "How do I know you'll let me live when this is all done? I mean, what if I told someone?"

"Then your sister dies."

"And what's stopping you from killing us both when I finish the job?"

He shrugged. "Nothing. I'm afraid you will just have to trust us. Obviously, we want you alive so you can do more work for us. Killing you doesn't serve our purpose."

She knelt and picked up the envelope. She opened and looked at the contents quickly. Then she nodded.

"Okay. I will leave for Marseilles on this flight." She tapped the envelope with the plane ticket. "And I will contact Melania every hour to make sure she is well. If I suspect anything the whole deal is off."

"Don't worry. Take care of your end, and we will do ours."

She turned to leave. He called out. "Oh, one last thing."

She waited.

"Don't even think about asking anyone for help. Especially your boyfriend, Dan Roy. He'll be dead soon, anyway."

*****

At the floor landing, Dan stopped, listening. The doors to the two bedrooms, and the bathroom remained closed. He heard no sounds. When he moved, his feet were a blur. In less than three seconds he had kicked down the door of the bathroom. It was empty. He repeated the process with the two bedrooms. They were empty too.

Either these guys had killed the Scorpion and then waited for him, or she left before they arrived. He doubted she was dead. There would be signs of a fight. Bullet holes in the wall. Tears in the carpets. There were none, and Dan hedged his bets Scorpion was out and alive.

He went back down and checked the men. They had suppressed handguns, rifles that were similar to Heckler and Koch 416 and radio's. He shone a light on their faces. Crew cut hair and hard faces. These guys were a far cry from the idiots he had seen at the factory in Champigny sur Marne. These men were ex-military, maybe even ex-Special Forces from France or Belgium. Dan was lucky that idiot came out for a smoke.

He frisked them quickly and took a rifle and three handguns.

Once outside, he saw flashing blue lights. Damn, that meant he couldn't cut across the front to get to the car. He moved fast. The last thing he wanted was get caught by French cops with three dead bodies.

Dan ran down the fence, past the bungalows, back the way he came. He was about to walk out into the open when another police car pulled in. Cop cars looked the same the world over.

Dan ducked underneath a fence. When the car passed, he jumped over and into another garden. He had to hide behind a trash can

239

when he saw the curtains move and a face peer out. The neighbors were wondering about the commotion.

A parked car got Dan's attention. It didn't have any alarms on. He had moved a block, and the car was down a quieter side street.

He took off his shirt and rolled it around his right elbow. Raising the arm high he smashed the window, then got inside. Tearing out the plastic case covering the steering wheel's base, he found the wires with some difficulty. After a few false starts, two wire heads clicked, and the engine started. A police car stopped at the mouth of the side street. Dan stared at it, his heart thumping. The gas was half full, and if it came to it, he would have to risk a chase.

A cop inside the car held a radio to his ears. He pointed ahead, and his partner moved the car.

Dan breathed a sigh of relief. He rolled out slowly, then picked up pace once he hit the main road.

He stopped when he saw the lights of the main drag. Parking the car and hoping it wouldn't get stolen again, he joined the pedestrians. People walked into a road called Rue Gabriel Peri, a broad avenue lined by shops of all sizes. French kids of all backgrounds hung around shops and bars, some playing with a soccer ball, like they did in the banlieue. Middle aged men and women shopped in small department stores. Dan found what he was looking for eventually.

A sign over a small, crappy store contained the sign: Jean Louis David Internet Cafe.

Dan went in, paid in cash for a terminal and connected to the web. He downloaded the Tor web browser and went into the Dark Web. The dark web was used by criminals, secret organizations, and many hideous, dangerous minds. But normal people also used it when they wanted to keep communications secret.

Dan scrolled to his mailbox. Only three people knew his address. McBride, Dan's brother Rob, and Scorpion. He had mail. It was from Scorpion. He breathed easier.

She had written down a cell phone number and nothing else. He knew it would be a burner phone to be discarded after a single use. It also meant she was alive.

Dan went out and brought a burner phone himself and six new SIM cards.

He put one SIM card in the phone when he was back inside the car. Scorpion answered on the first ring.

"Just listen. They got Melania. I need your help."

"Why can't you go?"

Scorpion told him. Dan listened, then asked, "Where are you?"

"In Marseille. I think they'll keep me hopping so I can't get to her."

Dan paused for a while. "What do you need me to do?"

"Bring Melania back here. When she's safe I can hunt down Borislov."

"Bringing her back won't be easy," Dan said.

"Please try. She's not safe in Bethesda. Cyclone has widespread reach."

"Okay. I'll let you know."

Dan hung up, then powered the phone down. He took out the sim card and crunched it under the heel of his boot.

He headed back to the car. He was bound for Charles De Gaulle and then back home. He just hoped he could reach Melania Stone in time. Otherwise a fate worse than death awaited her.

CHAPTER 44

Anna Ramitorva was going through the morning papers. Her understudy, First Lady Janice Ryan, had started a charity called Rise Up. For the launch, the First Lady had hired a hall in Washington and the press had turned up in droves. She was caught on camera posing with children from disadvantaged backgrounds. Anna noted her new hair style – a chignon and bob. Her dress was below the knee, a simple blue affair that still hugged her figure. She wore a pink cardigan that covered her arms and was tied at the neck. Blue heels with blue earrings and blue nail polish completed the ensemble,.

Anna read all the papers, and all of them had news about the First Lady. Anna knew the names and backgrounds of the First Lady's staff. Jennifer, her personal secretary, had been a paralegal at a law firm before applying to work for her husband's campaign. Michelle, her Social Secretary, used to work for a public relations firm which represented several politicians, including Bertram Ryan when he was a senator of Colorado. Now she worked for the White House full-time. These two women were always at the First Lady's side, Anna had noted. Janice Ryan had another three members of staff, including a Chief of Staff who was a man. Anna suspected Janice wasn't as close to her three remaining staff members, especially the two men. In fact, she felt this strongly. She didn't know why. But she knew Janice Ryan so well she felt like she was Janice herself.

There was a knock on the door, and Igor poked his head in. Igor was the SVR officer who was charged with the maintenance of the theatre. He set the stage and production, hired all the designers and props, even advertised for an audience. After the first couple of months, Anna had realized the audience was carefully selected.

Only the staunchest party faithful were allowed to attend. Everyone was sworn to secrecy.

Anna knew only what she had been told. Because she bore a striking physical resemblance to Janice Ryan, and the Party wanted to make a movie series about her, Anna had been chosen as the actress. The movie was being made to educate the people, to show them how the First Lady led a life of privilege and luxury, while the poor in America lived in run-down apartment blocks like so many did in Russia.

But the more Anna learnt about Janice Ryan and her life, the more she realized this was not true. Janice wasn't born into a life of privilege. Her parents had worked as school teachers.

Janice was a staffer in the House of Congress and met her future husband, Bertram Ryan while she was interviewing him. From what Anna could see, Janice worked considerably hard. She was aware of the tax dollars that went into the Office of the First Lady and used that money to raise awareness of the poor and marginalized in society.

Anna hadn't seen the Russian Premier do that for as long as she could remember.

Anna's total, complete immersion into Janice, from what she wore to how she talked, had also meant an immersion into western culture. It had aroused a secret, dormant desire she had. All her life she wanted to live in the West. It had never been possible for she was a school teacher and amateur actor from Podolsk. The more she evolved into her character, the more her desire grew.

The knocking on the door was louder. "Come in," Anna said, standing.

Igor came in. He was a handsome, broad shouldered man who wore the habitual black suit of the SVR. He was much younger than her, and she suspected he knew as much about this project as she did.

She also thought he was attracted to her. She didn't quite feel the same way. He was a good-looking man, but a bit too young for her and also one of those bland faced, eager Party workers who had little conception of what the outside world was like.

Igor smiled at her and came forward. "The Colonel would like to see you today."

He meant Borislov. She wondered what he wanted. Well, she had questions for him. All this time, she had gone along with his demands. But now she needed to know where this was headed.

Anna knew the First Lady was due in Paris in two days' time.

A flutter of apprehension ran through her. She suspected Borislov had something important to tell her.

"Is he coming here?" Anna asked.

"Yes," Igor replied. He looked at his watch. "In three hours. At 12pm."

That gave her enough time to do her morning reading and get ready. "Fine. Tell him I'll be waiting."

*****

Borislov arrived on time. Anna watched from the second-floor window as the familiar Zil limousine stopped on the tree covered avenue. Borislov wasn't on his own. Another man in uniform joined him as the driver opened the door for them. A knot tightened in Anna's gut.

Igor had set the TV up, and it showed a live stream of a speech Janice Ryan was giving on the subject of women in the workplace. Anna wasn't paying attention as the door opened and Borislov walked in. His hair was uncombed, and his shoulder hunched, as usual. His aide, in comparison, looked pristine. Borislov introduced him.

"This is Mr. Pushkin, my secretary."

Anna shook hands with the man who was in his forties.

"Shall we watch the TV for a while?" Borislov suggested. "Let's see what the First Lady looks like today."

Anna nodded, and they sat down. Soon, she was submerged in what Janice was saying. The content wasn't as important as the sound of her voice, the small tics she had like lifting her head slightly between sentences, and the way she shifted from one foot to another after a long pause.

Anna felt she knew this woman personally. She had been inside her bedroom and got to know the most intimate details about her. Anna had studied Janice so carefully, so deeply, she felt she was in the First Lady's head, aware of her thoughts.

Far from it being a weird experience, it felt warm, pleasant. On the TV, Janice looked up, and instantly Anna knew the speech she was reading at the lectern was finished, and she was going to start speaking freely.

Anna closed her eyes and murmured, *"Today we have more women who are millionaires than ever before. Yet, in the workplace the average woman earns 20-40% less than her male counterpart."*

When she opened her eyes, Borislov was looking at her in amazement. "How did you know that? She said almost exactly the same thing."

Anna shrugged. "She was preparing for this speech, right? I figured that–" She stopped suddenly when she realized she was answering back in English with an American accent.

The three men facing her had raised eyebrows, and Borislov was smiling. The smile faded, replaced by a distant, curious look in his eyes. It seemed Borislov was trying to look inside her mind, just like she had done with Janice Ryan. The moment passed, but it left her unsettled, like Borislov knew something she didn't. Like she was an experiment, and he was the doctor in charge.

He sat back in his chair, regarding her with a steady gaze. Anna met it, but her heart trembled inside.

"You must be wondering why I wanted to meet you today."

"I'm sure you're going to tell me what the purpose of this theatre is."

Borislov nodded, respect in his eyes. She could tell he was impressed. "Absolutely. The time has come for you to know. I thank you for all the hard work so far."

Anna waited. Borislov said, "We want you to impersonate the First Lady of the United States in real life."

The suspicion had gnawed away inside her for a long time. It wasn't a complete surprise. She had been partly expecting it. But to hear it loud was still shocking. Her nostrils flared, jaw clenched, and her mind went numb, like a cold block of ice was resting inside.

"What do you mean, *real life*?" she asked.

He took his time to respond. He pointed at the TV which was now turned off as the First Lady had finished her speech. "Could you imagine doing that speech yourself?"

The question startled her. She thought for a while. It was bizarre to think of herself standing there, addressing those people – but then, why not?

She looked the same as Janice. Talked the same. And she had just proved she was even preempting what Janice was saying.

Borislov said softly, "No one would know the difference. Trust me, Pushkin and I"—he gestured at his aide, who leaned forward—"have watched hundreds of hours of video tapes of your performance, then watched the First Lady on screen. It is impossible to tell you apart from her."

Janice murmured, almost to herself. "Like I am her."

Borislov seemed startled but recovered quickly. "Yes. I'm glad you think so." He coughed and looked away to his aide, exchanging a silent message with him. Anna didn't miss it, but she let it go.

Borislov said, "The US President is due in Paris in two days. You can be there too." He put his elbows on his knees and leaned towards her. "Anna, this is up to you. No one can force you into this. What you will be doing will potentially change the course of this country's future."

The silence was oppressive, but Anna found she couldn't speak.

Borislov said, "When the First Lady is here, I want you to take her place."

Anna felt her heart jackhammering against her ribs so hard they might break.

"How?" she croaked.

"Leave that to us. Janice Ryan will be incapacitated while she is in Paris. Before anyone knows she is missing, you will be in her place."

"And then?"

"Then you will carry on as the First Lady of the USA."

CHAPTER 45

Dan was sitting in the park bench not far from the Lincoln Memorial when he saw a man approaching. Back still straight after all these years, long black coat and fedora, despite the warm weather. In fact, DC was hellishly hot in the summer. The city forgot to breathe it seemed. But the man walking toward Dan didn't seem bothered. Jim McBride sat down next to Dan with a sigh. They stared at the ducks in the pond flirting with the weeping willow branches leaning over the water.

McBride took out a cylindrical object, flicked a switch on it, and put it between them. A soft hum came from it, hardly audible, but enough to mask any listening devices within ten feet.

"Who killed Grant Pearson?"

"I don't know. But whoever killed him came after me."

"That makes sense."

"Grant was in trouble. Rashid told him he would come after his family. I figure Grant told Rashid some stuff they're working on."

"Who's they?"

"Rashid and the Russians. I can't imagine how Rashid got hold of Grant's personal details. No terrorist can do that, it had to be the Russians."

McBride nodded. "That makes sense. But what do the Russians get out of it?"

Dan said, "Something big. They're onto Natasha. She's been told to do a job for them or Melania dies."

McBride frowned. "Melania Stone? Her sister?"

When Dan nodded, McBride said, "That has to be SVR intelligence as well. For them to be in so deep with Rashid, whatever they're up to must be worth their time."

"I agree. And the sooner we find out the better. But first, I need to help Melania. She isn't safe here anymore."

"She's a CIA agent, and she's at home. What makes you think she's not safe?"

"They killed one agent in London, right? I think this thing is big enough to kill another one."

"That's almost unheard of, Dan. Governments don't like killing each other's agents, you know that. Nothing's stopping us from taking out a couple of SVR agents as revenge. And then the whole thing escalates."

"I know. But the Russians clearly think the risk is worth taking."

They were silent for a while. Dan said softly, "I wonder what Grant told them."

"And they think he revealed it to you as well, hence they're after you."

Dan nodded. "Rashid also has a factory outside Paris. I don't know what he's making. But I'm worried. He's out for revenge. Against me, sure, but what if he takes it out against...." Dan's voice trailed off.

"Innocent civilians in Paris," McBride finished for him. "Have you told the French? Maybe the DGIS can shut the factory down."

"I wanted to. But Claude, my source, was killed." Dan told McBride about Claude.

The older man shook his head. "One by one, the links in the chain are vanishing, Dan. You know the CIA are looking for you? Susan Harris is pissed."

"Let her be, not my concern. I wish I could alert her about Melania, but I can't do that without giving Scorpion away. And even if I did, I don't trust the CIA to protect her."

Dan took a break and continued. "I need some creds. To get inside the McLean campus if I have to. Sure, I'll try to grab Melania outside. But the sooner I can alert her, the better."

"Anything else?"

"Yeah. Can you alert the French about this factory? They might not believe me but would take a retired 2 star general more seriously."

"Maybe not. This is the French we're talking about", McBride grinned.

Dan stood. "Try. Also press Susan Harris for what Grant knew. Might make our job easier. I need some weapons too."

*****

Dan took the metro to a car rental place and paid in cash for a Ford Taurus. He wanted to drive into McLean, the CIA HQ, but he wouldn't be allowed in without creds, and there was little chance of meeting her even if he could. So he decided to call Melania. He had kept her number from last year. It rang out, and Dan tried again. The response was the same, so he sent her a text. She didn't reply.

Dan drove to her address in Bethesda. Melania's apartment was in a converted mock Tudor five story house, built at the turn of the century. The kind of place Dan would like to live in himself. He parked at the end of the tree lined avenue and sat for a while. He could see the house from here. He drove past it after a while, went around the block and returned. He waited until sundown. He rang her a couple of times again. She didn't answer.

Dan knew she drove a black Audi A5, DC plates. He couldn't see her car on the street and the garage in the building had been converted into an extension.

Dan went to a local diner and had burger and fries, they tasted good after a few days of European burgers. He took up vigil again, but by 10 pm there was no sign of Melania. Dan called McBride.

"She's not here," Dan said. "Natasha hasn't spoken to her either. As far as I know, she's not abroad."

"Let me check with my contact inside McLean. Call me back in ten."

When Dan did, McBride's voice was grim. "She didn't turn up to work yesterday, or today, Dan. She's not on assignment overseas. She didn't call in sick, nor is she meant to be on vacation. I'm checking with the State Department about her passport."

"Call me back," Dan said.

He hung up. He took out the Colt M1911 that McBride had given up and made sure the suppressor was screwed on. He checked the K-Bar kukri knife, loosening the tie of the leather scabbard so he could grab it easily.

He walked down the street, checking for any movement. Lights glowed behind windows, yellow squares that showed an occasional human figure, or the blue screen of a TV. This was a nice residential street. Suburbia. Surely someone would have noted anything unusual. But Dan didn't have time for a police investigation. It made sense that Melania had been taken. After all, to make the threat viable, and to make Scorpion do as they wanted, it was important to have Melania in their hands already.

Dan got to the house. Some lights were on, but Melania's second floor apartment was dark. He looked around, then vaulted over the side gate. He was on a narrow path that led to the garden behind. At the end of the path he flattened himself against the wall and looked around. The garden was empty. He saw security lights on the wall and security cameras. He found a trash can, and stood on it, trying to reach the light closest to him. He was just able to get his fingers on it. The light was mounted on a metallic holder that was screwed into the wall. Dan pulled hard, and the light came off in his hand. The camera was too high up to reach. But he got rid of both the lights, then climbed up the fire escape.

On the landing, he paused in front of the back window of Melania's apartment. The glass was broken, wide enough to let a man through. Dan took the Colt out. He leaned in with one leg, and his foot hit something soft. A sofa maybe. He couldn't see well in the dark. He lowered himself inside, then dropped to the floor quickly, lying down flat, weapon raised. Shards of glass prickled his skin. After listening for a while, he stood. This was a small bedroom. The door was open, and he stepped into a small hallway. The lounge and open plan kitchen was in front. He peeked in. It appeared empty.

He checked the other bedroom quickly. Working swiftly in the darkness, he opened the dresser to find it full of clothes. No one hid under the bed. He cleared the bathroom and then the lounge. In a drawer next to the kitchen cabinets he found a flashlight. He turned it on, cupping the mouth of the beam and checked the apartment again. Nothing. No dead bodies. No sign of Melania. He breathed a little easier. It was his greatest fear as soon as he saw the broken window.

Dan pulled the curtains on all the windows, then turned the lights on. He searched every corner of the floor, windows frames, door jams. They came in through the window, but they must have left via the front door. Did Melania walk out, gun rammed into her back? Or was she knocked out?

Dan couldn't see any sign of blood. But the paint was chipped on the doorframe of her bedroom. The chair was on the floor, and the bed had been slept in. Dan knelt and examined the carpet. He touched it, and it came away damp. He sniffed – mud. Then he saw the faint boot mark. A man's shoes. Someone had come into this room to grab Melania. Maybe a two- or three-man team.

Dan went out to the front door and opened it. Another boot mark on the white door frame. His eyes picked up something on the doormat. It was a matchbox, white, with a black logo on it. Rodney's Bar. 7342 Woodmont Avenue.

Dan turned his phone on and pulled up the address on the map. It wasn't far, less than eight miles. He shut the front door and left. He jogged back to his car, turned the GPS on and drove out.

He went through an area called Chevy Chase with rolling hills and wide spaced houses on tree filled avenues. Traffic was nonexistent, and even when he hit the town, only a few cars were on the road.

It was 11 pm by the time he stopped opposite Rodney's Bar.

A waiter was lifting up a table from the sidewalk and taking it inside. Dan could see a couple inside, and a few men drinking at the bar. He locked the car and crossed the street.

The barman looked up as Dan walked in. He stopped scrubbing the counter and smiled at him.

"What can I get you?"

Thick accent, Eastern European. Dan glanced at the tattoo on the man's left wrist. It was in Cyrillic, but he could read it. *Bratva.*

The Brotherhood. Russian Mafia. Dan had dealt with them in the past down in Atlanta. They had a big chapter there, and it didn't surprise him they'd got this far north. The Bratva were all over America.

Dan knew bartender had caught him looking. The man was short, but burly and wide, with Pop eye wide arms.

Dan asked in Russian, "Atkuda Vi Idioche?" *Where are you from?*

The man's eyebrows lifted, then his eyes narrowed. "Pochemu? Kto ti?" *Why? Who are you?*

Dan knew his accent gave him away as non-Russian. He put his elbows on the smooth wooden bar and leaned over. He switched to

English. "I'm looking for a woman called Melania Stone. Know her?"

The bartender's eyes flickered. He paused for a little longer than usual. Then he shook his head. "No. No idea."

Dan said, "Did she ever come here? Dark hair, five six, 110 pounds. Attractive."

The man shrugged, flicked the towel off his shoulders, and made a show of scrubbing the counter again. "No."

"Then how does this end up in her place?" Dan held up the matchbox.

The man frowned at it then at Dan. "How do I know?"

Dan sucked a tooth. "Well, I'll stay here until you find out." He jerked a thumb toward the curtained exit behind the bar. "Why don't you ask someone in there? Kharasho?" *Okay?*

"No," the bartender leaned over, his shoulder muscles bulging. There was a snarl on his face. One of his bottom teeth was gold. He pointed to the door. "Get the fuck outta here?" His voice was a low menacing growl, and Dan supposed he used it a lot to sound intimidating.

But Dan didn't intimidate easily. He shook his head. "How rude." His right arm shot out and grabbed the finger that was still pointing at the door. He bent the finger backwards until the joint cracked. The man howled. Dan reached out, grabbed the man behind the neck, and slammed his face down on the counter. The entire bar rattled and glass rolled off, smashing on the floor. Dan pushed the bartender backwards, and the guy fell to the floor.

Behind him, he could hear chairs scraping as the guests got up to leave.

The curtains parted, and two men appeared. Both were Bratva wise guys, dressed in suits, one had a bent nose, the other a silver earring and a silver cross hanging from his neck. Both were thick at the neck and shoulders, flesh bulging over collars, jackets tight under packed muscle.

"Hello Madonna," Dan said to the silver cross guy. He didn't like it. Muttering an oath, he stepped forward.

"Hey, you," a growling voice said from behind Dan.

CHAPTER 46

Dan looked behind to see another suit, arms hanging loose by his side. He turned. "Nice threads. Sure you want to waste them? All I want to know is where the girl is."

The man was built like a linebacker with a beard on his face. He cursed at Dan and swung. One of the problems of size is the slowness that comes with it. Dan had expected the move, and before the arm was halfway up he had stepped inside the man's space, caught the arm, bent his back, and heaved the big guy over his chest. Dan did it in the blink of an eye, lifting the guy up and slamming him down over the bar counter.

The floor shook with the impact, the counter barely held up straight. Dan punched the guy in the side of the face, making his teeth fly out.

Footsteps rang out to either side. Madonna and the other guy were on either side of him. Neither had guns drawn. Presumably not wishing to shed blood in a nice neighborhood like this. Dan shared that sentiment. He did a quick 360, but saw no one else.

Silver chain flying, Madonna leaped at Dan. He didn't expect Dan to fall to the floor, and move towards his feet. Like a sliding tackle, but with steel pincers for legs. Dan swept his legs out, and the guy, off-balance already, fell heavily, cracking his head against the bar.

Dan felt a heavy kick land on his ribs and it hurt. He grunted and rolled over. The man rushed him, kicking him again, but this time Dan grabbed the foot and shoved him backwards. They fell over a table, breaking plates, cracking the glass top. Dan lifted his broad forehead and smashed it down on the guy's head. He howled in pain. Dan bent his elbow, lifted it high, and repeated the process. The scream was louder this time.

Hands grabbed Dan from behind. They pulled him back by the collar, and Dan let himself be dragged. His throat was grabbed in a chokehold, and Dan stumbled backwards. There was no knife or gun rammed in his spine.

Dan pushed himself against his attacker, and the man realized his mistake too late. By that time, Dan had rammed himself so hard against the guy they both fell backwards in a heap. Dan was the first up as he was on top. He twisted then straddled the guy's chest.

It was Madonna, the wearer of the silver chain. "Should've stuck to fashion and singing, dude," Dan panted. Then he brought his fist crashing down on the face, twin blows side to side.

Dan stumbled to his feet, chest heaving. Sweat was pouring down his ace. He wiped it with his sleeve and checked the three men. Reinforcements would be on their way soon, and so would cops. Dan needed to make himself scarce before either happened. He checked the men for weapons, found them, and ejected the magazines, putting them in his pocket.

Only one guy was still conscious, the one he had lifted onto the bar. He had slid down to the floor. Dan grabbed his collar with both hands, and pulled the guy to the back of the restaurant and then through the back door.

A chef with his white hat on poked his head out. He saw Dan and quickly withdrew. Dan kicked the back door open. He was in a small parking lot with large dumpsters everywhere.

He propped the linebacker against the wall and flicked open his knife. He slapped the guy hard until his eyes opened.

Dan held the knife up for him to see then put it close to his face. "An eye for an eye, right?"

The guy mumbled something in Russian. Dan put his palm against his face and slammed his head against the wall. The man grimaced in pain.

Dan held the tip of the knife and nicked the corner of the left eye. With his other hand he grabbed the guy's throat.

"I'll push this all the way in before your friends get here. Or you can tell me where the girl is held." He spoke in Russian. The guy gasped, swallowed, then nodded.

*****

The place was an abandoned retail park several miles outside Bethesda off a dark ramp on route 355. Graffiti covered the walls. A Target store lay in ruins, only the T of the Target logo remained standing. Dan didn't drive inside. He cut the headlights as soon as he drove off the ramps then parked further down the road. The locked gate was easy to climb. Dan had the gun in his hand now. He scooted across the wreck of a JC Penny and went to ground when he saw a shadow outside the drug store. Not one, two shadows. Both men were speaking in whispers. Dan couldn't hear from this far away, and his eyes were still getting used to the dark.

When the men turned their back, Dan crept closer. He was within thirty yards. Close enough to hit his targets. There was open space between them and him, but however quiet he was they would still hear him. The linebacker had told him three guys were holding the woman. They were told not to touch her. She was important.

Dan was on one knee, leaning against the wall, elbows ramrod straight. He was gripping the Colt with both hands. The gun jumped in his hand, twice. He aimed for center mass. Both bodies fell to the floor. He shot them both again, then ran forward, gun aimed at the two prostate figures then scanning upwards.

He was worried the sound of the two men falling would carry in the silence. When the door to the drug store creaked open, Dan knew he was right. He fell flat on the ground as the door opened further, and a shadow detached itself from the darkness. Dan didn't have time to aim properly, but he fired anyway. He hit the guy in the shoulder, spinning him around, hurling him back against the door. The man grunted, fired twice wildly, and began moving inside. His unsuppressed rounds shattered the silence.

Dan stopped running, knelt on one knee again, holding the Colt with both hands. He squeezed off four rounds, and two of them hit the man in the leg. He screamed. Dan ran forward, firing twice at the midriff. The body jerked, then was still.

Dan checked all three bodies, discarding their weapons. One of the men had a torch. Dan used it to shine it on the guy who lay at the door. Blood was frothing at his lips. A round must have punctured his lungs.

Dan used the door as a shield and shouted, "Melania? This is Dan Roy. Are you here?" He knew her mouth would be gagged, but he expected some sound. He got it. A clanging sound, like something was hitting a hollow pipe. The sound kept coming. That gave Dan confidence. It must be Melania, and she wouldn't be making that sound if a guard was standing over her.

He remained cautious still. The guard could be hiding, and Melania was trying to warn him. He went out of the door and ran around the outside of the building, stopping at the corners. There was a back entrance, but it was locked. A wrought iron staircase led to the upper floor. The door at the top was closed as well. Dan went back down and inside the drug store. He heard no sound this time. He scurried behind old counters, staying low. The sound came again from the back of the store.

There was a bank of counters at the far end, and Dan vaulted over them. He kicked open a door and sank back down against the wall. No shots were fired, but he could hear the sound much louder now along with a muffled noise like someone was trying to shout.

Dan shone the lights inside, and to his right, tied to a pillar, he saw a figure. It was Melania. Her hair was wild, plastered to her face. A cloth was tied around her mouth. Dan checked the rest of the room quickly. It was empty save some old desks, chairs, and computers.

He cut Melania free. She leaned on him, and he helped her stand. She clung to him, and he hugged her back.

"Let's go", Dan whispered. "The rest of the Bratva might be on their way."

"Who?" Melania whispered her voice cracked, lips dry.

"Don't worry. Did they hurt you?"

"No. They came in while I was asleep."

Dan nodded. "I figured as much. Shall I carry you, or can you walk?"

"I'm fine. Let's go."

Dan moved in front, Melania close behind.

Melania stumbled when they were on the road. Dan knew she was too proud to ask for help. He put his weapon away and pulled her up on his shoulders in a fireman's lift. He jogged back to the car and helped her inside.

He drove back the way he came, Melania directing him. They pulled up at a twenty-four hour gas station that had a McDonald's as well. Dan brought food back to the car.

Melania ate like she had never seen food before. Dan didn't have any appetite. He chugged on a drink instead, casting a critical eye over Melania. She didn't have any bruises on her face. Her hands had small cuts but nothing that needed stitching. She rested her head back and closed her eyes.

"So, where is my sister now?"

Dan had filled her in while they were driving. "In Marseille, south France, as far as I know. How long did they have you for?"

"This was the second day. It happened after I started looking at Grant Pearson's files. They're classified, but I managed to get access. That must've tripped up some alarms."

"Did you get in trouble?"

Melania nodded. "The director called me in. She wanted to know why I searched for Grant's files. Well, she wanted me to contact you as well since you were there when Grant died."

Dan listened in silence. Melania continued. "I told her I needed access to Grant's files to see if there were any clues. She shut me down." Melania glanced at Dan. "But not before I discovered Operation Nectar Flower."

Dan frowned. "What? Weird name."

"I know, but wait until you hear what it is."

Dan listened in silence, his eyes growing wider with each word.

CHAPTER 48

Randall Rann had his eyes closed. His mouth was open, and he was breathing in fast, shallowed jerks. His right hand was on Skylar's head as she kneeled in front of him. Randall had not felt sensations like this for a long time, hell, never. His ex-wife didn't believe in blow jobs. Like, at all. In the last two years of their marriage, she barely touched his dick.

Skylar was the complete opposite. A nymphomaniac, she practically ripped his clothes off as soon as they were alone. Anywhere. Randall got her a visitor's day pass to come into the White House. Randall was busy, and he couldn't leave the building until all the security arrangements for the First Lady's European trip was finalized. No problem, Skylar had said. She would skip work and come to him. After all, she wouldn't see Randall when he was in Paris.

And all because he was a such a fierce, dominant alpha male she couldn't keep her hands off him. She fantasized about him all the time and just couldn't stay away.

Randall couldn't believe his luck. The most beautiful woman he'd ever met was crazy about him. Who knew single life could be such fun?

Skylar's tongue and mouth moved faster, and Randall moaned softly. He was building up to the biggest climax ever. His balls clenched, buttocks tensed. He moaned again, but this time grit his teeth. They were inside a bathroom in the South Wing, and he couldn't make any sounds. Well, some. Like the strangled croak as he finally came, knees buckling.

Shakily, he sat down on the toilet as Skylar washed her mouth, then sat on his lap and kissed him passionately. He could feel himself hardening again.

What. A. Woman.

"Shh, slow down," Skylar whispered, as Randall's hands slipped underneath her blouse and started massaging her breasts. "Do you have a room here?"

Randall breathed. "Yeah, but it's being redecorated."

"Poor Randy," she purred, brushing her hand through his hair. "Why don't you show me your office then?"

They walked out. Skylar was a visitor from her magazine, the Woman's Weekly. Randall had tried to get her an appointment with the First Lady and failed. When they walked into Randall's office, two other secret service agents were present. Randall introduced Skylar, standing well away from her. Soon after, the two agents left, and they were alone.

Skylar sat down on Randall's chair. "Is this yours?" She said, smiling playfully as she opened up the laptop on his desk.

"Hey, that's restricted," Randall said gently.

She brushed his hand away. "Tell me you have a photo of me in here?"

"Nope. Not allowed," Randall said.

"Oh?" She frowned. "Really?"

"Yes," Randall said. She looked so disappointed he felt bad. God, he wanted to lean over and plant a kiss on those ruby red lips. Her deep blue eyes were full of hurt as she stared back at him. Randall felt his heart skip a beat.

She shrugged. "I guess you can't as it's your job."

"Yes. Exactly."

"I'm thirsty, baby. Will you get me some water, please?"

"Sure. There's a water machine right here."

Randall walked to a side door, and opened it to reveal a smaller room. Skylar's hands moved with dizzying speed. She pulled out a tiny black object from her purse. She lifted the laptop and clipped the black magnetic object, smaller than a dime coin, to the underside. It contained a file reader that could access any files on the laptop every time it was opened.

Skylar clicked on the email icon twice, and a page containing Randall's recent emails loaded. She closed it down when she heard Randall entering the room.

"Here you go," Randall said, giving her a plastic cup of cold water. He glanced at his laptop, then reached over and shut it.

"Why don't you show me round the rest of this wing?" Skylar said. Her eyebrows rose. "Maybe we can find another bathroom somewhere."

*****

On a fifth-floor office of the imposing building on Lubyanka Square, a phone started to ring. Borislov was smoking a Cohiba cigarette by the open window. He turned and snatched up the receiver. As he listened, his face creased into a smile.

"Good. Very good."

He went back to smoking. The view across the Square was majestic. The Lubyanka prison rose opposite, its foreboding yellow walls high, and the blue spire at top shining in the sun.

Borislov was in a good mood. Everything was falling into place.

265

The door to the side opened and Pushkin, his aide, walked in. "I have the itinerary of the First Lady's visit."

Pushkin had the file downloaded on his phone. "She will be in London for two days, Paris for two days, and one day in Brussels. In Paris, she's visiting this community center twenty miles outside the city, to talk about the effect of social media on children's health. She's due in Paris tomorrow."

Borislov squinted at the screen. Pushkin said, "This center has multiple entrances, and there's also a mosque attached to it."

Borislov smiled. "So we can insert Anna there, wearing a headscarf, covering her face."

"Exactly what I was thinking."

CHAPTER 49

The Scorpion was at Marseilles Port. She was leaning against the railings of the walkway that faced the emerald sea. Wind whipped her hair back, and she raised her face to the sky, enjoying the warm, saline breeze coming off the Balearic Sea. Enclosed by the southern coasts of Spain, Italy, and France, the sea was sheltered from the colder waters of the Atlantic. It was holiday season in southern Europe, but the last thing on Scorpion's mind was a holiday.

Right next to her stood three red and white telephone boxes. The man in Paris had been very specific.

The phone in the last booth will ring at 23.00.

She glanced at her watch. It was 22.45. She went closer to the booth, then saw a patrolling policeman. Their eyes met, and she looked away, transferring her gaze back to the sea. She had seen the cop once previously. He was on the beat, and though he was armed, she could see he was no more than an ordinary cop. Probably employed by the Port Authority. Another man walked past, but at this time of the night the place was more or less empty. Scorpion watched the cop turn once to look at her as he walked away.

She didn't expect any trouble from him. If he tried, she could neutralize him in the blink of an eye. She could pull off the tourist routine easily, but just hoped he didn't think she was a hooker looking for business.

It was 22.57. She moved closer to the telephone booth. The last thing she wanted was the cop to come back while she was making a dash for the phone. She stiffened when a man appeared, wearing a black trench coat. He moved fast with purpose, heading for her.

Instinctively, her hand went to her waist where the Glock was placed on her belt.

She was next to the phone booth now. The man came closer, then walked right past her and away. She watched him go, then breathed a sigh of relief.

The phone rang.

She was inside the booth immediately, snatching the receiver into her hand.

"Hello?"

There was silence on the other line, but she could hear the sound of breathing.

"I'm here as you asked," Scorpion said.

"Tomorrow," said a voice she hadn't heard before. There was a clear accent, and it was Russian, but he spoke in English. "Come back to Paris. Get to the tourist center of the Eiffel tower. Be armed and ready."

"I just came from Paris," she couldn't hide the irritation in her voice.

The voice was totally unconcerned. "I know. At the tourist center you will see a bank of pay phones. One is covered in graffiti, the last one on the right as you enter. That will ring at 11.00. Be there."

"Yes, but what if–"

The man hung up, and all she could hear was static.

Angry and frustrated, Scorpion walked back to the Metro station and took the subway train to the town center. Marseilles, despite its enviable location, isn't exactly a tourist destination. Those places are Cannes and Nice around the bend to the east. Marseilles has always been a hub for trade, and now trafficking of all types. Le Milieu, The French Mafia, have a strong presence in the city, as do the Italians.

Scorpion was staying in a side road off the main roadway, down a rabbit warren of twisting cobbled streets. Groups of men sat on doorways and several catcalled to her. She ignored them, and luckily for them, they left her alone. Her mind was busy with concerns for Melania, and what on earth she was going to do tomorrow.

She found a two-story boarding house where the manager wasn't fussed about ID. She paid extra to use the one desktop computer they had. On the dark web, she checked the email inbox she shared with Dan but never sent any mail to. There was still no news from him. She trudged back up to her room and tried to catch a few hours of sleep.

*****

Champigny Sur Marne

Outside Paris

Farouk Abdullah was a skinny, bespectacled twenty-eight-year-old whose round glasses and cord trousers made him look a nerdy academic. Which is exactly what he was. Farouk was a bio scientist who had graduated in the University of Baghdad, and then come to Paris to do his master's. After his master's, Farouk carried on to do a PhD at the University of Lyon, studying different ways of producing castor oil by changing the genetics of normal bacteria. Farouk was an expert in castor beans biology from which castor oil was made.

He had not been radicalized in Iraq. In fact, he was quite cosmopolitan in his outlook. His female friends wore western clothes like jeans and skirt with the obligatory headscarf. The 2003 war changed a lot of things, but like many Iraqis, Farouk hated Saddam and his cronies from long before that. His parents lived in Basra in southern Iraq close to the border with Iran. In Basra many Iraqis are Shia Muslims. Hence, they were closer to Iran, where the vast majority of Shia Muslims lived. Iran benefited from the 2003 Iraq war since it was against their worst enemy – Saddam Hussein.

The day before the first bombs fell on Baghdad, Farouk received his visa and student grant to study at the Biology Department in Sorbonne. Baghdad Airport was a tornado of activity the day he left with military jets taking off the same time as his flight. He wondered, looking back from the plane window, if he would ever see his country again.

He didn't. He heard of the war on TV and radio. It wasn't even a war, in his mind. A dog, no matter how loud it barks, cannot fight a lion. A part of him rejoiced when the CNN footage showed Saddam's glorious palaces lying in ruins, his statue being pulled down from the city square. A biologist himself, he had no doubt Saddam had used biological agents in warfare. He knew personally many of the professors at his University who were involved in the production of said weapons. But nuclear? He doubted that. Whatever the reason, getting rid of Saddam wasn't the problem.

The problem was what happened to his country after.

With a power vacuum in Baghdad, Al-Qaeda flew in like air being sucked into a low-pressure zone.

As Farouk carried on with his studies, Al-Qaeda, the foreigners, spread like an ulcer in his land. He tried to explain this to his fellow graduate students, who either didn't understand or pretended to. He wanted to show them his country existed from biblical times, it was the seat of Babylon, where Noah built the

Ark, where Adam and Eve were created, and where Jesus himself had roamed and preached.

But no one cared. Everyone saw Iraq as a terrorist country, ruled by an evil dictator for 30 years. Farouk didn't drink, and one night in a cafe he got into an argument with three drunk students, one of whom had a brother who was fighting in Iraq. It got ugly, Farouk was thrown out of the cafe. Farouk got arrested, despite not throwing a punch. He was called in to the Dean of his college and reprimanded. As the days went on, Farouk found himself increasingly ostracized from French society. He spent lonely evenings and weekends writing his dissertation and reading the Koran.

Being a pious Muslim, Farouk prayed five times a day. At his mosque in the 13th arrondissement, where he lived, he met a man called Altaf Bakri, also from Iraq. He introduced Farouk to a group of Muslims who were different to the moderates in the mosque where he prayed. This mosque was in Saint Denis, a deprived banlieue outside Paris. It was with these Muslims, many from North Africa, that Farouk found common ground. They looked at the world in a different light. They regarded the West as the ulcer ravaging the middle east, not Al Qaeda. Fiery preachers delivered sermons in this mosque.

Did Mohammed not lead great armies from Arabia into Spain? Was he not a great military leader? These preachers predicted the rise of the old Islam, when a new army of Muslims would take the battle to the infidels, the Kaffirs, the non-believers.

It was Altaf Bakri who introduced Farouk to a man called Waleed Al-Falaj. Waleed came and prayed with them, he became a part of their *Umma,* or brotherhood. When Waleed died, Rashid took over the financing of their cell in France.

271

Today, as Farouk looked over the collection of the castor bean mash left over after producing castor oil in, he felt a surge of pride. He moved down the warehouse in his green overalls, waving at the men in their Biosafety suits. Castor bean mash has to be handled with great care because it contains high quantities of ricin. Ricin in a natural toxin found in castor beans. It is also one of the most lethal poisons known to man.

Ricin stops the production of proteins in the body. Without protein synthesis the body couldn't function. Lungs stopped inflating. Hearts stopped beating. Guts froze and filled up with water. Within a few hours of ricin inhalation, the most potent way of poisoning, people struggled to breathe, their skin turned blue, blood pressure dropped, and they died.

Farouk stopped outside a steel door with rubber gaskets as locks. This was their laboratory, where ricin was extracted and weaponized. The CDC has four categories of Biosafety Labs. This lab was a crude, but effective copy of a category 4 lab.

Farouk could only go inside after changing into a biosafety suit and mask with visor. Inside, several of his colleagues were busy at the lab desks. All wore the same protective suits as him. They were dissolving the ricin extracted from the castor beans into weak hydrochloric acid. Once dissolved, the solution could be loaded into high pressure cans. When a nozzle was pressed, a spray would emit from the cans, just like hair spray, but more condensed, and releasing smaller particles.

These tiny particles could be inhaled. Those inhaling would die within hours.

Farouk walked over to the cabinet where Omar, a scientist, was working with a new aerosol can. They nodded at each other. Omar was working on an electrically activated aerosol can. Just like a ringing phone can detonate a bomb, it can also trigger the release of a spray from a can. But these cans have to be large, and the release of the spray has to be in an enclosed space, like a theatre hall, to be most effective.

Farouk was called to the door by a man. He got changed and left the lab. Rashid was waiting for him outside. Farouk shed his suit, then stepped inside the shower. He dried himself and emerged outside. Rashid embraced him. They walked around to the front, then outside to his office, where they could talk in peace. Rashid closed the windows firmly and shut the door.

"We have a location. Tomorrow is the ideal day. The Russians can help us. How far are we with the weapons?"

"Almost ready, sayidi. Tomorrow is a distinct possibility."

"Alhamdulillah," Rashid whispered. "We will release a wave of death on Paris."

CHAPTER 50

Anna Ramitrova was packing her things. It was her last day in Moscow. Her flight would leave tonight, and she would reach Paris close to midnight. The time was intentionally chosen to be outside of traditional tourist hours. The less eyes on her the better. She would be in disguise of course, but she would still have to pass as the Russian wife of a French businessman. That man was Igor, who spoke fluent French, courtesy of being a cultural attaché – or spy – in the Russian Embassy in Paris.

Borislov had been to see her in the morning, and with Pushkin and Igor, they had gone through the plan over and over again until she knew it like the back of her hand.

Before he left, Borislov told the other men to leave the room, giving him and Anna total privacy.

His hair was combed today, for once, but his eyes had the same dark, glittery fixation as always.

"Who are you?" he asked Anna.

The words slipped out of her easily, like she was speaking the truth. "I am Janice Ryan, wife of the 46th President of the United States of America and the First Lady of the USA."

Borislov asked her a few more questions about the President's habits, the names of his close aides, and the names of his cabinet. Finally, Borislov leaned back in his chair.

"There will be no going back once this is done," he said softly. "Are you sure you will be faithful to the motherland?"

The question took her aback, but of course, she had thought of it as well. Why did so many artists defect to America and never come back? Never mind the intellectuals. Even KGB officers did it. She was about to find out for herself why. And what would happen when she did?

But she didn't dare speak her mind to Borislov.

"The Imperialist traitors have ruined this world. They act like their shallow idealism and corrupt democracy can spread over the world. But they are wrong. And they are weak. We will show the next generation how muscular Socialism can be. We can make the world a better place."

After she finished, Borislov stared at her for a long time. "I taught you how to act. You're not pulling a trick on me, are you? Do you really believe what you said?"

"If I didn't, would I have the courage to carry out something like this?"

Satisfied, Borislov nodded. Then he said, "Just remember, if you do not keep supplying us with information when we need it, then we can tell the Americans the truth. Do you know what happens then?"

She said nothing, but stared back at him impassively. Borislov leaned closer. "The Americans won't put you on the next plane back. They will torture you until you will wish you were dead. Whatever we can do in the basement of Lubyanka, they can do a hundred times worse. Remember that."

His eyes were flat and cold. Anna's throat was so dry she couldn't speak. Borislov straightened. "Our agent in DC will be in touch with you once you settle down. She has a contact inside the White House. Her code name is Jackal."

Anna nodded. She had recovered her composure. "I shall look forward to meeting her. And to be of service to the Motherland."

After a little pause, she continued. "I am curious about one thing. What will happen to the real First Lady, Janice Ryan, after she is abducted?"

Borislov smiled. "She will be kept very much alive and under our control. If you ever get caught, we can do a swap."

Anna swallowed, a dread spreading inside her limbs like poison. A leaden weight pressed against her throat.

"That," Borislov said, "should act as another incentive for you to succeed, my dear Anna."

She breathed, and spoke with an effort. "I will not fail."

Anna watched Borislov close the door behind him.

Then she smiled, and whispered to herself. "I will not fail."

CHAPTER 51

Dan never slept well on planes. When he was operational as a Delta member, he used to take a Valium whenever he boarded a flight. Most of his buddies in the team did the same thing. But ever since he'd become a regular guy, *whatever that meant,* he didn't do that many long flights, and hence didn't have a stash of Valium he could use.

It was 9am London time, and they had been flying most of the night. Dan looked below as the Eiffel tower came into view, along with Paris, stretched out in patchworks of streets and greenery. Next to him, Melania Stone slept in peaceful repose. Dan couldn't believe it. He rubbed his eyes. It was going to be a long, long day.

The first thing he did after landing was call Scorpion. It went to voicemail as he expected. He didn't even know if she was carrying the phone with her. He checked into a hotel with Melania and called McBride's contact in the COS – the French Special Forces Command. Jacques was a retired NCO or non-commissioned officer in the French Army, the rank given to many special forces operatives in Europe, as the traditional hierarchy in the Army was more fluid in the special forces.

Jacques organized to meet Dan at the Tuileries Garden, next to the Louvre at noon. Dan needed weapons, and he needed some creds in case he got stopped by police.

He left Melania at the hotel and walked to an internet cafe. On the dark web, he saw the Scorpion had left a message for him in the inbox. He left one to notify her he had the package, and it was safe with him.

Paris was in a festive mood because it was summer and the sun was shining, but also because the city had just received a famous guest. The First Lady had arrived the night before. Posters of her standing next to the French First Lady, a former pop star who was popular in France, were posted all over the 1st arrondissement.

Dan stared at one of the posters as he walked back to the hotel. A frisson of fear slithered down his spine. He didn't know what was going down today, but he had the horrible premonition it would be a nasty surprise, and it might well involve the First Lady. Somehow, Dan had to alert the Secret Service, but he knew they wouldn't believe him. He had to try and stop this himself.

To do that, he needed to get hold of Scorpion and fast.

*****

When Farouk had applied to become a security guard at the Louvre Museum, he hadn't realized how easy it would be. He expected to fail at every stage. He thought they would check his school and college background – all in Lyon, France. The French authorities who run the Louvre only cast a quick eye over it. They did check his background as a policeman in Nice and Cannes, but for that too, he had a forged identity. They only made some phone calls which were intercepted by Rashid's contacts. They checked his resume, which was of the officer who didn't know all his details now belonged to Farouk. Luckily, this cop was of Algerian background, and he bore more than a passing resemblance to Farouk.

If Farouk was asked to explain, he would just disappear. They would never know his real identity, but they'd keep his photo. That was a downside but one worth paying. He convinced Rashid of this. Rashid was understandably unhappy about his chief scientist applying for the job. But without Farouk being there, the whole plan ran the risk of falling apart.

What if the cans were not placed in the right corners? What if the they were not set off properly? And most importantly, what if they were stopped at the airport style luggage check?

A security guard could help with all three, and hence was an indispensable part of the plan.

But that didn't mean it had to be Farouk. In the end, Rashid had agreed, but made Farouk promise he left before all hell broke loose. The cans would be set off by a timer device, but they had to be manually activated. Farouk couldn't do it all on his own.

When Rashid had mentioned a woman would be helping him, Farouk had balked. A woman for a task like this? This was going to be the 9/11 of France. No, even worse. The ricin particles being emitted would be invisible and odorless. By the time a museum full of people realized what was wrong, tens of thousands would be affected. It was summertime, and the Louvre would be packed.

Of course, the Louvre was a big place, and they couldn't cover every room. There was one room, however, where they would definitely get the best results. The room that would get rammed to the full in early afternoon, will be on the first floor, in the Denon Alley, between French and Italian period paintings.

The Mona Lisa Room.

Rashid had reassured Farouk this was no ordinary woman. Her name was Scorpion. In fact, chances were high if she wasn't working with them she might have dismantled their operation by now. When the operation was over, Farouk was to deal with Scorpion in the best manner possible.

Put a bullet in the back of her head.

CHAPTER 52

The plan was a simple one, as all good plans are. The micron-sized ricin particle matter released as a gas would cause a panic and mass evacuation of the Louvre and the surrounding Museums and galleries of the 1st arrondissement. One of Rashid's men would call and declare a terrorist attack caused by a biological agent in Paris. That would trigger a stampede of people trying to leave Paris, or at least as far from the center as possible. In the resulting chaos, the First Lady would be switched for her body double. The Secret Service agents would be too concerned with keeping her safe, and not realizing Janice Ryan was actually a Russian woman.

That was the ideal scenario, but as Farouk waited for the woman to turn up, he kept thinking of the hundred ways it could go wrong. He had the woman and another security guard who had been bribed to turn a blind eye. This guard was young, and he was told this was a prank that would be filmed by a TV camera, and the guard would be on the film finally produced. He had signed a document and was happy.

Eventually, the woman arrived. She rang Farouk on the number provided. Farouk was manning the staff entry gates. He looked at the woman critically as she approached.

*****

Scorpion felt the man's eyes roaming over her body. She acted nonchalant, but there was something about this wiry, bespectacled, intense looking man that gave her the creeps. He wore the light grey uniform of a Louvre security guard.

He pulled her to one side once she had come in through the check in.

"Are you Scorpion?" he whispered.

"You must be Farouk," she said, trying to hide her uneasiness. She was wearing a T-shirt, cardigan, and slacks, dressed casually to merge in with the tourists.

He nodded. She knew he had to be the right person, as his description matched, and he also had the phone. Still, they had to check.

As she expected, Farouk asked, "Where is the tenth Iman hiding?"

"In a cave, south of Basra," Scorpion replied.

Some of the tension dissipated from Farouk's face. "Come with me," he hissed.

They walked across the ground floor to the far end – a long walk down a straight stone flagged corridor. Farouk pushed open a large pair of double doors, and they were in the back of the museum canteen. Farouk spoke to one of the porters in Arabic, and he was pointed to one corner. They approached a row of food trolleys, and Farouk counted them until he came to number 342. He lifted the lid and looked inside. Scorpion could see it was good news. Farouk could barely hide his excitement.

They had planned it well, she had to admit. Food materials didn't go through the same rigorous checks as personnel or tourists. Whatever Farouk had smuggled inside had escaped the scrutiny of scanners and x-ray machines.

"Help me push this," Farouk ordered.

She obeyed in silence. Her mind was buzzing with the implications of what was happening. Clearly, Farouk had a team in place here. The porter in the canteen who must have helped getting the load off the trucks and into the right place. He spoke to the porter in Arabic, Scorpion knew that much, but she didn't understand what they said.

How many more did they have in the team?

She helped Farouk push the trolley into the elevator. There was more than food in this thing, she knew that much. She had never worked in a canteen, but she felt like she was pushing a dead weight around. She could hear metallic chinks from inside, a hollow, dull sound.

She didn't like this at all.

On the first floor, as the elevator doors opened another security guard was standing there. He had black curly hair and sandy skin similar to Farouk. His eyebrows lifted when he saw Scorpion, but he glanced over at Farouk then nodded in silence.

He guided them to the end of the wide hallway. A sign at the top said Denon Alley in French and English. They turned left to enter a huge room, works of art adorning the walls on either side. No tourists had arrived yet, but she knew in a few hours this room would be filling up.

Another guard stood by the doorway, and Farouk's friend went and spoke to him. Then he waved at Farouk, who approached with the trolley. The guards moved away.

"Help me take off the fire extinguisher," Farouk said. She did as she was told. When the red fire extinguisher was on the floor, Farouk kneeled and opened the lower section of the food trolley. Inside, Scorpion saw stacks of cylinders, all painted red. Farouk pulled one out. It looked just like a fire extinguisher cylinder with a black funnel at the top. But she saw a small object taped to the back. It was an old generation cell phones, small enough to fit in the palm of her hand. A red dot flashed on the top.

"On the wall, this way," Farouk instructed her. Together, they put the new fire extinguisher on its hooks the strapped cell phone at the rear, not visible to the casual eye.

They moved to the opposite wall and did the same. Scorpion wanted to ask what the extinguishers contained, but she knew

Farouk wouldn't answer. Together they pushed the trolley down the large room. The paintings on the wall were stunning, and she stopped moving when she saw the familiar, half smiling woman on a frame in the middle of the room.

Mona Lisa.

The picture was far smaller than she had imagined. A glass enclosure cordoned off the space close to the painting. She could see it from about ten feet away. As she had felt before, she didn't think the painting was a brilliant work of art. Maybe that was just her since the rest of the world went crazy over it.

"Hey."

She turned to see Farouk frowning at her. He said, "You're not here to gape at pictures. Do your work!"

Anger flared inside her. She bit back her response. She was at the back, doing most of the pushing with Farouk at the front, pulling.

They moved on, but she took her cell out surreptitiously and almost stopped breathing when she checked the screen. She had a text from an unknown number.

"Weather is nice, but I got the umbrella."

It was a code she shared with Dan.

Her mind raced as her pulse danced to a new, frantic beat. Dan had Melania. That's what he meant by *the umbrella*.

Which meant she was off the hook. Melania was safe, for now. But she was lacking details. Where were they?

Ahead, they passed through another set of doors, and Farouk stopped. Without a word to her, he went behind the giant doors. Scorpion followed. They unloaded two more extinguishers in opposite corners and fixed them up to the wall. The original extinguishers went to the upper chamber of the trolley while the fake cylinders stayed at the bottom.

The guard who met them at the elevator doors appeared again. He helped Scorpion push the trolley, for which she was grateful. Her shoulders and arms ached. She looked at his name badge. Jalal Bakir. When she looked at Jalal's face, he studiously ignored her.

After half an hour, and five more drops, they were done. Scorpion was sweating. While Jalal and Farouk spoke in half whispers, she approached them.

"Where are the toilets?" she asked. Jalal gave her directions. She walked back the way she came, through the huge, still empty rooms, centuries old, beautifully preserved paintings by old masters staring down at her as her footsteps echoed in the silence. She could feel the figures on the wall following her progress, watching, judging her.

What are you going to do, Natasha?

She gulped and hurried on. She wasn't easily bothered - violence and death had been recurring themes in her strange, chaotic world. It was her life. But she knew something major was happening here, a momentous event the world would read about in the papers and watch from their TV screens for days.

Unless she did something to stop it.

She found the ladies' restroom, right next to the men's, and went in. A maid was inside, cleaning. She smiled at Scorpion who returned the smile then locked herself in a cubicle. She took her phone out. Dan answered on the first ring.

"I'm at a hotel in Rue de Jardine in St Germain, Paris. Where are you?"

She breathed a sigh of relief. "Is Mel with you?"

"Yes."

She told him quickly where she was, and what was happening.

"Shit. You can't leave now. But you need to stop them."

"I know. I–"

She cut off when she heard a door open. There was a knocking on her cubicle.

"Are you in there?" a rough, impatient voice asked. It was Farouk. She switched the phone off, then powered it down. She flushed the toilet, then opened the door.

She was staring at the barrel of a gun. Farouk's eyes were hard, flat, dark. Behind him stood Jalal.

Farouk spat on the floor, a snarl crossing his face. "*Kaffir,* bitch. On your knees, and put your hands behind your head."

CHAPTER 53

The Hotel de Pontalba in Rue du Faubourg Saint Honore, Paris, is a massive, spectacular mansion designed by the famous architect Louis Visconti. Although labelled a hotel for its many rooms and lush green grounds, it is actually the official residence of the US Ambassador in France.

The 8th arrondissement, where the building is situated, is a quiet, wealthy area of Paris, too close to be a suburb, but far enough from the madding crowds of the center.

Janice Ryan awoke, stretched, then sat up in the large four poster bed. Light was poking in through the gaps of the curtains covering the floor to ceiling windows. She got up and parted the curtains slightly. A rolling green meadow met her eyes outside the rear walls of the mansion. She could see two fountains, surrounded by a gravel bank. Woods rose in the distance, and the well maintained green meadow disappeared into it.

Janice yawned. It had been a short journey from London to Paris, but she was still tired from the three speeches a day, meeting ambassadors, civil servants, Army officials, a relentless parade of people. All the faces had merged into one. She had officially come to promote wellbeing for women in a digital age, mainly the effect social media has on teenagers and young women, but her time seemed to be taken up on meeting men who had nothing to do with these issues

Stephanie and Michelle had both complained to Jeremy Dunstall, her director of policy, but to no avail. Janice herself had signed off her schedule weeks ago and had agreed to these meetings and functions.

She just hadn't expected them to be this exhausting.

Janice got ready. She had to meet the French equivalent of Girl Scouts and give out badges of honor, an event she was looking forward to. That was in the French Lycee, then she had a speech at the Pompidou Centre, followed by another low-key event close to Saint Denis to the north of Paris. This was planned, unless Stephanie had reason to change the schedule, which she knew could happen, depending on security alerts.

After lunch, she had more of the same in the afternoon, followed by dinner with the Ambassador and wife with selected guests.

Janice took her role seriously, but she didn't like playing the game. Talking lame politics with powerful men while keeping her own thoughts at bay behind a plastic smile. That's the way it worked when schmoozing abroad. However, she could let her hair down tonight at the Ambassador's dinner. George Wilson was a Texan with a southern drawl and had lived in Paris for the last four years. At tonight's dinner at least, she could speak her mind.

She called for Stephanie, who came up and escorted her down to the dining hall. Michelle and Jeremy were already there, and over coffee they went through her schedule for the day, once again.

"We have to leave in one hour," Michelle said, draining the last of her coffee.

"Okay," Janice said. "Meet you in the lobby."

"Do you need help getting ready?" Stephanie asked.

"Yes. I'll call you when I'm done."

Upstairs, and back in her room, Janice put on her below knee blue dress suit, handmade by Victoria Winslow, her British designer. Visiting Victoria's shop on Bond Street had been a highlight of her trip to London.

She knelt on the floor and opened a small suitcase. Inside, she had a notebook that her mother had given her, and also the blue box with the photos. Janice took out the photo of herself as a baby, and stared at the other faces in it, faces she had never known, and never would.

An emptiness resounded inside her, like the hallways of a ghost house, a derelict mansion. Her mind became a blank slate, devoid of color. A heaviness settled in her heart, like silt depositing at the bottom of a river, its flow forgotten.

She sat down on the bed.

Her eyes blurred with tears as she stared at the photo.

CHAPTER 54

Dan and Melania were walking down the broad central avenue of Tuileries Garden. The central avenue, or Grande Allee, was punctuated by two huge basins, or fountains, at either end. To Dan's left, as he approached it, lay the Musee de l'Orangerie, an art gallery in the west corner, close to one of the large fountains.

Dan left Melania by the impressionist paintings of Pissaro and Monet and strolled over to a large sculpture of the Nymphaea. Tourists came and went, but one man stood watching, his back to Dan. He wore a flat black cap, jeans, and brown shirt as promised.

Dan approached and stood next to him, staring at the statue rising above them.

"Jacques?" Dan asked.

"Yes. You're Jim McBride's man?" Jacques had a charming French accent, sliding over the vowels.

"Yes."

Jacques looked carefully at Dan then nodded. "This way."

The Tuileries Garden is divided into several small squares on either side of the Grande Allee.

They sat down on a bench behind a giant vase, sheltered by trees.

Jacques had a backpack, and he simply handed it over to Dan who took it. Dan didn't open it to look inside.

"Silencer?" he asked.

"Yes. For a Glock 22."

"*Merci.* There is something important you need to know about the Louvre Museum." Speaking quickly, Dan told Jacques the Scorpion's story.

Jacques frowned. "And what proof do you have of this?"

Dan shook his head. "You don't understand. I have a bad feeling about this. These guys have a factory in Champigny Sur Marne. I bet you they make these gas cylinders there."

Jacques took out a cell phone and stood. He walked a few steps and spoke into the phone in French then listened. He came back and shook his head at Dan.

"The Louvre is starting to admit its first guests. Nothing unusual is reported. Everything is working as normal."

"Ask them about the guards. Farouk and Jalal."

"Jalal is on duty, and there is no one called Farouk. Listen, Dan, if that's your real name. The Louvre Museum is a giant attraction. I can't just shut it down with a phone call, even if I was the President. And your source, where is she now? Has she called back to give an update."

Dan clenched his teeth. "No, she hasn't. What does that tell you? She could be in trouble. Maybe even dead."

Jacques shook his head. "This is too farfetched. An assassin chasing terrorists inside the Louvre? Look, I'm helping you because Jim is an old Army friend. But–"

"Why do you think I asked for the gun, Jacques? Not for target practice. There is some serious shit happening today, and if you don't do something about it, I will."

Jacques stared at Dan, his eyebrows pinched, grey eyes hooded.

Dan said, "Just tell the authorities to be on high alert. I don't know what's going to happen, but we might have to evacuate the Louvre at short notice."

Jacques still stared at Dan. "It's a lot to ask for, Dan. I need to call the divisional heads of the gendarme. Get them to mobilize their

291

units. Inform the Tourist Board, who are busy this time of the year. Then the chiefs of the DGES. Do you know how hard it is to convince these people? We hear of hoax attacks every day."

"Yes, but this isn't a hoax. Remember November 2015?"

Jacque's face tightened.

"Yeah, I thought so," Dan said. "This attack, if it goes through? It's gonna make November 15 look like child's play."

Jacques stood. "I'll do my best."

"Make sure it's good enough," Dan said, also standing. "This is urgent."

Jacques nodded, and they shook hands. Dan watched the old man walk away, and he had a sinking feeling in the pits of his stomach. French bureaucracy was slow and ponderous. There was little hope of him being taken seriously.

Dan jogged back to Melania. "Come on. We need to get inside the Louvre, now."

From the Tuilerie Gardens they crossed the Place de la Concorde then headed east to the main front entrance of the Louvre. It was still early, and only a few groups were scattered around. The glass pyramid in the middle glinted in the morning sun. Dan looked both ways, then pointed to the right, at the eastern face of the Louvre main facade.

"How big is this place?" Melania panted as she jogged harder to keep pace with Dan.

Dan had seen a map already. "It's very long. Stretches along the river bank for miles, and has loads of wings. The pyramid is just at the main entrance."

They jogged on, sweat flowing freely as their bodies warmed up. Dan could feel the weapons bouncing inside his backpack.

They were on the main road now, traffic to their right and the Louvre on their left. Another entrance opened up as a break in the main walls. The huge gates were open, and a truck passed through.

"This way," Dan said.

It was quieter here. Dan had no idea where they were, but it was still the palace. They were in a giant courtyard, four floors of French windows rising above them. The entrance was across the courtyard, and the guards in front were standing at attention.

Dan and Melania looked around. She tugged on his sleeve. One corner of the wing was under renovation. A scaffolding was built, and it lead up to the third floor. No workmen were visible. Plastic sheets covered two open windows on the second floor. A ladder was leaning on the side of the scaffolding.

"Well done," Dan said. He took the backpack off and looked inside. He had 2 Glocks with silencers, extra ammo, two maps, and a compass.

He gave Melania one of the guns. She didn't screw the silencer on like he did.

She grinned at him. "Diversion, right?"

*****

Scorpion had a gun pressed against her head, grinding her face to the floor.

"Who the hell are you?" Farouk hissed. Scorpion had her hands tied behind her back. Farouk had a knee on her back, pressing into her right kidney. The pain was excruciating, a dull ache eating into her spine. Nausea rose in her mouth, she wanted to retch. But she had tolerated far worse than anything Farouk could do to her.

His fist smashed into the side of her face. A yellow orange ball of pain exploded inside her skull, rocking her vision.

"I heard what you said, bitch. You told someone all our plans."

Jalal had left the bathroom. She assumed he was standing outside, not letting anyone in. This was the staff bathroom, and therefore less busy. Jalal must've put a sign outside to say the bathroom was out of order. But he couldn't leave it out there forever. She needed to play for time.

Farouk hit her again, and she felt her jawbone crunch. She grunted, blood trickling down the side of her mouth onto the floor.

"You called an overseas number. Who was it?"

He lifted his arm to hit her again. She croaked, "Stop. Please stop." His arm lowered.

Scorpion said, "I'll tell you."

She panted. Farouk bent closer until his face was closed to hers.

"Who sent you?"

"Your mother."

Farouk howled in rage. Scorpion knew he was running out of options. He must've called his boss by now. He would've vouched for her. She just prayed Melania was safe.

Another jolt of pain ran through her as Farouk stood and kicked her twice. She curled herself into a ball, but the kicks kept coming. He stomped on her shoulders and head. Light dimmed in Scorpion's eyes.

The door opened and someone came in.

It was Jalal. He said, "The place is filling up."

Scorpion shook her head and opened her eyes. Farouk and Jalal faced each other.

Farouk wiped the sweat off his forehead. He took off his glasses, wiped them, then put them on. Exertion made his chest heave.

"Did you get a fix on the number she called?"

Jalal shook his head. "No. Not possible from here."

"We have a leak. If she knows, Allah knows who else. How full is the room?"

Jalal said, "Getting fuller by the minute. It's going to be a busy day."

"Good. We cannot wait any longer. Prepare to blow the weapons now."

CHAPTER 55

Anna Ramitrova had never worn a hijab, or headscarf, before. Neither had she prayed in a mosque.

Today, she would have to do both because those were her orders. She had learnt Muslim women from different parts of Arabia wore the headscarf in different ways. In more conservative countries like Saudi Arabia and Pakistan, the hijab came down lower over the face. In Iran, the headscarf was mandatory of course, but it was okay as long as it covered part of the head. From her research, she noted that wealthy women in Iran wore a loose scarf on their heads, while they wore pants and shirts like western women. That was virtually impossible in countries like Saudi Arabia. She read that Iranians were Persians, culturally and ethnically distinct from Arabs, and most longed for their country to return to democracy.

None of which bothered her today, as she stared at the mirror and clasped the hijab over her chin. She had opted for the more conservative look, bringing the hood low over her eyes. Her face was still visible, but she would wear large sunglasses covering her eyes.

The shapeless black gown she wore was the rest of her dress. She didn't like what she saw in the mirror. It seemed she was having to hide herself from the world.

Which, in a way, she was. But soon the world would know her identity.

There was a knock on the door. Without waiting for a reply, Igor stepped in. He shut the door and leaned against it.

"Are you ready?" he asked softly. He was definitely attracted to her. She was going to use that to her advantage.

Igor took a gun out from his shoulder holster. He started to screw a silencer to it. They had come in a diplomatic flight from Moscow, and their luggage had not been checked, in-line with diplomatic privileges.

She turned to face him. "Do I look okay?"

"Like a good Muslim woman," he said, then grinned.

Despite the tension that was brewing a storm inside her, she smiled back. "You should see what I'm wearing underneath the robe."

He lifted himself off the door and walked toward her. "What's that?" he asked softly.

It was actually a blue business skirt suit, exactly the same as the First Lady was wearing. Live TV footage from the US Ambassador's office had been beamed into her room this morning. She didn't have a similar dress, so Igor had to go shopping.

"The suit you bought for me today," she said, as Igor stood close enough to touch her. She glanced at the Patek Philippe Nautilus watch on her wrist. It was a replica of the original, a fake made in Turkey. But the First Lady was never seen in public without her Patek Philippe, a gift from her husband.

"It's almost midday," she said. "We should get a move on." She touched his arm. "Are we going to be safe?"

He leaned in quicker than she had anticipated. She didn't want to kiss him, but she either had to move away, or kiss him for now. She chose the latter. She offered him her firmly pressed lips, and when she felt his tongue, she stepped back.

"Not now," she said. "Later."

His face was dark with passion. "I have dreamt of this day for a long time."

"Me too," she smiled like an actress. "But we have work to do."

His eyebrows met in the middle, and his lips quivered. A tenderness welled up in his eyes, warm and liquid. "But after today I might never see you again."

"Yes, you will. I will come back one day. You know that."

"Will you?" he smiled sadly. "Maybe we shouldn't have waited this long."

There was a knock on the door, and they stood apart hastily.

"Come in," called Natasha.

Pushkin, Borislov's aide, walked in. He looked from Igor to her, studying them both. He always had a unhurried manner. Nothing seemed to disrupt the calmness of his approach. It unnerved Anna. She imagined he wouldn't hesitate to put a bullet in her head.

"Everything okay?" he asked.

"Yes, fine," Anna said.

"Do you know the routine?" Pushkin asked.

"Yes. I wash my hands and feet and go inside the mosque. You listen to the First Lady's speech. Igor waits in the corridor. There's only one toilet at the venue. When she goes to the bathroom Igor follows her. One female agent, dressed as a maid, makes sure no one else enters the bathroom. Igor renders the First Lady unconscious by spraying a chemical." Anna paused. This was the part she wasn't clear of, but she knew murdering Janice wasn't an option. She carried on. "You ring me on the cellphone. I discard the cellphone, then enter the main hall, and carry on as the First Lady."

She guessed when the American agents had left the building, Igor and Pushkin would remove Janice Ryan from the premises.

"Very good," Pushkin said flatly, not a trace of emotion in his beady eyes. "And what happens if she doesn't go to the bathroom? It's highly unlikely, as she goes after every speech, no matter the location. But if she doesn't?"

"Then Nasirova meets up with Randall in the Ambassador's House. We find a way in, tomorrow."

Nasirova, or Skylar, was in Paris already. So was Randall, but he didn't know his paramour was here too, lying in wait for him.

"Excellent. Time to go." Pushkin marched out of the room. Igor was about to follow, but she reached out and caught his sleeve.

"I need a weapon," she whispered.

He raised his eyebrows. "What for? Both of us are armed, and we're not looking for a shoot-out. With all the American Secret Service agents around, it's only going to end one way."

"I know. But what if I have to defend myself? I won't shoot anyone, but I night have to point the gun to help me escape."

Igor was deep in thought. Then he nodded. "But you need to discard the weapon before you take the First Lady's place. If the Americans see a gun on you they'll know you're not her."

"Yes," Anna said. "Of course, I will."

CHAPTER 56

Dan walked very slowly. He stayed close to the stone walls and crossed the courtyard until he was close to the scaffolding. He snuck in behind it. The ladder was right next to him, but he waited. He looked at Melania across the courtyard. He bent down to tie his shoelace.

That was the signal.

Melania raised her Glock in the air and fired two shots. The unsuppressed weapon went off like a canon shot, the sound echoing in the courtyard. She put the gun inside her jacket and lay down on the floor. She started screaming.

"Help! Help!"

Heads turned. A few men came running to help. Dan watched as the guards left their position and ran towards Melania. He waited until they were close to her, then started climbing the ladder quickly. The second-floor window was covered by tarp, hammered in with nails. Dan cut a section with his knife and got inside. It was a building site, the walls smelling of fresh plaster. He picked his way around the tools on the floor. The power tools meant the builders were close by. He saw a hammer and stuffed in his pocket. Hammers always came in handy. A builder's hard hat and yellow high visibility vest lay on the floor. Dan put them on.

He opened the door and poked his head out. A builder rushed by to his left down the main hallway. Dan waited, then slipped out.

He came out in the hallway. Several people had gathered by the window, watching the scene unfolding on the courtyard. Dan knew Melania would spend as long on the ground as possible. He walked past slowly.

Scorpion had told him where she was. But Dan had no way of knowing if all the buildings were interconnected. If they weren't he was in trouble.

He set off a brisk pace. The floor to ceiling windows looked out on the courtyard, and he could see a police car pull up. Then he lost sight as he entered another section of the palace.

A sign above his head said Louvre Main Museum. Dan walked as fast as he could without drawing too much attention to himself. He hoped he looked like a builder.

Pretty soon he came up against a wall. A huge framed painting of some king, with his subjects around him, took up the majority of the wall. A staircase went down to his left, and another hallway to the right.

Dan didn't want to go down the staircase. The exit lay that way, which meant he would have to walk to the main entrance, which meant leaving his guns behind.

He went down the hallway, but all it did was curve around. He was walking back to the same spot. There was no way through.

In desperation, he looked out the window. Melania lay in the external courtyard. But the circular hallway that Dan was rotating in looked down at another, smaller, internal courtyard. It had a little pond, shaped topiary's and statues. Dan knew the whole of the Louvre palace was made up of small sections like this.

Presumably, if he could get down to this courtyard, then climb the wall…

He ran. Scorpion hadn't called him back. She hung up abruptly. He had to fear the worst for her.

He came across a wide doorway that opened into a staircase going down. He descended, then found himself in a quiet colonnade that circled around the internal courtyard. It was empty, and even at this moment, with the fire of danger burning in his veins, he appreciated its timeless charm. He was isolated in a courtyard of history, a little capsule of time. French Queens must have roamed this garden once, chatting to their maids of honor.

The moment passed quickly.

He moved to the far wall. He planted a foot against a statue, the other on a section of the wall, and could just about reach the top.

Windows looked down on this courtyard. Anyone looking would see a builder climbing an ancient wall.

Well, shit. Take a photo.

Dan thrust himself upwards, levering off against the statue, and his fingers grabbed the top edge of the wall. He hung for a while, then lifted himself.

For a few seconds, he could see across the next courtyard. Several beautiful gardens opened up in a line, all bordered by a wall. In the distance, he could see the main garden of the Louvre with tourists milling around.

Dan dropped, bending his knees. It was a ten foot fall, but his ankles took it. He had a choice to make. Did he keep climbing walls and get through, or try and find another way?

He opted for the wall route. This way, he knew he was moving in a straight line, and was guaranteed to get there. But he ran the risk of being seen. He had taken far worse risks than this.

It meant he could have to be fast, and his clothes were wet with sweat already. But his blood was warm, and he could smell that old heat burning in his blood. He ran across the courtyard.

When he dropped down into the next courtyard, he felt the phone buzz in his pocket. Relief ran through him. It must be Scorpion. He answered immediately.

"Natasha?"

"Do you want to speak to the bitch?" A male voice growled.

Dan came to an abrupt halt. "Who is this?"

"Your worst fucking nightmare. The woman is about to die, and the Louvre will burn to the ground."

A shock of fear whipped against Dan's spine. His mouth went bone dry. "Listen–"

But the line was already dead.

CHAPTER 57

Rashid Al-Falaj was furious. Against his better judgement, he had let Borislov talk him into using Scorpion. And now she'd turned out to be a traitor.

A woman would arouse less suspicion, Borislov had said. And she was one of his best operators.

Rashid's Daimler SUV was speeding down the Champs-Élysées, and his cell was held tight to his ear.

"Who else has she told?" Rashid raged. He was speaking to Borislov.

"I don't know. But when she was held by the DGES, she called a man by the name of Dan Roy."

Rashid's jaw went slack. Dan Roy. The man who had killed Waleed, his cousin.

Bismillah.

Rashid put the phone down and muttered a prayer, eyes closed. Allah moved in strange ways. Rashid knew enough about Dan. Dan would come to save the woman. And when he did, Rashid would get them both.

Even if this had to become a suicide mission. Farouk had weapons hidden inside the canteen in Louvre. They would come in handy.

He got back on the phone to Borislov. "I'm heading down to the Louvre. Whatever happens there today, I want to be present when the woman and Dan Roy die."

He hung up, and called Farouk. He didn't answer, but called Rashid back.

"Salaam Aleikum," Farouk said.

"Walaikum Salaam," Rashid said. "The woman knows the killer of Waleed. He is on his way, I think, if she did speak to him."

"I think he is. I just had a word with him." Farouk chuckled. "He wasn't expecting to hear from me."

"Let him come. Make sure he is dead before you leave the place. I will see you inside."

"Yes. I have the gas masks, if needed. We will unleash hell today, my brother. The world will remember us forever."

He hung up and tapped the driver on the shoulder. "Hurry up."

*****

Dan slowed down as he scaled off the last wall. This garden was wider and much bigger, and the shuffle of hundreds of feet was close by. His shirt was sticking to his back, sweat poured off his face. He had discarded the high visibility vest and hard hat already. Standing behind a statue, he checked his weapons. He slid the magazine out, then slapped it back in. He had two more clips of ammo. He screwed the silencer on.

He walked out slowly, trying to look more composed. His heart was beating wildly, a staccato rhythm against his ribs. He had to find Scorpion and fast.

Dan merged with the people milling around on the courtyard. He found the directions for the Denon Wing and Mona Lisa. Women and children were climbing the stairs, the holiday crowds building up to a peak. Dan's chest tightened. He didn't know what the fire extinguisher canisters held, but it had to be some form of gas. Wild guesses made sweat break out on his forehead.

Sarin gas?

Anthrax spores?

VX nerve gas? The one that killed King Jong Nam, the North Korean's dictator's stepbrother.

All would be lethal, causing thousands of deaths. Dan's blood ran cold. This was a better plan than he had expected.

He ran up to the wide hallway of the Denon Wing, the only person who was moving fast. He knew he would attract the attention of a security guard soon. He didn't care.

Dan jostled against people, trying not to push a woman or child. Ahead, he saw a sign for *La Giaconda.* The Italian name for Mona Lisa.

People were streaming in that direction like they were borne by a current. A security guard was standing at the door of the chamber that housed Mona Lisa, among other paintings.

Curly black hair. Shifting, roving eyes, head moving sideways. Most security guards were silent and watchful. They watched people's hands to see if they were reaching inside their jackets. But this guy was nervous. On edge. His eyes had fire in them.

He looked in Dan's direction, and their eyes met. They stared at each other for a while, and Dan knew.

Shit. *Shit.*

He didn't want to do this. The panic would cause a mass stampede. People would get hurt. But he had no choice.

He saw the guard's hand reach for his weapon, his eyes fixed on Dan. Dan was close enough to make out his name, sewed on the top of his uniform. Jalal. One of the names Scorpion had told him.

"Get down," Dan screamed. He took the Glock out and fired twice in the air.

Pandemonium ensued.

Screams filled the air. Bodies rushed for the stairs, knocking each other down. A man slammed against Dan, but he was rock solid, advancing despite people hurling themselves past him.

He aimed several times but couldn't fire. Too many people in the way, and Jalal had vanished from his post.

Scorpion had said the extinguishers were behind the doors on wall hooks. He had to get them before...the sharp burst of a weapon came behind him, whizzing past his ear. A man's face burst into blood and bone, and he collapsed. Dan crouched and turned around.

The chaos was worse now. It was a real stampede, people crushing each other in their blind panic.

It was a total nightmare. Dan seethed, jerking his weapon around. He could barely see for the rushing people. Rage and frustration were boiling in his blood.

He saw a security guard, ducking and diving. He looked similar to the description that Scorpion had given him. Glasses, thin, Arab. But there was no way Dan could fire back.

Biting back a scream, Dan turned back and barged past people to reach the doors of the Mona Lisa chamber.

He found Jalal behind the door standing next to the fire extinguisher. He was unhooking a gas mask that hung from his belt. He saw Dan, dropped the mask and reached for his weapon. Dan shot him in the chest then followed up with a headshot.

He kicked the dead body aside, then took the fire extinguisher off the wall. An old generation, tiny cell phone was fixed to the back of the extinguisher. Dan ripped off the black tape with his knife. He held the phone and saw the two wires descending from the phone and disappearing inside the black funnel of the extinguisher.

The phone started to ring in Dan's hand.

CHAPTER 58

Anna was in the back seat with Igor driving. Pushkin sat next to Igor. Anna watched as Pushkin answered his phone. Anna watched him listen, then say something inaudible.

When he hung up, Igor asked, "Any problems?"

"The operation at the Louvre hit a hiccup. We progress as normal."

Anna didn't know about this. It sounded strange to her. "What operation at the Louvre?" she asked, leaning forward.

"Nothing," Pushkin said. "Focus on what you have to do."

Anna frowned. The car turned soon, entering a building that looked like a school. She could see the minarets of the mosque, and its large central dome to the left. She checked her watch. The First Lady was due in two hours.

Igor parked, and they alighted from the car. They went their own ways. She crossed the courtyard separating the community center from the mosque. A small fountain gurgled before the mosque. Men and women washed their hands and feet, then went into segregated chambers for their prayers. Often, Scorpion knew, the mosque was used as a place to sit and talk as well. Something she would have to avoid.

She performed the *Wudhu*, as the cleaning process is known, then entered the mosque. She went through the narrow hallway, taking her glasses off, but keeping her face lowered. She sat down cross-legged in one corner. The large room had women scattered all over. Most were sitting in groups, chatting. A few had children with them. A few of the women turned to look at Anna. All wore the headscarves, and some wore a *niqab*, the total face veil with only a mesh allowed for the eyes to see through. In France, wearing this outside the mosque was banned.

Shame, Anna thought wryly. It would've been one hell of a disguise.

She closed her eyes and visualized what Janice Ryan was doing right now. Her motorcade wouldn't be far away. She was going through her speech in the car. Reading it once to make sure she remembered all the major points. She would come in, meet and greet the welcoming committee, see the children and their artwork. Then she would go up on the stage and deliver her speech.

Then she would go to the bathroom. Janice always went to the bathroom after a speech. That routine had never failed.

Anna hoped like mad it wouldn't fail today.

Time passed quickly. Then her phone beeped. A text from Igor.

It's time.

She called him back as she hurried out of the mosque.

"Meet me outside," she whispered. "There's an alcove between two buildings opposite the fountain."

She had spotted the place before going in. It was secluded, and no one would see her.

"Why? Is there a problem?"

"I think so. I might have been spotted. I'm scared."

"On my way."

She hung up and rushed over to the alcove, heart hammering against her ribs. Igor arrived soon. She beckoned him inside the alcove. She leant back against the wall, allowing him to move close to her.

Igor was frowning, a puzzled expression on his face. But his eyes softened when he got closer to her. A smile appeared on his face. He looked around, but walls covered them on both sides, closing them in.

"Is this why you called me?" he asked, stepping into her space. His face moved down to kiss her.

She held his waist and pulled him closer, opening her mouth.

Her right hand emerged, holding the silenced Makarov. She thrust it against his abdomen, and pulled the trigger.

CHAPTER 59

The sound of the silenced weapon was like the hiss of a bicycle tire letting out air. The bullet shot clean through Igor's belly, severing his abdominal aorta and crashing into his spine. His mouth fell open, and his face contorted with pain. Before he could stumble back, she hardened her grip on his waist.

She angled the gun up and shot him in the chest, then let him go. He collapsed, his eyes staring up at her, but already glazing over, light fading. Blood pooled beneath his body, spreading out in a crimson wave.

Anna ran inside the community center, through the side door that connected it to the mosque. She approached the bathroom. The female agent was standing there, dressed as a maid. She had put a sign on the floor which said the bathroom was out of order.

Which meant the First Lady was inside.

The agent looked surprised as Anna rushed towards her.

"Igor is dead," Anna whispered breathlessly. "The Americans know. Tell Pushkin to abort the mission."

The agent's eyes widened. She nodded, then walked off quickly.

Anna entered the bathroom. She ripped off the hijab, then took off the robe. A toilet flushed, then the cubicle door opened. Janice Ryan stepped out. She looked to her left and saw Anna. Janice froze.

Anna felt the ground slip beneath her feet. Her retina's dilated, absorbing, searching Janice's face. Air was stuck in her lungs. Her heart stopped beating. Sometimes, a moment can last a lifetime. An eternity passes by unnoticed.

She had copied every aspect of Janice Ryan's life for more than six months, but the shock of seeing her in the flesh was staggering. Anna had her nose reshaped, her breasts lifted, fat sucked out of her tummy – all to make herself a replica of the woman standing in front of her.

And Anna knew she was a replica without even trying.

Janice looked barely able to stand. Her hands clutched the sink, and her back was pressed against it. Her eyes were wild, bulging. They moved up and down Anna's body like she was a ghost.

Then her mouth opened, her eyes narrowed, and a new light danced into Janice's eyes, the light that we see when dawn breaks over the night sky, the light that heralds a new morning.

Anna stepped closer. She was gasping, but was the first one to speak.

She dug into her pocket and took out a photo. It was old and faded, corners folded. It showed a woman holding two babies, one in each hand. The woman, obviously the mother, was beaming happily.

"I am Anna," she said. "I am your twin sister. We were separated at birth."

Then her voice broke, and tears blurred her eyes.

CHAPTER 60

Dan stared at the phone screen as it rang.

Then he burst into action. He knew if he ripped the phone off the canister might explode anyway. But if he didn't then the canister would definitely be weaponized. And if it blew up when he ripped the phone, he would be first in line to get blown off. Maybe his body would shield a few others. Maybe not.

People were still rushing past him screaming. The chamber was almost empty now, which was a blessing.

"Move!" Dan shouted. He ripped the phone off, and it took two tugs to do it. He hurled the phone as hard as he could across the room. Then he flinched, expecting a blast to smash him to pieces.

Nothing happened.

Dan looked down. The extinguisher stood silently. It didn't explode, or even burst into flames.

But he could hear a sound. A very soft sound, barely audible. It was like a hiss, and it was coming from the black funnel on top of the extinguisher.

Shock erupted inside his skull. He covered his mouth, stopped breathing, and snatched the gas mask off Jalal's dead hands. He put the mask on his face. He took out his knife, and cut a portion of Jalal's shirt. He wrapped the cloth around the black funnel.

The chamber was empty now, and he heard the sound of running footsteps. Dan dived for the ground even as a round whined above his head.

No. Not here.

Dan remained on the ground and raised his weapon. A security guard was running past him, firing as he ran. Dan squeezed off two rounds, aiming for the legs. The guard stumbled and fell.

Dan fired again, got up, and ran closer. The figure was barely moving now. He was hit in the chest and belly, and blood was turning the wooden floor dark red.

Dan kicked the weapon out of his hands. With his feet, he turned the man over. Dan could see the guy was dying. He had lost too much blood.

"Farouk?" Dan said.

The man nodded. Dan knelt by him, after making sure he had no other weapons.

He ripped the mask off his face. "Where is the girl? Scorpion?"

Farouk smiled. His eyes were hooded, and blood speckled his saliva as it dribbled out of his mouth. The bullets had punctured his lungs.

He opened his mouth to speak, but his eyes closed, and he stopped moving.

The sound of gunfire came from below. Rattling, heavy, the sound of an automatic rifle. He slipped his magazine out and put a fresh one in, then ran for the doorway. The sound of gunfire was louder, and it came from the lower floor.

Blood slicked the tiles in the hallway, where the innocent man lay face down. Dan stayed under cover and scanned with his weapon. He focused on the broad staircase. Sure enough, a figure bounded up, holding an AK-47 in his hands. The man looked odd because he was dressed in an expensive suit. His dark hair was slicked back, and he looked like a model rather than a terrorist. An older model in excellent shape for his age. The guy ran toward the room, jumping over the dead tourist.

"Dan Roy? Where are you?" the man shouted.

"Here," Dan said, stepping out of the door's shadow. "You must be Rashid."

Rashid spun around to face Dan. His eyes dilated, face creased with hate. "You killed my cousin. Waleed." He spat the words out.

Before Dan could speak, Rashid pointed the AK-47 at him and pulled the trigger.

Dan jumped backwards and the stream of bullets hit the door, chipping off wood, but the old thick door held, giving Dan protection.

The barrage stopped, and he could hear the trigger clicking. Rashid was out of ammo. Dan stayed on the floor and peered out. Rashid was frantically trying to insert a new magazine. Dan streaked out like a bullet, and slammed into Rashid, tumbling on the floor. The AK-47 went flying out of Rashid's hands.

Dan straddled Rashid's chest and punched him twice, rocking his face from side-to-side. Teeth flew out of Rashid's mouth. Dan heard commotion behind him. He turned quickly and saw uniformed men with guns pointed at him.

Dan raised his hands. "Seal the room," he shouted. "The extinguisher is leaking out gas. Get out of here!"

Dan picked up Rashid's unconscious body. The soldiers followed him as he ran out, then closed the massive doors shut.

Dan explained to them quickly what had happened. He showed them the creds Jacques had given him.

The cloth he had tied around the funnel of the extinguisher might have saved his life, but he didn't think it would hold for much longer.

With the soldiers, he ran down the stairs. A few dead guards lay on the floor along with a few tourists. Pain wrenched in Dan's heart.

It was like a war scene. A bloodbath. These innocent bystanders had done nothing wrong.

Sirens were wailing, getting closer. Dan looked around him. The soldiers were from an elite unit, probably from the COS, France's Special Forces Command. He approached the man wearing combat fatigues who was barking out orders.

"I need to go back upstairs. My friend is still up there."

"Negative. You said yourself the place is contaminated."

"Closing the doors secured it somewhat. I also have this." Dan showed him the mask. "Get more masks and protection suits," Dan said. "We're going to need them."

Dan raced up the stairs, mask on his face. Scorpion had been able to tell him she was in the staff bathroom before the phone cut off. He followed the signs until he found the tourist office on the Denon Wing. Alarms were blaring, the sound muffled behind his mask.

He finally found the staff bathroom and kicked the door open. Inside a cubicle, he found Scorpion, awake, but hogtied so carefully she couldn't even move a finger.

CHAPTER 61

"We should move out of here quickly," Anna said, clutching Janice's hand. Janice looked down at their entwined fingers in wonder then gazed at Anna.

"My mother told me about you," Janice whispered.

"I know," Anna nodded. "I looked up my adoption papers to find our real mother. She had died. I went to the adoption agency, and found I was one of twins. An American woman called Sylvia came to adopt my twin sister."

Janice still couldn't believe it. She gaped at Anna, seeing herself. But she knew Anna was right about getting to safety. She didn't know what was happening, but Anna did.

Janice allowed herself to be led by Anna out into the corridor.

Footsteps came from behind them. Janice thought how odd they must look, two women dressed exactly the same and looked the spitting image of each other.

"Let's head for backstage," Janice said. "The secret service agents are there."

The agent at the door almost fell over in astonishment when he saw the two women. Janice held Anna's hand firmly.

"This woman is my twin sister. She just busted a plot to kidnap and replace me."

The agent's mouth fell open.

"Your boss is called Randall Smith, right?" Anna asked.

The agent nodded, dumbfounded. Anna turned to Janice. "Randall is sleeping with an SVR agent called Skylar. Through her we get a lot of information."

Janice didn't hesitate. "Arrest Randall. That's an order."

"But ma'am, he's the chief—"

"Are you questioning me?" Janice said, standing up to the agent. The man, in his late forties and a seasoned agent, stepped back.

"No, ma'am."

"Good. Arrest him and call the President immediately. Alert the Ambassador. Let's get the hell out of here."

*****

Paris was in uproar. The roads leading up to the Arc de Triomphe were clogged with honking cars. Helicopters buzzed overhead, and two jets flew higher above, thundering.

Janice's car had its siren on and traffic parted to let them through.

The President's call came through, and Janice filled him in as they drove.

Bertram Ryan sounded aghast. "Is this really happening?"

"Yes, Bertie. It is. I'm sorry I never told you. I only found out I had a twin sister when I went see my mom two weeks ago."

Janice hung up and looked out the window at the chaos on the roads. Anna was doing the same, and they both turned at the same time to look at each other.

An hour and a half later, they were sitting in the lawn of the Ambassador's residence. Janice was drinking coffee while Anna sipped on tea.

Anna put the cup down gently. "I searched for this woman called Margaret Chandler. Her husband's name was also present – John Chandler. This American couple's name was on the adoption certificate for my sister."

"But you can imagine, from Podolska, where we lived, this wasn't easy. It took a good few months for me to find out where they were now. I actually found John first because he had a death certificate that came up in my searches."

"From there I moved on to Margaret. She was shocked to hear from me, of course. I told her I was adopted. She didn't know much about my mother." Anna looked up at Janice. "But I found out."

"Yes?" Janice asked eagerly. This was all so weird. So strange. But she had been wrestling with this ever since she found out from her own mother. Her *adopted* mother.

Anna closed her eyes, like she didn't like what she was seeing. "Our mother was a servant. She worked at the mansion of a very wealthy man. He is now a member of the Soviet Politburo. His name is Leon Mikhelson." Anna opened her eyes.

Janice was having trouble speaking. "Do you think he's our...."

"I don't know. But I heard of one thing, a rumor from those days. Illegitimate children were killed at birth to make sure they didn't stake a claim to the family's fortune in the future."

Janice sat back in her chair, feeling sick.

Anna kept going, "I can only think of that as a reason why our mother gave us away. She would never see us, but at least she would know we were alive."

A tear drop ran down Anna's left cheek, then the right. Janice reached over and held her hand. "Do you know where her grave is? I would like to pay my respects."

"No," Anna said, wiping her eyes. "I searched, but she died shortly after giving birth. So would I if I had to give my own children away." Her head lowered to her chest.

Janice hugged her, and they wept in silence for the cruel fate that had befallen their mother, and that had separated them.

After a while, Anna stood. "Let's walk," she suggested. Four Secret Service agents came down the stairs and escorted them.

"When Borislov and that man, Rashid, came to ask me if I wanted to impersonate you, I thought this was my chance. I never contacted you, although Margaret gave me your details," Anna said.

"I know," Janice said. "She told me. It was part of the reason I was so keen to come to Europe. I wanted to make a brief visit to Moscow, but you know how hard it is for me to go there."

"I know. I went along with the SVR's plan, but all along I knew that you knew about me because Margaret told me she told you. And I knew if I appeared in front of you–"

"I would know," Janice interrupted.

"Exactly."

One of the agents came up to them, He was holding out a phone. "Ambassador Wilson wants to speak to you ma'am."

Janice took the phone. "There's a CIA agent here called Melania Stone who wants to see you. There's a man called Dan Roy with her. Melania says the CIA knew about your twin," Wilson said.

"Let them in," Janice said.

They watched as a tall, muscular man, and a slim, petite woman came down the stairs and walked across the lawn to meet them. The man looked like a giant next to the woman. Janice couldn't help but stare at him. His shoulders went on for miles, and he was pure muscle. He moved with the grace of a panther, his head swiveling around like he expected danger any minute. He let the woman approach them first, standing behind her.

The woman, dressed in a cardigan and tee shirt, extended her hand. "Melania Stone, CIA agent."

They shook hands. "The CIA has an operation called Nectar Flower. It's highly classified, and it looks into the members of the First family. They ran checks on you. Found out that you were adopted way before your mother told you. One of the agents in charge, Grant Pearson, was captured in Dubai. Rashid Al-Falaj tortured the truth of Nectar Flower out of him. He told the Russians who started this."

Anna exclaimed, "So that's how Borislov knew about me."

Janice shook her head. "That is unbelievable."

Melania nodded. "I know. I'm sorry. On behalf of the CIA, I apologize."

Janice waved her off. "That apology has to come from a lot higher than you, Agent Stone. No offence."

"I understand." Melania nodded. "By the way, I wouldn't be here today without the help of this man, Dan Roy. Apart from saving me and getting us here, he just foiled a terrorist attack on the Louvre."

Melania waved at Dan. Dan looked at the Secret Service agents then stepped forward.

He gaped when he saw Anna before he looked at Janice again. Janice extended her hand. "Thank you, Mr. Roy."

Dan shook her hand. "I couldn't stop them in time. But we did our best."

"You saved thousands of people," Melania said. "I'd say your best was pretty darn spectacular."

"Maybe," Dan said quietly. "But there is still work to do."

CHAPTER 62

London

United Kingdom

The towers of the Houses of Parliament seemed to glow in the setting sunlight. The muddy waters of the Thames were choppy, restless in the rising tide, slapping against the bulwarks of the stone embankments. Traffic was grid locked in the rush hour, but the side streets of Westminster were empty. The imposing Victorian terraced mansions, just across Parliament Square, used to be the dwellings of Members of Parliament in days gone by. Now, in the shadow of Westminster, they rot away quietly, too expensive to rent, or to buy.

Dan Roy walked down one of these streets, eyes sharp on the few pedestrians and cars. Thames was a narrow river, but a gust of humid wind blew across it from the end of the street. It carried the acrid stench of gasoline. Dan extracted a phone and spoke on it briefly before returning it to his jacket pocket. He came to the address specified, a magnificent four story constructed of the same sand colored limestone that makes Westminster Palace bask in an ethereal light in early morning and sunset.

Dan knocked lightly on the black front door, and nothing happened. He pushed it, and it fell open. He looked around on the street to make sure it was empty, then went in.

The hallway was wide, and a yellow bulb glowed in the ceiling. Cobwebs hung on the corniches, and between the banisters of the broad staircases. Rooms opened up ahead of Dan, and he had seen enough English homes to know this could be a spacious residence, regardless of the constricted look from outside.

He moved in, shoes creaking on ancient floorboards. He had no gun on him. After landing in London, from Paris, he didn't have time to see Sparky. But he did have his kukri, strapped to his right ankle. And his bare hands.

He remembered a quote from Sun Tzu. One of McBride's favorites.

The supreme art of war is to subdue the enemy without fighting.

The first room, to his right, was huge, a living room that looked out on the streets. It was devoid of furniture, and of curtains. Dan didn't go in. He stopped and looked down the hallway. Daylight came in from the back, presumably from curtainless windows. But it would be dark soon. He walked down the hall, and into the back room, that opened out into a small, overgrown garden. A white garden table lay rusting, derelict, weeds growing over it. He opened the back door, and left it ajar.

He walked back to the staircase

He heard a sound from upstairs, and his eyes shot up to the ceiling. Someone was walking on the floor above. Then he heard the voice.

"Dan?"

A pair of legs appeared on the landing. Dan put one foot on the staircase, and squinted up.

"Jeff? Is that you?"

"One and only. Come up here. The view is better."

Dan went up the creaking stairs. Jeff Pearce walked down the hallway into a room that looked out at the Thames.

"We are alone, Dan. Come on in," Jeff said.

Dan followed. Jeff was dressed in a black work suit, the tips of his shoes gleaming, like the bald pate of his skull. He extended his arm and they shook hands.

"Busy time in Paris, right?" Jeff smiled. His hazel eyes moved up and down Dan's body, then settled on his face. "Still in one piece, I see."

"Looks can be deceiving," Dan said, moving closer to the window. Darkness was claiming the distant horizon. Closer, sunlight still glimmered in a purple and gold sky, tinged with diesel colored clouds.

Dan watched the grey waters of the Thames for a while. A black, RIB cut its engine, then drifted closer to shore. A figure hopped off the boat, and climbed the rungs of a ladder on the pier.

"Did you shut down the rest of Rashid's operation in London?"

"When we stormed his house, it was mostly clean. The Russians had advance warning, of course. Most of the evidence was gone. No laptops or phones. But we got fingerprints. Lots of them. Something for the database."

"Most of them now belong to dead terrorists."

"Thanks to you."

Dan said, "And the Scorpion."

Jeff shrugged. "I guess."

"Which leaves the man Scorpion met in Paris. The man who, to my mind, is in the center of this whole plan. He forced Scorpion to carry out the mess in Louvre. But it backfired, of course."

Jeff looked puzzled. "What man?

Dan allowed himself a smile. "The same man who tracked every move Scorpion made, and relayed it back to Rashid and Borislov."

"This guy was in Paris?"

"I think he's everywhere. He moves around, slippery as an eel, as you Brits say."

Jeff frowned, and stroked his chin. "I don't get it. Why did Scorpion go to Paris to meet him? And how did he know about you?"

"Scorpion came to London to kill a terrorist called Marutov. Dagestani national. This man wanted him dead because Marutov had learnt his identity. He was threatening to go public with it. That would be disastrous for him, but also for Borislov and Rashid, because this man fed them so much information."

Jeff blew out his cheeks. "Where is he based?"

Dan didn't answer the question. "You asked me how this guy knew about me. I reckon he's the same person who sent the goons after I met you the first time."

Jeff's brows met in the middle. "I wondered about that, too. How could anyone know you were here, apart from McBride and me?"

Dan said, "The same person told Rashid I was coming to Paris, hence Rashid was waiting for me outside the DGES prison. If it hadn't been for the safe house that Claude got for us, we might be dead now."

A light flickered and flamed in Jeff's eyes.

Dan nodded. "Yes, that's where you slipped up, Jeff. You shouldn't have given me Claude's details. He was a good guy. He gave me weapons and a safe house. He was becoming too useful to me, hence you had to kill him."

Jeff's face didn't change. His hazel eyes were dull and flat. "You're mad, Dan. Why would I call you all the way from the States if I wanted you dead?"

"Because your master, Rashid, wanted to kill me. You also wanted to know how much I really knew about Grant Pearson. All that stuff about Grant asking you about me was bullshit, right? Because if I knew about Grant, through McBride's contacts in the CIA, it meant Borislov and Rashid's grand plan to substitute the First Lady was in trouble."

Jeff smiled. "Dan, this is nonsense. Come on, admit it. It sounds farcical."

There was a thud from downstairs, followed by a crash, then two sharp, soft sounds.

Dan's eyes never left Jeff's, and he saw the corners of Jeff's eyes narrow slightly, and his lips press tighter.

"It's not so weird when you consider Susan Harris, the Director of CIA, formed Intercept with McBride, and a few others. Susan might have told McBride about Operation Nectar Flower. If they wanted to send a black ops agent over, McBride would have sent me."

Footsteps sounded downstairs.

Dan said, "By calling me over, you killed two birds with one stone. But I didn't know about Nectar Flower, and I got too close to Grant. That's why you had to kill him. Did you use one of the Russians to finish Grant off?"

Jeff said nothing. The footsteps came up the stairs. They stopped on the landing.

Dan said, "Nothing went to plan for you. You called me here today so you could kill me. But the men you had hiding downstairs are dead."

Jeff took a deep breath. "Scorpion?"

The footsteps came across the hallway, then a figure materialized on the door. In the fading light, the tight black neo propylene outfit was visible, but the mask was off the face.

Natasha Karmen, the Scorpion, stepped into the room. "Yes, me," she said. She came closer to Jeff. "You do one hell of an American accent, you know that? When I saw you in Paris, I believed you were American. One of your many gifts."

Her jaws clenched. "You took my sister. She could have died."

Jeff's eyes slid past her, towards the empty hallway.

"All four are dead, Jeff. Your insurance policy is gone."

In a quiet, steady voice Jeff said, "Think of the team we would make. My intelligence, and your operational skills. I have twenty-four million USD in a Swiss account. We could share that." He looked over to Dan. His right hand, inside his coat pocket, twitched slightly.

Dan moved like lightning. Jeff had barely removed the small gun from his pocket when Dan's hand closed over his. Jeff fired, but the bullet went low, chipping off wood from the floorboard.

Dan hit Jeff with an uppercut to the chin, and one was enough. His head snapped back. Dan held him by the collar while Scorpion patted him down. She removed another compact Beretta handgun from an ankle holster.

Dan propped Jeff against the wall. He jammed his elbow against Jeff's throat, making him choke.

Sirens wailed in the distance.

"Guess who's on their way, Jeff? Her Majesty's Secret Service. And Martin Shaw, the head of CIA in London. The Director of MI6 is waiting for you in Vauxhall. You're better off alive to them than dead."

Scorpion stepped forward. Dan moved aside. She removed a needle shaped stiletto from her waistband, and held it under his right eye.

"You'll remember me. And you'll never again do what you did to my sister."

She buried the needle into his cheek, ripping through flesh into the bone. She dragged the needle down, opening up a gash. Jeff screamed and kicked, but she held him against the wall.

She let him go, and he slumped to the floor, still screaming, holding his face.

The sirens were getting louder. Scorpion and Dan raced downstairs, then out the front door. They crossed the street, dodging the few cars on the road. They jumped over the grey stone bulwarks that separated the pavement from the river. It was a drop of six feet, but the landed on the jetty. It shook, but took their combined weight.

The RIB was close, its shining black nose rising up as the water bifurcated in waves behind it.

Cars were screeching to a halt on the road, footsteps running.

The RIB came right next to the jetty, and the driver, an ex-Navy officer and friend of Sparky's, reversed the boat closer to them.

Scorpion jumped into the boat, followed by Dan.

With a roar of its engines, the RIB took off. Dan gripped Scorpion around the shoulders and she slid her arm around his waist. They hung on to each other, close as they could be with clothes on.

Wind and froth rushed against their faces.

Scorpion raised her lips to Dan's ear. "Where are we going?" she shouted.

"Shall we get lost somewhere? Like nowhere at all?"

She nodded. "Sound good to me."

THE END

HAVE YOU READ THEM ALL?

ALL BOOKS AVAILABLE IN AMAZON ONLY – VISIT
AMAZON ONLINE

(Each book can be read as a stand-alone)

*Special offer: Save 40% when you get the box sets!! 3
full length novels in one book!*

*VISIT AMAZON ONLINE TO BUY BOTH
PAPERBACK AND EBOOK*

The Dan Roy Series Box Set: Books 1-3

The Dan Roy Series Box Set: Books 4-6

Individual titles:

Hidden Agenda (Dan Roy Series 1)

Dark Water (Dan Roy Series 2)

The Tonkin Protocol (Dan Roy Series 3)

Shanghai Tang (Dan Roy Series 4)

Scorpion Rising (Dan Roy Series 5)

Deep Deception (Dan Roy Series 6)

Scorpion Down (Dan Roy Series 7)

Code Zero (Dan Roy Series 8)

Enemy Within (A stand-alone thriller)

AUTHOR'S NOTE

If you enjoyed this book, would you mind leaving a review?

Mick is a nice kind of guy, and he would really appreciate it!

A review takes 2 minutes of your time, but guides other readers forever.

Just visit Amazon online, and write the review.

Thank you

Mick.

Made in the USA
Coppell, TX
01 July 2020

29950791R00194